Published by Author Level Up LLC.

Version 4.0

Cover design by MiblArt.

Editing by BZ Hercules and Audrey Weinbrecht.

Special thanks to Zachary M. Chisenga (consultant on rodent biology) and Toni Hyman (general beta reader).

Very special thanks to the following patrons who support the author on Patreon: Stephen Frans, Jon Howard, Michael Guishard, Beth Jackson, Megan Mong, Lynda Washington, and Etta Welk.

"My life's blossom might have bloomed on all sides
Save for a bitter wind which stunted my petals
On the side of me which you in the village could see.
From the dust I lift a voice of protest:
My flowering side you never saw!
Ye living ones, ye are fools indeed
Who do not know the ways of the wind
And the unseen forces
That govern the processes of life."

— EDGAR LEE MASTERS, SPOON
RIVER

CHAPTER ONE

Don't screw this up, don't screw this up, don't screw this up…

In the bathroom, Cyrus dabbed a giant blot of red wine on his new blazer with a tissue and cursed. The room, a tiny European-style toiletry with velvet fleur-de-lis wallpaper and oil paintings of romantic countrysides, seemed to close in.

A beautiful woman was waiting for him in the dining room of the restaurant, and that made his anxiety worse.

That was the last time he would ever crack a stupid joke with a wine bottle in his hand, at an expensive restaurant…on a date.

Someone pounded on the door.

"Occupied!" Cyrus shouted.

"There's a line out here, you know," an irritated voice said. "There's only one bathroom in this place."

Cyrus balled up the tissue and tossed it into the wastebasket. It might as well have been covered in blood. The next person coming into the bathroom would see the clump of red-stained tissues in the trash and get the wrong idea.

He stared at himself in the mirror. With the stain on his blazer and red dots on his white button-up shirt, he looked like he had been stabbed in the heart. The wine penetrated his undershirt too, and it was sticky against his skin.

He hated this blazer anyway. Beige pinstripes with gold buttons and brown elbow patches. He found it at the thrift store, and he looked like a kid wearing his dad's country club blazer. It was all he could find at the last minute. Even his sister had hated it.

"Please tell me you aren't wearing that on your date," Becca said.

"What's wrong with it?"

"Where the hell are you taking her? The Ritz?"

"The new French bistro that opened up."

"Seriously, Cy, you couldn't think of *anything* more creative?"

"What's wrong with fine dining?"

Becca had rolled her eyes and returned to the counter at the Wicked Cat and mixed a coffee.

He closed his eyes and took a deep breath, thinking of Becca's advice. Yep, she was right. She'd never let him hear the end of it. ("See? I told you not to wear that ugly thing…")

He could turn into a rat and find a way out of the place. Then he wouldn't have to show his face to his date again. But no. He wasn't going to let this ruin his night. This *was* the dating life. He was bound to embarrass himself somehow.

He gave a deep sigh and opened the bathroom door. A line of five people—a mix of men and women dressed in fancy clothes—stared at him angrily. One woman's anger softened to pity when her eyes dropped down to the stains. Cyrus tried to ignore the stares as he walked up a narrow flight of stairs into the restaurant.

The bistro was bustling in a Saturday night rush. Servers in white uniforms carried trays of food around linen-covered tables lit by candlelight. A pianist played jazz standards at a grand piano in the center of the floor, accompanied by an accordion player.

Next to the window, Marisol was waiting for him, watching the passing cars, cradling a bulbous glass of wine that was almost empty—another painful signal that he had taken too long. The flickering candlelight on her face reminded him of why he'd been so attracted to her in the first place. Long, curly brown hair pulled into a ponytail, piercing brown eyes, and a warm smile. Elegant white dress with her back showing. Quiet, but intelligent. Unlike a lot of women on the dating apps, she looked like her profile.

"I guess your blazer is toast, huh?" Marisol asked.

"It lived a nice life," Cyrus said, sitting down, "I'll give it a proper burial tonight."

She laughed softly, but he couldn't tell if she pitied him or if he had told a genuinely funny joke this time. Cyrus laughed nervously, sighed, and tried to figure out what to say next. But no words came. Just the same thought circling through his mind: *Don't screw this up. Don't screw this up...*

"The waiter changed the tablecloth," Marisol said. "I think the food will be here soon."

Thank God. At least with the meal at the table, she wouldn't have to look at the stain. He'd already taken the date from zero to awkward. Maybe the universe would finally give him a break and let him get to know her.

They listened for a moment as the jazz duo finished a song, and they clapped along with the other diners.

"So," he said in the quiet intro of a new song, drumming his fingers on the table. "You're an analyst, right?"

"Yep. I got into it because I've always thought that data was really fun," she said.

"Ah," Cyrus said. "I've never heard 'data' and 'fun' in the same sentence."

"You're not alone," Marisol said, sipping her wine. She let out a shy smile, which made Cyrus smile.

"When I went to college, my mom gave me three choices: doctor, lawyer, or something with a classy title," Marisol said.

"It's an immigrant parent thing. It took her a while to come around to a career in data sciences, but hey. It worked out."

"Nice," Cyrus said.

"What did you say you did again?" she asked, tilting her head.

"I just started working for a pest control company," he said. "Fontanelli & Son. Heard of them?"

Marisol shook her head.

"It's probably a good thing you haven't heard of us. We specialize in rats."

Marisol choked and coughed into a fist.

"I'm sorry," Cyrus said, eyes widening. "I didn't mean to—"

"It's okay," she said, dismissing the comment with a quick wave of her palm. "It's just…that's not what I expected you to say."

"I know, I look like a college student," Cyrus said.

"You look like a programmer," she said.

"Now *that's* a compliment," Cyrus said. "If this job doesn't work, I'll look into it."

She smiled and looked away for a moment and cleared her throat. They shared an awkward silence.

Of course, he couldn't tell her about his work with the Regulators. It paid way better than his extermination work, but he couldn't exactly tell non-paranormals about the seedy, magical underbelly of the city…

A waiter wheeled a cart of cloches to the table. He nodded to Marisol and placed her plate, removing the cloche and revealing a salad niçoise—tuna, green beans, hard-boiled eggs, anchovies, and tomatoes. He placed a patty of steak tartare in front of Cyrus—raw steak with an egg yolk on top, garnished with chives.

The food normally would have smelled delicious, but ever since he'd turned into a rat shifter, his senses were keener, even when he was in human form. The dishes smelled divine. He wondered what they would smell like if he shifted. He didn't blame rats at all for living lavishly on human garbage.

"You're adventurous," Marisol said, craning over to get a look at Cyrus's plate. "I have no idea how you can eat raw meat like that."

"Me either," Cyrus said, laughing. "I saw it on TV once. If I die from food poisoning, it'll make for a humorous story."

"Well, good luck, Cyrus," Marisol said. "And if that happens, it was nice knowing you."

Marisol cut into her salad with her knife and fork. She speared an artichoke heart, and it was halfway toward her mouth when a tremendous shadow darkened the sky outside.

It's already nighttime, Cyrus found himself thinking in slow motion as a giant tree slammed into the window, turning it into a wall of ragged triangles. Then the tree fell back and he glimpsed burning purple plasma and giant yellow incisors for a split second before the tree branch reared back and descended toward the glass again.

He grabbed Marisol and pulled her away from the window as it shattered.

Glass rained on Cyrus's back and ear-splitting screams erupted across the restaurant. The jazz music stopped.

The silence was only interrupted by the sounds of people moaning intermittently around the room.

Footsteps crunched on the broken glass.

Cyrus stayed on top of Marisol and kept her down. Her intoxicating sweet floral perfume drifted into his nostrils, mixing with what was left of her salad on the floor.

Whirling energy in the corner of his eyes drew his gaze to a humongous tower of rats. Hundreds of rats writhed over each other, aglow with smoke and fire. Their red eyes flashed like lightning, their squabbles grated against Cyrus's ears, and they moved together in one form—a big rat standing on its hind legs. It held an ash tree that it had ripped from a nearby tree square. The giant rat hissed, all the rats within making the same gesture at the same time.

Cyrus cursed as the giant rat jumped into the air, wielding the tree like a sword, aiming directly at him.

CHAPTER TWO

"Quincy, I'm firing you today."

In her office at the Wicked Cat Coffee & Brew, Becca Grant sat at her tiny desk overgrown with stacks of papers, clasping her hands together with a slight frown.

A muscular forty-something man sat on the other side of the desk in a folding chair. He wore a leather vest, a white apron, and an asymmetrical haircut with a comb-over, black hair buzzed to near bald on one side. Despite his tough-guy persona, he looked like he had just been slapped.

Becca's office was the size of a janitor's closet, barely big enough for a desk, and it was stuffy and hot in the summer. A pink fan blew cold air across the room, barely helping. The staff of the Wicked Cat clanged around in the kitchen outside.

"Here are your termination papers," Becca said, handing him a yellow envelope. "And the pay I owe you. Would you like to discuss it? This shouldn't be a surprise."

Quincy regarded the papers, then looked up at Becca with sad eyes. "I tried my best."

"Let's talk about that," Becca said. "This isn't the first time we've had this conversation. I explained to you that I have standards."

She felt a twinge of guilt every time she fired someone. A pit in the bottom of her stomach opened up, and even though she knew her exterior was calm with no sign of weakness, she couldn't help but feel sorry for the guy as he regarded his final paycheck at the Wicked Cat.

"I appreciate the work you've done," Becca said. "But let's be honest: you're a better bounty hunter than you are a barista. You're a natural with my customers, but you constantly get orders wrong, you've broken at least three of my porcelain plates, and you've been late on too many occasions. I have rules, and if I don't enforce them, is that fair to everyone else?"

Quincy didn't expect the question. "Well, uh, no."

"Do you think my customers like it when their orders are wrong?"

"No."

"Then I hope you can understand where I'm coming from."

She stood and extended a hand. "I wish you the best. Leave your apron on the chair. I'll walk you out."

How many times had she let underperformers go? Dozens, if not more, but never a paranormal. Ever since she met Desmond, he encouraged her to hire paranormals in exchange for protection since she and Cyrus were exposed to the magical world now. As a human with no powers, she was especially vulnerable.

But while regular humans were predictable, paranormals were anything but. Some were weird. Really weird. She thought she knew how to handle weird until she started working with *them*.

A little voice told her to be careful and extra polite. So far, so good. She walked to the door and opened it with a courteous smile. That was her first mistake.

"Fuck this," Quincy said under his breath.

"Excuse me?" Becca asked.

"I said fuck this!" Quincy shouted. He threw the papers up and they fluttered in a dazzle around him. "You think you're better than me? I spend my nights hunting vampires and shit, then I come and work in your stupid coffee shop, and you think you can order me around like you own me?"

Becca sighed. So much for the ceremonial firing.

"This was just a transition job anyway," Quincy said. "I'm trying to build a steady business of clients, and I thought I was doing you a favor. Fuck you, fuck Desmond, and fuck your little gourmet drinks!"

Becca's face hardened. If he attacked, she could have taken him, but this was a legal matter. Paranormal or not, he could still sue if she wrongfully terminated him. On a deeper, human level, she would have been mad too. Mad at herself for not performing.

"Quincy, our conversation is done. Please leave."

"I'm too good for this job," he said, laughing derisively.

"I'm not asking you again," Becca said, more sternly this time.

"You're just a human," he said. "You ought to be working for me. If it weren't for us paranormals, you wouldn't be able to walk home at night without being ripped apart by something."

"I'll take my chances," Becca said, not taking her eyes off him.

Quincy stewed in the chair, chewing his bottom lip, then he got up and charged past Becca and into the kitchen.

The kitchen staff stopped to watch the exchange.

"If I never work here again, I'll be grateful!" Quincy cried. "Don't ask me or any of my friends to bail you out when the supernatural world comes calling. I'll laugh! You're just arrogant and high and mighty. I'll be SHOCKED if this place isn't out of business in two years."

He pushed the back door open and slammed it behind him. The impact knocked a few soup ladles onto the floor.

Becca let out a sigh of relief.

"Thank the Lord, Hallelujah," a voice with a Spanish accent said.

Cristián, her assistant manager, leaned against the wall to her office. He wore a coffee-stained apron and his chestnut-brown hair was styled in a thick pompadour. He flashed her a tired, winsome grin. The ladies were probably going to be crazy about him tonight. When he was sarcastic, his accent was extra Spanish-y.

"Let me guess," he said. "He didn't take it well."

"Telling him he was fired was the nicest thing anyone said to him all day," Becca said as Cristián followed her into the office. She plopped down on her chair, threw her head back, and closed her eyes as the fan pointed cool air on her.

"What did you do to trigger him?" Cristián asked.

"Absolutely nothing," Becca said. "That was the problem."

"Maybe it was your hair."

Becca snapped her eyes open and gave Cristián a look of annoyance. Of course he was smirking.

Becca became self-conscious of her hair. She'd tried to dye her hair purple, but the color came out several shades darker than she wanted, and uneven. Cyrus said she looked like the unicorn mascot for the cereal they used to eat as a kid. She could have killed her little brother…except he was right. She adjusted her bandanna and checked herself in a small mirror on her desk. Her bandanna should have been extra tight today, with NO strands showing.

"Maybe purple is the trigger color for paranormals," Cristián said.

"Will you drop it already?"

"Come on, it's not that bad."

"My hair is the same shade as Barney. That qualifies as bad."

Becca looked at her reflection in the window again and

pursed her lips. She tucked in a rogue strand and surveyed her tiny office.

"Anyhoo," Cristián said, shrugging, "the wait staff is going to want a group hug when they learn of your valiant deed today. They've been waiting for you to do it for the past two weeks."

"If you don't want me to get sued like it's 1993, then you'll have to put up with my...protocols," Becca said.

Becca adjusted her bandanna a final time and picked up the remnants of Quincy's papers. She'd have to mail them.

"Desmond owes me big time for hiring Quincy," Becca said, scooping papers off the floor.

"You'll be able to tell him tonight," Cristián said. "A bunch of shifters are having a conference later."

Becca groaned. "As long as the wolf pack doesn't come. They're obnoxious. If the alpha hits on me one more time, I'll punch him."

Someone knocked on the door. It was one of the baristas. She hesitated at first.

"Becca, there's a man here to see you. He says it's important."

"It's not one of Quincy's friends, is it?" Becca asked.

"I don't think so. He said you'd be expecting him."

Becca glanced at the calendar on the wall. No appointments or reminders today. The only thing she had was an appointment with a coffee roaster later in the week. It was evening now—the waiters on the swing shift were cleaning up and getting ready for the dinner rush of patrons wanting beer, pretzels, and spirits. She never booked meetings this late.

Becca shrugged and handed Cristián the papers. "You're on mail duty," she said.

"I will execute the final affairs of that pompous asshole dutifully," he said, placing his hand on his heart.

Becca rolled her eyes momentarily as she walked onto the dining floor.

A few customers were trickling in. In the corner, underneath a constellation of mason jar lights, a man sat with his back to her. He looked out the window nervously, and his black windbreaker was still on. His jet black hair was slightly balding with a small bald spot in the center of his head. This had to be the guy that was waiting for her.

"Can I help you?" Becca asked.

The man turned, relieved upon seeing her. He was a Latino man with a clean-cut goatee and a small paunch.

"I'm so glad to see you," he said.

Becca recognized him and froze. He was Gilberto, the healer who had saved Cyrus's life by concocting an antidote to rat poison. She saved her brother, but it ended with Becca getting squeezed by an evil nymph, breaking several ribs, and being freaked out of her mind. Her ribs had just now barely healed. She had dyed her hair purple to celebrate the recovery. Boy, was her botched dye-job a metaphor for her life at the moment.

"You got a nice place," Gilberto said. "I knew we'd be working together sooner or later."

"Excuse me?" Becca asked, growing more skeptical about the unannounced visit.

"The promise, remember?" Gilberto asked.

When Gilberto saved Cyrus, Becca had promised him a favor to be disclosed by him at a later date. She never gave him her address.

"You have terrible timing," Becca asked. "Unless you're asking for a job. I have an opening."

"No," he said. "I need your brother. Where is he?"

"He's not here," Becca said.

"Where is he?"

"I don't know," Becca lied, trying not to think of her brother and the super awkward date he was sure to be having right now.

"Damn it," Gilberto said, glancing out the window.

"I'm in the middle of my evening rush," Becca said. "I'm happy to hear you out, but can you come back a little later?"

"If I wait any longer, I'll be dead," Gilberto said.

Becca's heart thumped. "Then you should call the police."

"Great idea," Gilberto said.

"My brother and I aren't looking for trouble," Becca said. "We appreciate what you did for us, but we may not be the right ones to help you right now."

"When they come hunting for your brother, you'll rethink *your* decision," Gilberto said. "I need my favor now, and I can't wait."

"Look, Gilberto, I—"

He grabbed her with a pleading look. "If your brother doesn't help me, then I'm screwed, and it'll be on your conscience."

CHAPTER THREE

Cyrus ripped Marisol out of the way just as the giant rat smashed the tree into the floor, leaving a massive crater.

He pulled her up. She saw the beast for the first time and screamed.

The giant rat—rather, a swarm of rats in the shape of a giant rat—roared as it plucked the tree off the floor. All the rats bared their incisors are the same time. A fetid odor hit Cyrus that reminded him of garbage and mold.

"We've got to get out of here," Cyrus said.

Customers were pouring out of the restaurant. He took Marisol's hand and they ran for the door.

The ground quaked behind them, and Cyrus instinctively let go of Marisol's hand and pushed her against the wall.

A branch lashed Cyrus's cheek.

The tree slammed into the doorway, blocking them from exiting.

"Oh my God," Marisol said.

Fire erupted across his skin and he brought his hand to it. Blood.

Cyrus grabbed Marisol's hand as they stared at the giant rat. Only the three of them remained in the restaurant.

The beast towered over them, rats swarming its body. It laughed with shrieking rats underscoring its voice.

It raised a ratty fist to strike, but Cyrus and Marisol dashed out of the way. The punch brought a wall crumbling down. Rats flew into the air after the impact but regathered on the arm, shrieking more intensely.

Cyrus led Marisol to the middle of the restaurant floor. The giant rat followed, shaking the ground with each step.

Cyrus looked around for something, anything to fight with. He spotted the kitchen in the corner of his eye and moved strategically toward it. Marisol's hand was slippery in his, and she clung close to him, panting.

The rat picked up a table and heaved it at them. They ducked as the table exploded in a bang of wood, metal, and ripped linen.

Cyrus grabbed a chair and chucked it at the rat. He missed by a long ways. The chair bounced on the floor.

Marisol threw a wine bottle and connected, bathing the rat in glass shards and Pinot Grigio. It didn't faze the beast.

"We have to make it to the kitchen," Cyrus said. "That's our best way out."

Marisol nodded. They wove across the floor as the giant rat crashed after them, throwing tables and roaring.

In the kitchen, a crisp smoldering filled the air. A skillet full of chicken breasts was burning on the industrial stoves.

He swiped a chef's knife off a counter and threw it. The knife stuck in the rat's shoulder and it cried out in pain as several rats fell off it and went limp on the floor.

Cyrus grabbed a fire extinguisher off the wall, pulled the pin, and smothered the giant rat in foam.

The beast recoiled, and Cyrus charged forward, his finger on the trigger of the fire extinguisher. Soon, the kitchen was covered in a semi-circle of foam.

Then Cyrus threw the extinguisher and hit the beast in the

head, knocking it backward. More rats spilled to the floor and went limp.

Cyrus took Marisol's hand and they dashed for the back door. He told her to go first, and Marisol pushed the door open and ran into the night.

The fresh air whipped around Cyrus and he imagined himself further down the alley, free from the giant rat.

Then something grabbed him at the last second and dragged him into the kitchen inferno.

Suddenly, he was airborne. Through the kitchen. Into the dining room.

He crashed into a table, breaking it. He landed hard on his back and the impact sucked the wind from his lungs.

The foam-covered beast stomped toward Cyrus, grinning, rats writhing in its mouth.

Rats poured off the beast's body, squabbling on the floor. In a flash, the single beast was gone, replaced by a wave of smoke-covered rats with red eyes and wispy bodies, who all stood on their hind legs, grooming themselves and bruxing their teeth.

Cyrus stood, gasping.

"What do you want?" he asked quietly.

A wave of squeaks filled the room.

His instinct told him to shift.

He shrank, his bones reducing themselves to rat size. Brown hair sprouted from his skin, and his incisors inched out of his jaws. The beautiful bistro blurred into a fish-eyed view of a landscape strewn with rubble. Soon he was a rat, staring at the others.

The rotten smell from the rat intensified against his little nose. Whatever this thing was, it was vile. The garbage and rotten undertones took on new, sicker nuances now. If his rat body could vomit, he would have.

A soft song echoed around the room. He hadn't heard it

before. A woman's voice, singing in simple, long syllables. Operatic and siren-like.

He froze with terror.

Murgalen. The tree nymph who turned him into a shifter. His maker.

Her voice was emanating from the rats' bodies.

But Murgalen was dead. Cyrus had watched her commit suicide at the Damen Silos. Yet her faint voice carried through the air as if she were with him.

The nymph's face flashed into his mind—skin mixed with wet bark, a mouth full of wooden, gnarly triangular teeth, and a crown of thorny branches. She spoke lines from his memory.

"I can be benevolent," she said. "Your existence will serve as proof of that in light of what's to come."

Cyrus squeaked in protest.

"If no one will stand up for nature, then I must," she said.

Murgalen's face tilted at Cyrus and grinned, full of malice. "Let's send a message to all these big, bad paranormals, shall we?"

Her face turned to dust and swirled away from his vision.

Cyrus shrieked in fear. The rats shrieked in response, then scattered around the restaurant. They scrambled over each other, dissipating into a dull smoke that lingered in the air. Their squabbles faded until the room was silent.

In the kitchen, Cyrus smelled another smoke. Burning smoke.

Flames erupted from the stove, and this time, an arc of fire set the sprinklers off. Water spilled on the tables and floor like heavy rain. The water stuck to his rat nose, and it was brown and sticky.

Cyrus took shelter under a table.

Bright lights washed across the room, followed by sirens, which were ten times louder to his rat ears.

Several voices shouted, and footsteps shook the floor.

"Police!"

Cyrus swept along the floor silently, navigating destroyed tables and chairs.

The flames were spreading despite the streams of water falling from the ceiling. A wall of heat blocked the kitchen. He relied on his whiskers as they led him to the door blocked by the tree.

Several boots thudded near the window.

"I don't see anyone," someone said. "The place is on fire."

A column of water crashed into the flames. More dirty city water. Droplets landed on his face.

He ran faster now as more water washed into the restaurant. The crackling flames and water collided and danced amid firefighters shouting over the noise.

He slipped under the tree that blocked the door and ran onto the street.

A woman screamed at the sight of him. Instinct kicked in as he wove between people's shoes. Someone tried to stomp on him but narrowly missed.

Soon, he was in the shadows of an alley, barreling along the walls. Smoke was thick in the air, forming a thousand different textures on his whiskers—amazing but burnt French food, linens ablaze, fire engine exhaust, and an intense duo of ash and soot threatening to choke him.

He found a dumpster.

Behind it, he shifted back into a human. The warm, flame-kissed summer night enveloped him as his vision sharpened and he grew taller.

He ran through the darkness, nose into his elbow to protect his lungs from the thick smoke.

He emerged into the street where police were herding people across the street behind yellow tape.

Siren lights swirled and the police had the building barricaded.

A hand clapped on Cyrus's blazer and lifted him by the collar.

"Hey!" he cried.

A police officer half pushed, half threw him across the street. He stumbled to get away from him.

"Behind the tape!" the officer yelled.

Cyrus spotted Marisol in the crowd. Part of her dress was ripped, and she was visibly shaken. He straightened his blazer from the cop's assault and dipped under the tape.

"Are you okay?" he asked.

She nodded.

"What happened to you?" she asked, her eyes widening with concern.

"I got away," he said. "Somehow."

"What the *hell* just happened?" Marisol asked. "Was that thing…a ghost?"

Cyrus shook his head. "I don't know," he said quietly. "But we should leave."

"I want to give a statement to the reporter," Marisol said. "You should too."

Cyrus gulped. A shadow flew overhead and he ducked. A raven with blue-tinged wings perched on a nearby streetlight, surveying the scene.

Luna.

It was probably taking everything in her power not to shift into a human, hang from the light and make a snarky comment about how Cyrus's first date had gone.

Another raven swooped over him and landed on a nearby car.

Rocco.

"It might be dangerous here," Cyrus said, gaze lingering on the ravens. "Maybe we should leave. I don't want you getting hurt."

"No way," Marisol said. "We're as safe as we'll ever be.

Besides, if we don't tell the police what happened, they'll never catch that thing."

"Yeah, I'm telling them everything," another person said.

"Hey, there's the news," another said.

A crowd started for a news van that was slowing to a stop at the end of the street.

"Come on, Cyrus," Marisol said.

Cyrus wanted to groan, but he couldn't leave her. Not until he knew she'd be safe.

Together, they walked to the news van, and Cyrus wondered if this night was an omen for his dating life.

CHAPTER FOUR

Kirk MacLeod sat on a bench in Logan Square Park, pretending to read a book.

The book, which he'd bought at an airport book stand years ago, was a space opera. An old mass-market paperback with a spaceship and an exploding planet on the cover, yellowed pages with coffee stains here and there, and a spine that had been cracked many times. It smelled like an old basement, but that was part of its charm.

From the few words he read over the years, the book was mildly interesting. A stranger on a jungle planet fighting assassins. He expected aliens but there hadn't been a single one in the book yet.

He could relate to aliens. Pretending to read a book made him feel like one. He never was much of a reader, but he sure played the part. To a passerby, he was just a black man quietly enjoying his time in the city in the declining evening.

The wind rustled the tall oak trees, stirring up the summer smell of humid air and freshly cut grass. Not a bad place to spend time, but not his first choice.

A woman with earbuds in a t-shirt and jeans walking a bulldog passed, and the dog sauntered over to him, sniffing.

Kirk instinctively reached down and let the dog smell the back of his hand. The dog licked, but when the woman said its name, it veered back onto the trail. Kirk gave a quick smile to the woman. She nodded back to him.

It never failed to amaze him that he could fit in everywhere. People always said he had a familiar face, yet he didn't look like anyone *he* knew. He'd stared at himself in the mirror many nights, wondering if he'd ever find his doppelgänger. The day he did, his time as a hunter would be over.

He settled on the uncomfortable bench and turned the page, tilting his head with fake intrigue. He stole a glance across the street, at the Wicked Cat.

He hadn't expected to end up casing a coffee shop. This wasn't the type of place Gilberto Sanchez frequented.

Kirk's head filled with static as his secret earpiece buzzed to life.

"I've got a good look at him," a voice said.

His stepbrother, Aidan, was in a nearby tree on the other end of the park. Between the two of them, they had the Wicked Cat covered. His brother was probably looking through a pair of binoculars. How he made it into the tree without being seen was one of their many trade secrets. Besides, it was better for Aidan to do the odd tasks—no one would suspect a white guy climbing a tree. A black man? Maybe. That was why they made a dynamic duo.

For kicks, Kirk wondered if Aidan could climb the tall eagle monument in the park. The stone eagle perched on top of a giant Greek column, watching over the street. Yep, his brother might be crazy enough to climb it sometime.

"He's talking to a woman," Aidan said. "You ought to see the hipster vibe on her. I'd bet she's the owner."

"Give me the deets."

"Crazy-ass purple hair," Aidan said, puffing. "The color is like a sickly eggplant. Anyway, she's wearing a camouflage tank, red bandanna. She's about five-six. Ponytail. Stud in her cheek. Looks like a dragon tattoo on her arm."

"Gilberto likes his women weird, eh?"

"Nah, she's not into him," Aidan said. "Her body language is saying 'get me away from this guy.' Can't say I blame ya, sister. He's being extra cautious. Keeps looking out the window. We'll have to give him some space or he'll spook if he sees us."

"I'm enjoying a nice book," Kirk said. "I have all night."

A few moments of silence passed between them.

"What do you see on the street?" Aidan asked.

"Looks like he came alone," Kirk said. "I thought he might seek protection. He must not be thinking clearly."

"Let's make a bet," Aidan said.

"You want to lose again?" Kirk asked. "You don't learn your lesson, do you, brother?"

"I'll bet you five bucks he takes a long way home," Aidan said. "You know, the circle-every-block maneuver."

"He's going to visit someone else before he does that," Kirk said. "From what we've seen so far, he's a little too mousy to go home yet. The night's young."

"So, no bet?" Aidan asked.

Kirk went quiet as a couple holding hands strolled by. When they were safely out of earshot, he said, "Is he drinking a coffee?"

"They're talking," Aidan said. "She doesn't like him, it seems. Trying to get him to leave."

"Bless her heart," Kirk said. "Maybe she'll make our job easier."

"Yep, he's leaving," Aidan said. "He'll be out the front door in about five seconds."

Kirk tucked his book into the inner pocket of his denim jacket. He cracked his neck, stretched his arms, and let out a refreshing sound.

"Over to you, brother," Aidan said.

Aidan Macleod slid down the oak tree. After making sure no one was watching, he hung on the bottom branch for a moment before dropping to the ground. He quickly crouched into exercise stretches, glancing around to see if anyone noticed him.

Negative.

He shook the wrinkles out of his sweatpants and blue nylon training jacket. He adjusted a small runner's backpack on his shoulders, and he jogged to the nearest path.

Just a jogger. That's all he was now. He passed a woman in yoga pants walking a bulldog who didn't even look at him, though he looked twice at her. Three times. He couldn't help himself.

He passed a giant eagle monument. A column jutted at least fifty feet into the sky. He eyeballed it as he passed. Yeah, he could scale that thing one day.

"Don't go get any ideas about climbing that monument, brother," Kirk said.

Aidan laughed to himself. His brother knew him too well.

He passed a black man with a low haircut, sunglasses, a denim jacket, and black boots sitting on a park bench as if he were relaxing. Kirk didn't even acknowledge his existence.

He ran to the edge of the park, at a busy intersection.

A pedestrian light blinked on and he crossed the street, running away from the Wicked Cat. Once he was a block away, he ducked into a shaded alley.

"Whaddaya got?" he whispered, dipping between two dumpsters.

"He's out of the shop and headed east," Kirk said. "I'm trailing him."

"Slow down when you figure out where he's going,"

Aidan said. He pulled his backpack off, unzipped it, and produced a stainless steel case. He unlatched it and revealed a human skull set in black foam. Its plates were covered with swirling tattoos and runes. Aidan had a tattoo sleeve of similar designs on his left arm, and Kirk had them on his right.

Aidan held up his father's skull and blew into it. His breath turned into a wisp of smoke and golden particles of light. The skull's eye sockets glowed with distant pinpoints, and the mouth hung open. A voice spoke from the skull, but the jaws didn't move.

"Can't you two do anything without my help anymore?"

"Love you too, Dad," Aidan said.

Even though his father had been dead for years, his cantankerous but charming voice sounded the same as if he'd never left. How many people were blessed enough to talk to their dead parents whenever they wanted?

Aidan still radiated pride every time he thought of adopting the Macleod last name. The old man didn't have to take him. If it weren't for Bruce and Maggie, Aidan would have probably been left for dead as a baby. But the couple insisted on foster children.

"Are you working?" Bruce Macleod asked.

"Always."

"Are you tired?" Bruce asked.

"Yep."

"Are you following your passion?"

"What do you think?"

"Good. Then your mother and I are still proud."

"We need some assistance," Aidan said. "We'll cash in two requests."

"Good God, Aidan. You know the consequences."

"We've got a good feeling about our odds," Aidan said. "Kirk is willing to risk bondage with a succubus for a week in exchange for what we need."

A quiet laugh emerged from the skull. "He doesn't know that yet, does he?"

"Come on, Dad, let's have a little fun."

"Well?"

"We're on a job, and we've got bad vibes," Aidan said. "Something doesn't seem right, but we're not ready to join you and Mom yet. I need to know exactly how, why, when, and how hard Axel Valentine is going to screw us."

"That damned nephilim again?"

"He hired us," Aidan said. "The money's good, and normally, he's a good client, but we don't trust him this time."

"You better hope he doesn't find out about this."

"That's why we're asking the best, smartest, kindest, and most kickass spirit we know," Aidan said.

"I'll see what I can do," Bruce said. "What else?"

"What can you tell us about the owner of an establishment called the Wicked Cat Coffee & Brew?"

"I suppose I could ask around, maybe explore the place myself."

"Thanks, Dad."

"Settle up and I'll get started," Bruce said.

Aidan closed his eyes and thought the darkest thoughts he could in rapid succession across his mind's eye. He thought them so hard he could feel them. Someone realizing they were being murdered and strangled before their very eyes as the crazed killer gritted their teeth. Dead bodies lying in a field with their eyes open, torn apart by crows. Blood-curdling screams. Gunshots. Frenzied news reports. He recalled across the dark canvas of his mind sirens, evil laughter, jagged knives, blood, bullets, tombstones under a full moon, and nothing at all. His mind went blank, and still.

Suddenly, a twist of shadow appeared on the dumpster next to Aidan. In the corner of his eye, he detected a faint contour of horns, claws, and swirling shadows. He dared not look. To glance upon the face of a demon with no reason was to invite eternal bondage.

Whoever died and made demons in charge of the dead did the supernatural world a disservice. They never cared if you talked to dead spirits, but the moment you wanted something, you had to pay, and they had no need for currency.

"You are sure about this transaction?" the demon asked in a distorted, staticky voice.

"Lay it on me," Aidan said.

The demon smashed into him, crushing him against the wall. He screamed in pain as the shadows ravaged his insides. He floated into the air, his arms and legs stretched like a human anatomy picture.

The demon laughed and filled Aidan's head with a foreign language in a grunting unlike any he'd heard. Then the voice faded, and he dropped to the ground, gasping.

How many demons did he and his brother carry within them now? They incubated the demons like babies to be born into this world, the wicked things crawling out whenever it was convenient. Sometimes it took days. Most demons took years to emerge. And when they scurried out, Aidan and Kirk had to do whatever they demanded. Sometimes, it was as simple as murder. Other times, it was more subtle, more devious. The brothers never asked questions. But when the deed was done, the demon was finally in this plane, with free will, with the ability to form a physical body. Whatever they did after that was their business.

Bruce's skull stared at him from the dumpster, its eye sockets glowing. A column of smoke streamed from the eyes, forming into a hazy silhouette that hovered above Aidan.

His father waited patiently.

Aidan mustered the energy, pulled himself to his feet, and locked the skull in its case.

"What's up, Kirk?" Aidan asked.

Kirk gave him an intersection.

Aidan would have to jog at a good pace to catch up, but he was up for it.

He walked through the alley, savoring a few last moments with his father's spirit before exiting onto the street.

Bruce circled him and then floated down the street toward the Wicked Cat.

CHAPTER FIVE

"I never thought talking to someone would be so cathartic," Marisol said.

Cyrus waited with her on the corner as the police investigated the scene at the bistro. Officers and firefighters streamed in and out of the building, stepping delicately over broken glass. Remnants of burnt food lingered in the air. The fire was mostly extinguished now, with only a few hotspots blazing in the kitchen.

Most of the crowd had dispersed, but the news van remained on the corner, with a black female field reporter speaking in front of a camera and lights.

"I can't wait to see the report," Marisol said. "Maybe we'll be famous."

"Hopefully not," Cyrus said, rubbing the back of his head.

He didn't give a statement to the media, but he had stood listening nearby as Marisol spoke to a field reporter. The last thing he needed was his face all over the news.

"I was on a date, and we were just talking and eating dinner," she had told the reporter. "A monster showed up and tried to kill us. We barely got away. It's a miracle no one was hurt."

He just wanted to go home. Now he was on the clock as a Regulator. It didn't seem right to mix romance and work, even though he was still attracted to Marisol.

He couldn't stop thinking about Murgalen's face and her message. It was impossible to think about entertaining a date when his maker sent a message from the grave. Marisol wasn't paying much attention to him anyway—she was too fixated on the crime scene.

The first stars of the night blinked into the sky. He was never taking a woman on a date at twilight again. Nothing good ever happened in the evening, not since he had become a rat shifter.

"Sorry our date didn't go so well," he said. "If I had known this would happen, I would have—"

"It's not your fault," Marisol said. The breeze grew slightly cooler, rippling her white dress and blowing a tangle of curly hair in front of her eyes. She rubbed her shoulders.

A red car with a rideshare sign on the dashboard pulled up to the curb. The driver waved, and Marisol held up her phone to confirm the ride.

"Cyrus, it's been great," she said. "As great as it could have been, I guess."

Cyrus laughed. "Most memorable first date ever."

She laughed and tucked a strand of hair behind her ear. She waited for a moment, and they stared at each other. Then she broke the gaze and started for the car.

A little voice shouted at him, *Don't screw this up.*

"Hey, Marisol."

She turned.

"Can I call you tomorrow and check in?" Cyrus asked. "Just to make sure you're okay?"

"I'd like that," she said, grinning.

Only when the car rounded the corner did he realize he hadn't helped her get in. He definitely lost gentleman points for that. He dug his hands in his pockets, shook his head, and sighed.

His phone rang. His mom. He slipped his earbuds in and paced the sidewalk.

"Cy, I couldn't remember if your date was tonight or tomorrow," Aurora Grant said.

"I'm on my way home."

"Oh, good," Aurora said. "I don't know why, but I had a weird feeling and had the urge to call you. Are you okay?"

Cyrus knew that if he hesitated, his mother would bleed the truth out of him. Ever since Murgalen turned him into a rat and he disappeared for three months, his mom kept a closer eye on him, and he didn't blame her. Especially because he never told her the truth. It made phone calls like this one inconvenient.

"I'm fine, Mom," he said. "And the date went okay."

"Just okay?" Aurora asked.

"Yep."

"You're not going to tell me anything else, are you?"

"What's up, Mom?"

She paused, allowing him to hear her displeasure, yet he still said nothing.

"I was thinking about what to do for my birthday," she said finally. "I haven't cleared this with Becca yet, but she'll just have to find someone to replace her at the shop for a few hours, so too bad if she doesn't like it on such short notice…but there's a new theater that opened up in Lincoln Park and they're doing a one-act play night. Doesn't that sound like fun?"

Glass shattered, drawing Cyrus's attention to the bistro. Firefighters were knocking out what was left of the front window and sweeping it up.

"Cy?" Aurora asked.

"Sure, sounds good," Cyrus said absently.

He'd almost forgotten about his mom's birthday. Every

year, he and Becca always spent the evening with her. Last year, they played board games and drank beer on a restaurant rooftop. The year before that, they got lost in the Chicago Botanic Garden.

"You don't like the idea?" Aurora asked.

"It's good, Mom. I'm just super tired," Cyrus said.

"Great. I'll meet you and Becca at the Wicked Cat tomorrow morning at eleven-thirty."

He couldn't hurt his mom's feelings by declining or suggesting another time. She would take it personally. "Sounds good, Mom."

He told her he loved her and terminated the call. He hung his head. He was supposed to be happy about his mom's birthday, but it was hard to concentrate right now.

"Sooooo, tell me everything," a female voice said.

His raven shifter friend, Luna, was sitting on a car behind him. She was wearing her trademark pink flannel shirt with a white midriff-baring shirt below. She also wore ripped jeans and golden high-top sneakers.

"I want every single detail of your date," she said.

"I don't feel like talking about it," Cyrus said.

"Okay, so it was super awkward," Luna said, hopping off the car. "But it's not every day that you get attacked by a giant rat thingy."

Together, they watched the scene. Several police officers ducked under a line of caution tape and rushed to a nearby squad car.

"Putting aside the fact that we're going to have a long night ahead of us," Luna said, "did you at least connect with her?"

"To be determined," Cyrus said. "Just when the conversation was getting good, I spilled wine on myself."

"Oh no," Luna said, inspecting his blazer. She tugged at one of the stains. "Looks like your blazer's ruined."

"At least I only spent twenty dollars on it," Cyrus said.

"Would you see her again?"

"Sure," Cyrus said.

"Ouch."

"What?"

"All you can say is 'sure'?" Luna asked. "No chemistry, huh?"

"I told you I didn't want to talk about it," Cyrus said.

Luna shrugged.

"Maybe you can take your mind off the date by preparing a statement for Desmond," Luna said. "He's going to have a thousand questions for you."

Cyrus thought of Desmond, the werehyena shifter and precinct captain for the Regulators. His boss. He was a man of few words, so whenever he spoke, everyone listened. He was going to have some strong opinions about the giant rat. But at least he'd know what to do.

"Now that the entire world is going to know about the existence of paranormals," Cyrus said, "what do we do?"

Luna dismissed him. "Don't worry about that. This sort of thing happens all the time."

"Really?" Cyrus asked.

"Totally," Luna said, dismissing him with a wave of her wrist. "A few years ago, a werewolf went berserk and started killing people randomly. He tore through Navy Pier too, and thousands of people saw it and posted videos on social media. It never made the local or national news."

"Why?"

"We have…fail-safes to stop that from happening," Luna said. "The Valentine family has a pretty firm lock on the city."

"Let me guess," Cyrus said, rolling his eyes. "Vampires."

"More like angel and demon spawn," Luna said. "It's best to avoid them when you can. Rocco and I had a bad run-in with Axel Valentine a while back. I don't recommend it. I was really scared for Rocco."

A whistle drew their attention down the street. Rocco,

fellow raven shifter and Luna's boyfriend, walked toward them. He wore a leather jacket and skinny jeans. His black hair was perfectly pomaded as usual.

"Whoa, what happened to you, bud?" Rocco asked, glancing at Cyrus's blazer.

"Long story," Cyrus said.

"What'd you find out?" Luna asked.

"Not much," Rocco said. "I was able to sneak in as a raven for a minute before a cop shooed me out. I didn't see any clues. What did you see, Cyrus?"

"The same thing we saw the night we fought Murgalen," Cyrus said. "Lots of magic-infested rats. They looked like rats and acted like rats, but they had a hive mind. And super strength. They fused into a giant rat. It swung a tree like it was nothing. And I saw Murgalen."

"Murgalen? But she's dead," Luna said.

"She wasn't alive," Cyrus said, remembering the nymph's face. "It was a flashback. She said something about sending the paranormals in the city a message."

"Sounds like her plan is finally taking shape," Luna said. "Desmond was right that it wouldn't take long."

"Desmond called an emergency meeting at the Wicked Cat," Rocco said. "He wants us there now."

"Cy, how about you shift and we'll carry you," Luna said.

Cyrus shook his head. "Nope. I'm walking. I need some fresh air."

"Suit yourself," Rocco said.

"I'll come with you," Luna said, hooking her arm underneath his. "Look at you. Accompanying two women in one night."

"I guess I better make sure to treat her extra right tonight, eh, bud?" Rocco asked, grinning. "We've got some time anyway. I'll fly ahead and help Becca get the place ready. Desmond'll probably make her close early."

"She's not going to be happy about closing early," Cyrus said. "Grouchy Becca is also not what I need tonight."

"Moody Cyrus isn't what anyone needs either," Luna said.

Rocco ducked into an alley. A few seconds later, his raven form flew over the rooftops.

"I'm at your command," Luna said as they started their night stroll. Despite the warm summer night, it was quiet. It was a long walk down Armitage Avenue to the Blue Line at Damen Avenue, plenty of time for Cyrus to relax before the shifter meeting.

"I'm proud of you," Luna said. "I wasn't sure if you'd ever get back into the dating scene."

Cyrus didn't say anything. Even though he still felt some pain when thinking about his last adventure and how much trouble a broken heart caused him, he had moved on.

"You deserve to be happy," Luna said. "Rocco and I want that for you."

"Thanks," Cyrus said.

They passed a Latino grocery store with a giant Mexican flag painted on one wall, an art gallery, and a funeral home where people were gathered in a parking lot for a wake.

"How'd you meet Rocco?" Cyrus asked.

"A few years ago, at a shifter party," Luna said, smiling as she reminisced. "An apartment party. He happened to open the door, and it was love at first sight. He made sure that he asked me out on a date."

"Sounds like Rocco," Cyrus said.

"He's not afraid to ask for what he wants," Luna said.

"Are you two ever going to get married?"

Luna laughed. "We've talked about it. We worry about our work with the Regulators. It's so dangerous, you know? But yeah, one day, he better put a ring on this finger."

They passed another Latino grocery store with a giant Mexican flag painted on one wall, another art gallery, and another funeral home with a crowd gathered in the parking lot with a wake. Cyrus looked around, confused.

"Didn't we just pass by here?" he asked.

"I think so," Luna said, unhooking from his arm.

A quick glance at each other without speaking told them to hurry their pace.

They rounded a corner and changed streets.

Again, they passed by the grocery store, the art gallery, and the funeral home.

"Excuse me!" Cyrus cried, waving to the funeral home crowd. No one responded.

"Hey!" he cried again.

Still no answer.

"Shit," he said. "Why can't I catch a break?"

A breeze blew, rustling several leaves into an arrow pointing across the street between the grocery store and the art gallery, where a narrow, vine-covered pergola led to an alley with an ornate cobblestone brick path. The pergola glowed, beckoning them in.

"Looks like we don't have a choice, do we?" Cyrus asked.

They passed under the gateway and into the brick alley, which opened into a public space with two tree squares with small trees and metal patio tables. The space was covered with the intoxicating scent of wildflowers. Cyrus cursed again at the realization of what was coming.

The trees came alive, moving like creepy clay animations until they morphed into two beautiful women. One was an older Caucasian woman—probably in her fifties. Thin strands of gray hair hung down on her face. She reminded Cyrus of Murgalen, but older. She wore a brown raincoat and blood-red high heels. The other was a light-skinned Asian woman who looked to be in her twenties, wearing a leopard print dress. She gazed at them with fierce black eyes.

He knew these nymphs. During his last adventure, they had accosted him and Desmond on a train. They escaped the women's wrath by sheer luck. This time, he and Luna might not be so lucky.

"Do you have any idea what you have done?" the older woman asked.

"I haven't done anything," Cyrus said.

"He isn't aware that his very existence is the problem, Oleandra," the Asian woman said.

"We've already told him, Rue," Oleandra said. "I hope he was listening."

"I'm right here," Cyrus said. "And I was listening. Maybe you ought to listen to me for a change: leave me the hell alone."

"We should have finished you when we had the chance, rat shifter," Oleandra said. She and Rue circled them.

"If you had, then he wouldn't have stopped Murgalen," Luna said. "You ought to be thanking him."

"*We* would have stopped her," Oleandra snapped.

"What do you want?" Cyrus asked.

"The monstrosity that appeared tonight was your doing," Oleandra said.

"Like hell it was," Cyrus said.

"If you had died like all the other rat experiments, none of this would have come to fruition," Oleandra said. "Why didn't you die?"

"Great choice," Cyrus said. "I'll remember that if I buy a time machine."

"Murgalen unleashed the souls of the failed dead rat shifters on the city," Oleandra said. "As one of the oldest nymphs in this area, her magic was unrivaled. She did not have the blessing of the other nymphs in the city. She acted on her own and we were not organized enough to stop her. While we oppose the abuse of the city's natural resources, and we resent paranormals for their complicity in the destruction of nature, we would not have taken her actions, namely initiating you into the paranormal world. We would rather see you dead, but it's fortunate for us that you're alive."

"If you don't like the giant rat, then hunt it down and destroy it," Luna said. "You have the magic and the strength to do it. Leave us out of it."

"That's why we're here," Oleandra said. "Cyrus, *you* will help us hunt this creature, and *you* will destroy it."

"Why me?" Cyrus asked.

"You are Murgalen's last living descendant," Oleandra said.

"She's not my mom," Cyrus said.

"Her magic lives within you," Oleandra said. "That is the same as motherhood. You must pay for the sins of the mother."

"Bullshit," Cyrus said. "I don't owe you anything. I'm just trying to live my life."

"We thought you might refuse," Rue said.

"So this is a threat," Cyrus said.

"The nymphs of Chicago will not be blamed for this disaster," Oleandra said.

"The Regulators will take care of it and it'll be over soon," Cyrus said.

"That monster is more than just a beast," Oleandra said. "It is infused with Murgalen's last wishes. And she wanted blood. Not of humans, but of paranormals. It is our preference that this be resolved without any further nymph involvement. Our position is already tenuous and in decline. We cannot afford for paranormals to target us for revenge. We ask for a one-time favor helping us in exchange for not destroying everyone in your life who you've ever held dear."

"Do it, and I'll destroy you," Cyrus said. "You leave my family and friends out of this."

"No, that is not how we operate, rat," Rue said.

The wind blew, gathering a column of leaves around the

two women, and they were gone. Oleandra's voice carried on the wind.

"It is Saturday night," Oleandra said. "If you have not eradicated this threat from the city by tomorrow at midnight, we will forever break your heart, Cyrus Grant."

CHAPTER SIX

A_ROUND_ 8:30 P.M., Cynthia Longvale received a text message about the attack at the French bistro in Bucktown.

The message sent by her boss only had minimal details.

Giant rat-like creature in Bucktown. No one was killed. We have no idea what this story might become, but kill it. About 100 people were exposed. Thx.

She yawned as she rolled out of bed and parted her sheer curtains, revealing a multi-million dollar panoramic view of downtown and Lake Michigan from her swanky apartment in Streeterville, right on Lakeshore Drive. Traffic moved in small beads of gold and red down the winding river road. A cluster of pristine white sailboats eased across the rippling waters. The Ferris wheel at Navy Pier blinked on, coloring the sky with spokes that strobed with blue and purple lights. The sun, a fiery phantom of energy, sank over downtown, glinting off the reflective glass of nearby high-rises.

Waaaay too early to be waking up on a Friday night, but duty called.

She slipped into a magenta robe neatly folded on an ottoman at the foot of her bed. Yawning, she trekked into her ultramodern kitchen replete with a granite island, floating range hood, subzero wine cooler, and hanging pots and pans. She grabbed a tea kettle off the wall, drew water into it, and turned it on.

Her phone buzzed again.

Couldn't she just drink some tea first before Axel worked her like a dog? It was not like the world was going to end in five minutes.

She wasn't complaining, of course. That was part of her unique job description as a technomancer. It sometimes required her to sacrifice a Friday night or two.

Yawning again, she checked her text messages. Axel sent her screenshots of social media profiles where people were sharing images of a giant…rat?

Jesus Christ, what was that thing? Why was it wielding a tree?

Cynthia had never liked rats. The things she saw on the job sometimes were enough to give her nightmares. It was the main reason why she no longer slept at night. As a paranormal, it was better to be awake when the things that went bump in the night were bumping. Then maybe you could stay alive and defend yourself.

She strolled into her office, with built-in bookcases and a large standing desk covered with computer monitors. She often did her best work while looking out over the harbor, when the waters were black and the horizon was a line of empty sky, clouds, stars, and possibility. The depths of the lake, which might as well have been an ocean, reminded her of the depths of the paranormal, depths which not even she knew.

As a major city in the Midwest, Chicago got a little of everything. She'd seen dream mages that ripped people's minds apart while they slept. The photos of the casualties were never pleasant, and she was happy to run interference to make sure the general public never, ever saw them. She'd seen Kelpies who chose Lake Michigan for their effrontery, harpy sightings in the suburbs, lupine activity in the city's parks, and rogue spirits that possessed people and needed exorcisms that took the life of the host. She saw things that no one should ever have to see, but at least she got paid for it.

She held her palm over her phone and blue energy pulsed from it. With a fluid motion, she gestured to her computer, and all the images that Axel sent her appeared on her monitor. The computer worked on its own accord, searching, searching, searching…

As a technomancer, her mind interfaced with technology and allowed her to search, interact, and edit content with her thoughts. She was paid handsomely to run interference any time a human tried to share the paranormal world on the Internet.

They called her the "battering ram." She could make even the most ardent believer of ghosts doubt themselves and everything they ever believed. She'd manipulate content, trace it back to people's devices, and doctor it at the source, and then she'd use some good old hacking and stealth to send an army of bots after the person to gaslight them. She did this in seconds without leaving a trace. Not even the best hackers in the world could detect her magic. The result was that her marks suffered a dizzying decay of mental health, anxiety, and self-doubt. She didn't care about the damage—clean-up was someone else's problem.

On each of her monitors, a social media profile appeared. She leaned in and looked at one: a Marisol Garza in the Ukrainian Village.

Cynthia blinked and every social media profile that Marisol ever owned appeared on the screen in cascading windows. Cynthia flicked through them until she found a post on a network that said, "Gonna be on the news tonight. You won't believe what I saw. Monsters in the city!"

Cynthia puffed. It sounded so ridiculous when humans

described their encounters with the paranormal world. They often sounded childlike.

She identified a picture on Marisol's profile. A restaurant. Looked like a fancy French bistro. The windows were blown out and a crowd of people was gathered around.

"Nope," Cynthia said, waving a finger. Instantly, the photo went blurry, like Marisol had taken the image with a finger accidentally over the lens. The location data on the post disappeared, and Cynthia tagged it with a curse so that it wouldn't show up in other's feeds even if Marisol tried to share it. Next, she edited the post by misspelling the word "monsters." Now the post had the words "edited" in parentheses, which would undermine Marisol and raise doubts about what the original post said.

She rolled over to a laptop and blinked Marisol's profile onto it. She spoke a few words, and they appeared on the screen.

"Are you kidding me?"

"This is a joke. Stop posting bullshit on here."

"People like you shouldn't be allowed to reproduce. Do you seriously think there are monsters in Chicago? Get OUTTA here!"

Then the computer took over. Dozens of fake people replied to her post. One even sent her a threatening direct message.

Cynthia wheeled back over to her main monitors.

"Next," she said, yawning.

Marisol's profiles disappeared from the computer and another person's appeared.

A text message interrupted her work.

Progress?

Geez, Axel…

She beamed a response to the phone.

Paranoid much?

Three dancing dots appeared as Axel replied.

Got a bad feeling about this one, that's all. Thanks for your work. God/demon bless, whichever you're feeling tonight.

In the kitchen, the water in her kettle began to hop. She had about a minute left before it steamed. She could wipe out the next person in that time, so she started battering another person's profile.

A scratching sound came from the kitchen, and she paused. She turned her head and looked out of the office.

Scrrrssh…Scrrsssh…eek!

She jumped in her chair.

"Hello?" she asked.

She crept into the kitchen and glanced around. Nothing except the kettle on the stove.

She flicked the lights on in the living room. Her expensive leather furniture and wall-mounted television sat in silence.

She did a lap around the apartment, turning on all the lights. She wondered if the sound had come from a neighbor's. Even though she lived in a luxury high-rise, the walls were thin.

The next profile was waiting for her when she reentered the office.

So was a brown rat. It stood on the desk, studying the profile. The monitors bathed it in a pale glow, and smoke emanated from its body.

She yelled and pointed her hands at the rat, blasting it with a wave of blue energy. The rat shrieked as it struck the window. It lay on the floor, unmoving.

"What the hell?" she asked.

In the kitchen, her kettle was ready to blow. The fact that it was going to steam gave her even more anxiety.

More scurrying came from beneath the desk. Her kettle blew.

Whooooooooooooo….

Slowly, she crouched and screamed again as she beheld dozens of rats chewing the wires underneath her desk. They pulsed with purple plasma and smoke, their eyes glowed red, and they munched on her computer equipment as if it were a feast.

The kettle subdued her scream.

The floor creaked behind her.

She turned around just in time to see a giant rat laughing at her.

No, not a rat—an amalgamation of them in the shape of one, walking on hind legs. Rats scurried all over its body. All of them emanated smoke and their eyes were red. The rat might as well have looked like it was bleeding because of the many red eyes within its depths.

She held out her hands to fight, but a fistful of rats slammed into her, knocking her into her desk. Her monitors crashed to the floor.

Tiny little rat jaws tore into her skin and she screamed, trying to pull them off, but the fist of rats closed around her throat, followed by rat teeth, which sliced her skin.

The fist lifted her into the air, and the teeth let go, tearing her.

She broke through the window and sailed into the sky in a screech of broken glass.

The last thing she saw before nose-diving toward Lakeshore Drive was the giant rat, which seemed to be laughing as her tea kettle whistled madly, and the little rats under her desk who had stopped briefly to regard her fate. Then they started chewing again, and she fell thirty-two stories.

CHAPTER SEVEN

FUMING, Becca hung a "closed for a private event" sign on the front door of the Wicked Cat. Even though she had an agreement with Desmond to shut the shop down whenever the Regulators needed it, this was horrible timing—right before her busiest hours.

A couple wandered up to the door.

"What do you mean you're closed?" a man asked. "We made plans to hang out here tonight."

"Private event," Becca said. "We forgot to put it on the calendar on our website. I'm sorry. If you wait a moment, I'll give you a voucher for two free drinks next time."

The man swatted at her and walked away with his girlfriend.

As the sign swung on the window, Becca wondered how many more customers she was going to lose.

She wasn't losing money, though. She got Desmond to agree to pay her for lost revenue any time he made her shut the shop down with less than 24 hours' notice. He'd never asked her to close early before, so this was the first test to see if he would honor the contract. There was the small question of how much revenue she would lose, but that was simple math.

She watched the couple cross the street to another bar. She tried not to think about the terrible service that place provided, along with terrible domestic beer choices and rude waitresses.

Suddenly, the wind blew, knocking the sign against the window repeatedly. It came out of nowhere, and it ruffled Becca's bandanna, making her self-conscious about her hair. She felt a slight shiver as she adjusted the bandanna, tightening it. Then, the feeling as if something were passing through her. Her heart beat faster and she looked up and down the street.

No one.

She adjusted the sign, pulled a roll of scotch tape from her apron, and taped it to the window.

When she opened the door, she hesitated as resistance pulled her back, like something was pushing her and trying to stop her from passing through.

The door chimed, and Cristián, who was mixing a screwdriver, glanced at the door.

"You all right?" he asked.

Becca stepped in. "I think so. I had a weird feeling just now."

She closed the door quickly behind her and joined Cristián at the bar. He slid her the screwdriver.

"Maybe you should ask Desmond about it," Cristián said, spearing a lime wedge with a toothpick. "Nothing seems to be normal around here anymore."

"Tell me about it," she said. She sipped her drink, relaxing as the alcohol burned her lips, then replaced itself with sweetness.

She could have done with something harder, but something told her not to drink too much tonight; she would need as much brainpower as she could muster. It had taken every excuse she could manage to get Gilberto to leave. But she wasn't going to go back on her word. She had agreed to meet him in two hours at a church address.

"If you think I'm lying, give me a chance to prove you wrong," the nervous man had said. "I know I sound like a crackpot, but I promise that I wouldn't have asked you for help if I didn't need it."

"There are millions of people in the city," Becca had said. "And you came to me? How do you expect me to help you? I'm not even a paranormal."

"You and your brother are just what I need," Gilberto said. "I won't take no for an answer. We had a deal, remember?"

"What are you so afraid of?" Becca asked.

"I can't tell you here," Gilberto said.

"If not here, come to my office," Becca said, gesturing toward the kitchen.

But Gilberto shook his head. "No. Not here. It has to be somewhere safe. I'm taking a risk by even coming here."

His voice faded, and she stared into the brownish-orange liquor, lost in her thoughts.

"You're not okay," Cristián said.

"Says who?" Becca asked, taking another sip.

"When you start acting like Cyrus, that's never a good sign," Cristián said. He leaned on the counter, staring at her with a look of concern.

"Cyrus and I are nothing alike," Becca said.

"You both get this far-gone gaze whenever you're thinking about a problem," Cristián said. "Remember when Cyrus was strung out over Jules? Whenever I spoke with him, he might as well have been on Jupiter, even though he was standing right in front of me. I'm talking to you right now, but I'll be damned if you're processing a word I'm saying."

Becca set down the drink and met his eyes. "I'm sorry. I just have a lot I'm dealing with right now, okay?"

"You don't have to do it alone," Cristián said. "You and Cyrus act like you're bearing crosses. We're a community, Bec. And with the paranormals here, we ought to stick together more than ever."

She was touched, but she didn't know what to say. Instead, she took another swig of her drink.

The door chimed, and a black man in a long leather trench coat, black shirt, a gold chain, and sunglasses entered the Wicked Cat. Desmond flipped his sunglasses into his hair and looked around at the coffee shop that was empty save for a few waiters, Becca, and Cristián. He furrowed his mustache and said, "No one's here yet? What a night."

Cristián waved. "Want the usual?"

Desmond wandered over to the bar. "No, just some ice water. I prefer to stay sharp tonight." He looked over at Becca. "I figured we'd have to do this at some point, but I didn't think it would be tonight."

"Just as long as you're paying me, we're fine," Becca said. "Oh, and the next time you recommend an employee to me, would you please avoid narcissistic assholes?"

A sly smile spread across Desmond's face. "I heard about Quincy. Can't say I'm surprised. Sorry, Becca. What did he do?"

Becca frowned. "He couldn't get an order right even if his life was at stake. When I fired him, he threatened to kill me and said that he would relish in my destruction if I was ever wanted by a bounty hunter service. Suffice to say I kicked him out. Other than that, he was a wonderful hire."

Desmond sat down. "Don't worry. He won't be a problem."

The tone in his voice was final, and she knew that he would take care of it. She never had to tell him twice about bad clients.

"Our friend also came to visit," Becca said.

"Friend?"

"The healer."

Desmond winced. "I don't need any more shit tonight."

"You think *I* do?" Becca asked. "I don't know what he wants, but I'm probably going to need help."

"All right," Desmond said. "If I'm alive, I'll help you out."

Becca's eyes widened. Desmond wasn't one to crack jokes.

Several people entered the shop. She recognized them as shifters who frequented the Wicked Cat. They were regular people, and you would've never known that they could turn into animals.

"It's about time y'all showed up," Desmond said. "You'd think there was an emergency or something."

"Sorry," a middle-aged man said. "Lotta police out. Some of the roads in Bucktown are blocked off. The L isn't running on time either."

Becca hopped off her stool and pushed two tables together, and told some of the shifters to sit down. Then she started taking orders, grateful for the opportunity to take her mind off the problem at hand. Before long, she was mixing drinks, pouring beers, and passing back and forth between the bar and the dining floor as if on autopilot.

The door chimed as Rocco entered.

"Cyrus and Luna will be here shortly," he said, looking at Becca. "They decided to walk."

Becca stopped and put her hand on her hip. "Cyrus is on a date," she said. "You didn't seriously interrupt the first date he's been on in months, did you?"

Rocco's jaw dropped. "Hey, I didn't make the rules."

"I don't need my brother being grouchy tonight," Becca said. She paused to think. Why was Rocco commenting on Cyrus's whereabouts? Why was Cyrus with Luna?

"Desmond!" she cried.

"Maybe you want to tell her what happened," Rocco said to Desmond.

Desmond sat at the bar cradling his ice water. He opened his mouth to speak when the door chimed again and an entourage of people walked in, making all the shifters stop and turn.

A man wearing an unbuttoned sky-blue polo, and khaki shorts entered. He had a well-manicured beard that was so long, it was almost biblical. If he wasn't at the Wicked Cat, Becca would have mistaken him for an extra in a Bible movie.

A teenage boy with a baby face followed him. He couldn't have been older than fifteen or sixteen. Though he didn't have a beard, he looked like the man's son. He even wore a matching polo.

A woman with cropped brown hair accompanied the man as well. She looked like a personal assistant the way she followed the man around. She ran to the tables that Becca had pushed together and snapped her fingers. Three people sitting at the head of the table scrambled out of their chairs. The woman pulled the chairs back and gestured to the man.

A shadow drew Becca's eye toward the kitchen. Rocco was standing next to the swinging door as if he were making himself small. His eyes tracked the man across the room as he sat at the table.

"Desmond, thanks for the invite," the man said. "I appreciate you gathering your folks on such short notice. Let's get this going."

He glanced around and settled on Becca. "Hey, you. What's on the drink menu?"

"Why don't you try another less insulting greeting if you're looking for a drink," Becca said. "You can have one more chance."

Silence spread across the bar. A mischievous grin spread across the man's face. "Okay, well played. I'll take an energy drink. One for me, one for my son Ezekiel, and another for my assistant Johanna."

"I don't carry energy drinks," Becca said. "Can I get you a coffee instead?"

The man stared at her for a moment and his face went flat. "Well, hey, you're useless, aren't you?"

Then he ignored her, addressing the shifters at the table. "Let's get to work!"

The assistant stared at Becca incredulously, like it was a crime to be insulted by the guy.

Becca sensed fire rising in her chest. Suddenly, she couldn't see straight as she stared at this asshole who had just insulted her in front of everyone.

"Since she can't take a hint, translate for me, Johanna," the man said.

"He doesn't want to order from you anymore," Johanna, the assistant said.

"Obviously," Becca said.

"I'm waiting on an important associate," Desmond said, breaking the awkwardness. "He'll be here shortly."

"I don't care who you're waiting on," the man said. "I don't have all night."

Turn around, Becca. Turn around…

She turned and walked to Rocco, who gave her a look of pity.

"Who the hell is he?" she whispered.

Rocco motioned for her to be quiet.

She shrugged, then dragged him into the kitchen.

"Start talking," she said as the swinging doors shut.

"Be quiet," Rocco said.

"You're normally a tough guy," Becca said. "Why are you so scared of an arrogant asshole with a beard?"

"He is not just any arrogant asshole," Rocco said. "He's one of the most dangerous and powerful paranormals in the city."

Through the swinging door windows, Becca studied the man again. "Come on."

"Seriously," Rocco said, pulling her deeper into the kitchen. "He has very good hearing."

They made it to the back door before Rocco relaxed a little. Becca folded her arms.

"That's Axel Valentine, of the Valentine family," Rocco said. "Don't screw with him. Don't even speak to him again unless he speaks to you."

"I don't care who he is," Becca said. "If he talks to me like that again, I'll put him through the fucking window."

Rocco shook his head quickly. "Becca, please, please, *please* don't do that. Not even Desmond will cross him."

"What, did he beat you up or something?" she asked.

Rocco glanced nervously toward the dining room. Becca smirked, taunting him to reply.

"I asked him a question," Rocco said.

"Like what he had for breakfast?"

"No, I questioned one of his plans," Rocco said. "It was on a mission a few years ago. His orders didn't make sense, so I asked him to clarify. He took it personally. He made my life miserable. Sent his goons to intimidate me afterward."

"You are completely ridiculous right now," Becca said. "In case you've forgotten, you're a grown-ass man. Luna doesn't put up with this, does she?"

"Luna says the same thing, but I'm the one who has to pay the consequences," Rocco said. "Becca, I know you are a straight shooter. You like to deal with people as they are. And with any other paranormal, that's fine. But—"

"But what?"

"He's not what he seems," Rocco said.

"Neither am I."

The door chimed again, and out of the corner of her eye, Becca spotted Cyrus. She started for the dining room, but Rocco called her.

"Becca, I need you to trust me. Desmond will agree with me."

"We'll see," she said.

Cyrus and Luna sat at the table next to Desmond. Cyrus

looked like crap; his blazer—the thrift store one she hated—was stained red, and he had that sullen look on his face that she hadn't seen in months.

She sat at the bar and listened in on the conversation.

"Whatever this thing is," Axel said, "we have to take it out. Do we have any news?"

Silence.

"Who's the one that saw it?" Axel asked.

Desmond glanced at Cyrus. Soon, all eyes were on him.

Luna took Cyrus's arm and whispered something to him. His eyes widened at what she told him.

He hesitated at first, but then he told his story.

Becca leaned back on the stool, closed her eyes, and pressed her fingers against her temples.

Giant rat… Murgalen…

It was going to be a long night.

CHAPTER EIGHT

Marisol Garza had never received a death threat before. She had always thought it was something that someone did on a piece of paper that they dropped in a mailbox and shipped halfway across the country with no return address.

This death threat arrived in the inbox of her favorite social media app in the form of an instant message shortly after the attack.

Keep posting about monsters and maybe you'll wish a monster had killed you after I'm done with you.

It came from a Caucasian woman in Morton Grove. Her photo was a sunny selfie in a bikini on the beach, with a dog's snout at the bottom trying to bomb the photo. Somehow, the fact that the threat came from someone who didn't look like a loon made it even more intimidating.

Marisol stared the woman in the eyes. If someone could do something this brazen with a public profile, there was no telling what they would do in person.

She couldn't stop staring at the screen. Her hands trembled.

She didn't deserve this!

All she'd done was post about her experience at the French

bistro. Why *wouldn't* she share her experience with a giant rat monster that crashed through the window and tried to kill her? What was so wrong with that?

The rat monster was real—she'd seen it with her own eyes. Surely she couldn't have been the only one. And this…bitch felt the need to threaten her. It's not like she was spouting UFO conspiracy theories.

Anger numbed Marisol as she swiped back to the post that had started it all. At least, how she remembered it:

Gonna be on the news tonight. You won't believe what I saw. Monsters in the city!

She read the post incredulously. "Monsters" was misspelled and the post appeared edited, even though she never did that. She most definitely did not misspell monsters.

Someone had manipulated her words.

How?

She checked her email app. When someone logged in from an unverified location, the social media company was supposed to email her.

Her email inbox was empty, like usual. She tapped on her spam filter and trash folders, and they were empty too. Just how she liked them.

But how could this happen?

Someone had changed her words just now. Was her phone hacked? She would have to make all of her social profiles private now. What about her address? It was public record online…anyone could find her if they wanted. She didn't use an alias on her social media profiles.

A lump formed in her throat.

Was she being watched? She darted out of her chair and rushed around her apartment, drawing curtains over her windows. A quick, furtive glance out the window showed her street below, a busy avenue with tons of foot traffic and swaying trees.

She noted every car in front of her apartment building.

They were all empty. Or maybe someone was hiding in the back…

She closed the curtains again quickly and rested against the wall, her phone in hand.

Who would have the gall to do this to her, send her a death threat and change her words? Why not just *delete* her words? That would have had a better effect.

She swiped over to the woman's profile. Other than a location in Morton Grove, it was blank. The woman off-line.

Marisol kicked off her flats and settled at her desk. She was still wearing the clothes from her date. Her hair smelled like smoke and she desperately needed a shower. She almost died on a date with a handsome but super awkward guy. Her night couldn't get much worse, or so she thought.

She swiped back to her inbox and took a deep breath.

She had watched a motivational video on the Internet once about how the only way around a problem was through it. She tried to channel that courage.

She wasn't one to back down from a fight. Once, at work, she'd worked on a project to reconcile data from seven different sources. She worked on a solution for several months, only to be told by her boss that the project was scrapped. Boy, did she let her boss have it. The project was reinstated by the end of the week.

Transferable skills, she told herself as she typed a response to her new enemy.

Last I checked, death threats are illegal. Maybe you'd like to explain your message to the police?

She wanted to tell her *"órale."* Bring it on.

She fished deep into her purse for a business card for the reporter she spoke with at the scene of the attack. Letitia Frankland. She was a dark-skinned black woman with long curly hair, red lipstick, and a bright purple dress.

Marisol dialed and waited, walking around her tiny apartment with her cell phone cradled against her ear.

The reporter answered. Wind obscured her voice.

"This is Letitia."

"Miss Frankland, hi, my name is Marisol and you interviewed me earlier about the monster attack."

Letitia hesitated. "Oh, hi."

"I have something you may want to add to your story."

Letitia told her to wait a moment. When she returned, the wind noise was gone and her voice was clearer.

"What can I do for you, Miss Garza?" Letitia asked.

Marisol paced as she told the reporter everything.

CHAPTER NINE

Letitia Frankland leaned against a brick wall in a dark alleyway and took notes as Marisol told her about the death threat. She listened with concern, letting Marisol do all the talking. The woman spoke quickly, her voice trembling with fear and anger.

Letitia scrawled chicken scratch on her detective pad as Marisol spoke. She resisted the urge to roll her eyes.

Rat monster. Interview. Death threat. Blah. Blah. Blah…

"Thanks for letting me know," Letitia said after Marisol finished. She was in the middle of a wiry doodle that she had grown quite fond of. "Have you called the police?"

"Not yet."

"I would highly recommend it," Letitia said.

"Are you going to cover this story?" Marisol asked. "I can visit you for an interview."

Letitia frowned. All humans were the same every time this happened. They got a death threat and felt the full force of Cynthia Longvale's "cyber battering ram," and suddenly, they were scared for their lives.

As an empath, she sensed Marisol growing more frustrated, and desperate. Letitia could have used her powers to connect with Marisol, to drive her to calmness. But instead, Letitia turned cold.

"I'm sorry, but I can't cover this story," Letitia said, faking a smile. Marisol let out a puff of air and Letitia started to reply, when a car horn startled her. She peeked around the corner of the alley and spotted the news van. The driver, her partner in crime, leaned out of the window and motioned for her to hurry up. Down the street, firefighters were still dumping water on hotspots in the French bistro, and a small crowd of people was still watching behind barricades.

"Why won't you take the story?" Marisol asked.

"Miss Garza," Letitia said, "I'm just a field reporter."

"But it's your job to report stories!" Marisol cried.

Anger. Frustration. The little voice in Letitia's head yelled at her now. The words that she could have said to defuse the situation: *Here's a number you can call. Tell them I sent you…*But Letitia forced them out of her mind.

"It's my job to cover the news, not criminal instances," Letitia said. "I strongly recommend that you call law enforcement and report this incident to them. They'll know what to do."

"If I get killed, you'll cover the story, right?" Marisol asked. "Then will there be enough sizzle for you?"

"I've got to go," Letitia said. "Miss Garza, please take care of yourself."

Letitia hung up.

If only this woman knew that she was never in any danger.

She pulled up her text messages and sent a note to her colleague, Cynthia Longvale.

Hey, Cynth. Your hammer is working mighty well tonight. Maybe go a little easier on folks? You're making my night difficult.

She stuck her phone in her pink leather wallet and jogged over to the news van.

"Another death threat victim?" Kedron asked. He wore a purple striped polo, thick glasses, and had Japanese tattoos down one arm. "Cynthia's crushing it tonight."

Kedron's cool, easygoing spirit helped her shake the residue from her interaction with Marisol. He was only a little peeved for having to wait so long. That she could deal with.

Letitia laughed as she hopped into the news van. The air-conditioning died a few weeks ago and the station hadn't repaired it yet. A wall of heat settled around her and she fanned herself.

"If it weren't for us, the city would be freaking out right now," Letitia said. "Hopefully, Cynthia can keep a handle on social media."

Kedron backed the news van up and inched onto the street. "Come on, do people even trust social media?"

"Not me," Letitia said.

They drove a few blocks in silence. Letitia rolled down the window and let in a cool night breeze.

They had a long, long shift ahead of them, but at least they could drop the news van off and do the rest of their shift in the office. This heat was going to kill her. It was hotter in the van than outside.

"I win the bet," Kedron said.

"Bet?"

"You forgot that soon, eh?" Kedron asked. "I told you that we'd have another paranormal incident before the air-conditioning got repaired." He nudged her. "I want a soda and a hot dog on Monday for lunch."

Letitia harrumphed. "If we don't die in this heat, maybe I'll keep my promise."

As two paranormal suppressors, they did a lot of waiting around. Mostly, they covered typical news stories: house fires, shootings (God, she hated shootings), corporate ribbon-cuttings, and heartwarming stories of neighbors helping each other. Reporting wasn't glamorous, but it paid her rent. It was her first paycheck.

Her second paycheck came directly from Axel Valentine himself, and it was for "paranormal events." Once or twice a month, they'd get the call to speak to people about an encounter with the paranormal.

Letitia would hold her microphone in front of the interviewee, look concerned, ask questions, and even stand in front of the camera and report on the story.

Except the camera wasn't rolling, and they weren't broadcasting. And the executives were in on it too. It was the biggest scam she'd ever heard of.

"You're a glorified therapist," Axel told her once. "Your job is to make people feel heard."

"And when they don't see themselves on TV?" Letitia had asked.

"We'll handle that," Axel said, laughing.

She still heard his asshole laugh every time she hung up with another human who thought they were going to expose the paranormal to the world. Ha. Ha.

Just another night in Chicago…

WHAM!

An impact slammed Letitia against her seat.

"Kedron, are you okay?" Letitia asked, rubbing her neck.

"What the hell?" Kedron asked. The impact had knocked his glasses off, and he was fishing for them. He put the van in park and a sickening crunch came from the floor.

"Goddamn it!" he cried. "I broke my glasses!"

Letitia checked the side-view mirror. She didn't see another car.

"Stay here," Letitia said. "I'll find out what happened." Her head was spinning and her neck stiffened.

She opened the door to the van and climbed out, grabbing her wallet. A red car approached and the driver motioned to her, twirling his wrists as if he were telling her to hurry up. Then he sped past.

Fear radiated from the car—gut-grabbing, blood-chilling fear that sent her empath senses into survival mode.

More cars sped past faster than normal. No one wanted to stick around.

"Kedron, call the station," Letitia said. "I'll look at the damage and call the police."

Traffic flowed around the van as Letitia stumbled toward the rear, her head spinning.

She expected to see a car stopped behind them, but there were none—just a steady stream of cars passing by.

The rear bumper of the van was crumpled in as if something had kicked it.

More cars zipped by, honking their horns. Every horn elevated her senses.

Run! Run! her empath voice shouted at her, but her mind told her to keep investigating.

She crouched further to observe the damage to the bumper, but her foot landed on something, and it cracked.

A twig.

All around the back of the van were twigs. And leaves.

A rat darted beneath her feet and she screamed, jumping to her feet. The rat stood up on its hind legs and stared at her with red plasma eyes.

A giant roar ripped across the street. The ground shook. Letitia stumbled toward the side of the van. She needed to call Axel.

First, she saw a giant tree rise over the top of the van as if it were growing out of the ground.

Second, the tree slammed down on the driver's side of the news van, pancaking it. Letitia screamed Kedron's name.

Third, the tree went flying and landed in the middle of the road, blocking cars from passing.

Fourth, the giant rat stomped on what was left of the van, using it as a springboard into the air.

Her empath voice screamed, *Pure hatred and malice!*

As the giant rat barreled toward her, she could have sworn she heard someone singing underneath the rat's screeches.

CHAPTER TEN

"You're the rat shifter everyone's been talking about," Axel Valentine said.

Axel established eye contact and didn't break it. Looking at the man was like being an ant under a magnifying glass.

He glanced at Becca sitting at the bar. She looked irritated, just as he expected. Something must have been bothering her because her lips were turned in a slight scowl.

"Help me understand something," Axel said, stroking the end of his long, biblical beard. "You took a girl out for French food on the first date?"

He pounded the table and laughed. His muscular arms jolted the table and nearly toppled the drinks on the table. No one else laughed.

Cyrus glanced at Luna, who shook her head slightly, telling him not to speak.

Cyrus stared at him. Who the hell was this guy and what was so funny about that?

"I'm sorry," Axel said. "Looks like you had a bad night. What else can you tell us?"

"Nothing," Cyrus said. "Other than that nymphs want the giant rat dead. Immediately."

"Noooo," Axel said. "Who bothered you? Oleandra?"

Cyrus was surprised that the man knew the nymph's name.

"I bet she was serious too," Axel said. "I can take care of her. If she knows I'm involved, she'll back off. At least, she better. We've got history, me and her, but I don't have time for any nymph bullshit tonight. I'm already cleaning up Murgalen's mess."

He regarded Cyrus again and softened. "Rat kid, how many people were in the restaurant?"

"My name is Cyrus."

"How many?"

"A few dozen," Cyrus said. "They were all taking pictures."

"I've got a gal working on that," Axel said. "My team is working to suppress this from the public. But I need to know where we might be able to find it next. There's too much we don't know."

"I have no idea," Cyrus said. "I was hoping everyone here could help."

"Help we can," Axel said. "Desmond, I need your shifters to divide the city up."

"I'm already working on that," Desmond said.

"I knew you would," Axel said. "I'll suppress this from the media. The next time the thing appears will hopefully give us enough information to track it down. But it would be nice if rat kid could talk to it."

"Cyrus," Cyrus said.

One of the shifters spoke nervously. "Uh, Mr. Valentine…"

Axel's gaze went to a television over the bar playing the news on mute.

He snapped his fingers at Cristián. "Put the sound on!"

Cristián unmuted the TV, where a male news anchor in a studio gave a report.

"Authorities are investigating a mysterious string of deaths across the city tonight," the anchor said. "Eyewitnesses say that a woman may have jumped from the thirty-second floor of the Smyrna Condominium Tower in Streeterville. In Skokie, a man was found dead in his home. Sources say he was a police officer for the city of Chicago. At city hall, an aide was found dead in her office."

"What the hell," Axel said under his breath. He pulled out his phone and sent several quick text messages.

"In other news," the anchor said, "authorities are working extra hard tonight investigating an attack at a Bucktown restaurant..."

Axel rose and knocked his chair over.

"That's my team," he said quietly.

"Your team?" Desmond asked.

"The ones who were supposed to contain this," Axel said.

He snatched a glass off the table and flung it on the floor, shattering it. "Ladies and gentlemen, our lives just got ten thousand times harder," Axel said. He dialed on his phone and took a call outside. Everyone else at the table watched the news report in silence.

Becca curled her finger at Cyrus.

Relieved to get away, Cyrus joined her at the bar.

"We need to talk in private," she said.

He followed her into her office, where she quickly shut the door behind him.

"Crazy night," he said.

Becca paced around the office. "That's one way of putting it."

"What's wrong?" he asked. "I'm not having a good night either."

Becca closed her eyes and sighed. "Remember when you got turned into a rat, we took you to that healer in Hermosa, and he made us both promise to help him out in the future in exchange for an antidote?"

Cyrus exhaled. He didn't have time for this right now. "Can't it wait 'til tomorrow?"

"Apparently not," Becca said.

"What does he want?"

"He didn't say," Becca said. "I have no idea how he found me because I never gave him my address or my name. But he found me. He kept looking out the window, like someone was following him. He wouldn't give me answers, but he insisted that if we didn't help him, he was screwed."

"How is that our problem?" Cyrus said.

"Cy, I promised him," Becca said. "If it weren't for him, you'd be dead. We owe him, and we can't go back on our word."

"This is the worst timing ever," Cyrus said.

"I don't like it either," she said. "I told him that I would meet him in an hour at a church in Hermosa."

"A church?"

Becca shrugged. "Cy, I don't want to go alone."

The fear in her voice made him pause.

"I just don't know what's normal with these paranormals yet," Becca said. "Ever since Gilberto dropped by, I've felt unsettled, like the time when I had to save you, but worse."

"All right," Cyrus said. "We'll leave now. Desmond will have to manage."

Becca lightened and forced a smile as she tugged at his blazer. "Let me guess: you tried to crack a stupid joke while you were pouring wine, and you spilled it all over yourself."

"Don't remind me," he said. "Might I say that your hair is looking phenomenally violet today?"

Becca punched him on the shoulder. "When I promised Gilberto that I would help him out, I didn't promise that you would live long enough to complete the deal," she said.

They returned to the dining room floor, where Axel was standing at the front door.

"Where the hell have you been?" he asked.

Cyrus was really starting to hate this guy. He chose not to answer.

"We need you, rat kid," Axel said.

"I have another engagement," Cyrus said. "I'll catch up with you later."

Axel acted like Cyrus said something in a foreign language. "Excuse me?" he asked, leaning forward. "*This* is your engagement."

Desmond rose. "Cyrus, is there any way your affairs can wait until tomorrow?"

Cyrus shook his head. "Desmond, I'll tell you later."

"I recommend you reconsider," Desmond said slowly and quietly. "I'll tell *you* later."

"Cy, this can't wait," Becca said.

"I'll let you ride with me, rat kid," Axel said, motioning to the door. "Ever rode in a Bentley before? It'll blow—"

"Excuse me," Becca said, interrupting sharply, "since you haven't noticed, my brother and I both have self-respect, and we won't let you boss us around. Leave us alone."

"Do you know who I am?" Axel asked.

"Honestly, I don't care," Becca said. "And since you are on your way out, get the fuck out of my bar and don't come back."

Silence. Cyrus swore he heard someone gulp.

"Oh, you made a big mistake," Axel said, staring at Becca. "A big mistake."

"I asked you nicely," Becca said. "I suggest you leave before I start throwing things."

Axel puffed, gave Cyrus and Becca a lingering sneer, and walked out. Before shutting the door, he stopped and said, "Rat kid, if I didn't need you tonight, your sister would be a very sorry woman."

He snapped a finger. "My associate Johanna will text you the address. You better show up, or Oleandra will be the least of your worries."

He slammed the door behind him, making Cyrus jump.

"That was unwise," Desmond said.

"You've known me long enough to know that I don't take crap from anybody," Becca said, staring after Axel.

"Well, who was so important that you had to make my life hell tonight?" Desmond asked.

"Gilberto Sanchez," Becca said. "And if you don't mind, he's waiting on us right now."

CHAPTER ELEVEN

CYRUS AND BECCA took a bus to Hermosa, the next neighborhood to the west of Logan Square.

Cyrus was so exhausted that he could barely think. His feet just led him, one step after another alongside Becca. At least his sister still had focus and energy, but she was more anxious than usual tonight.

"Cy, what did we get ourselves into?" she asked, folding her arms. She stopped next to a green space.

"I'm sorry, Bec, but I'm brain dead right now. Can we not talk about this, please?"

Becca ignored his comment. "That Valentine guy is bad news."

"Yeah, especially after you ripped into him," Cyrus said. "He's a huge asshole. This isn't going to end well."

"I keep wondering if I made a mistake in doing a deal with Desmond," Becca said. "He tried to warn me that things would never be the same at the bar."

"He would have kept an eye on you anyway," Cyrus said. "Better to get something out of it."

They continued walking and crossed a street that stretched into mature trees and houses.

"I've been thinking about Dad a lot," Becca said.

"Really?"

Cyrus thought about his dad, smiling, adjusting his thick Coke-bottle glasses, sitting at the dining room table amid a stack of papers at tax time. It was the warmest thing he'd thought about all night, and a welcome distraction.

Becca shrugged. "No idea why. I mean, I always miss him."

"I wonder what he'd say about all this," Cyrus said, laughing.

"He'd probably be logical about it," Becca said. She imitated his voice. "Now, Bec, what do you think is the right thing to do?"

"He always loved turning questions on us," Cyrus said.

Becca laughed and then sighed. "Cy, we better be careful." She extended a fist.

"Yeah," Cyrus said, bumping her. "Hopefully, this time next week, we'll be relaxing and laughing about this."

They continued the rest of their walk in silence.

La Iglesia del Espiritu Santo was a three-story, stately but rundown brick building on a tree-lined street. The building had historic brickwork, with red and white bricks that formed crosses between the windows.

The parking lot was empty, but through wrought-iron gates on the first floor, a single light flickered.

Cyrus and Becca stood at the entrance, a double cedar door with a black cross on each door.

Cyrus glanced across the street at a giant red-brick elementary school with Chicago flags flying on the roof. Cars were parked along the street, but they were all empty.

"Why a church again?" Cyrus asked.

"No idea," Becca said. "He wouldn't meet me anywhere else."

"Is he going to meet us outside or inside?" Cyrus asked.

"Inside," Becca said.

Cyrus gestured toward the door. "After you. Just in case there's a bad guy inside, he can pick you off first."

"Absolutely not," Becca said. "You're the one who's supposed to protect *me*. You're also the one who speaks Spanish, remember?"

Cyrus's face went long. "That was in a past life. With Jules. Besides, I speak like Tarzan."

"Are we going to argue or are we going to get this over with?" Becca asked. "I can think of a million other things I'd rather be doing right now."

Cyrus tried the brass door handle. The door was so heavy, it could have withstood a battering ram. Made sense given the crime in the city.

He poked his head into a foyer. An old, musty odor hit him hard. A lot of historic buildings had a certain smell to them—Cyrus called it the smell of distinction.

A stairwell led up to a set of brown doors that opened into a barrel-vaulted sanctuary with stone walls and cedar beams.

Cyrus held the door open for Becca and they walked into the sanctuary, where posters with psalms in Spanish hung on the walls. A backlit golden cross hung in the center of the stage.

In the corner of the room, a Latino man in a black windbreaker sat staring up at the cross. He had an air that was both relaxed and reverent. He must have heard them enter because he spoke without looking back at them.

"I was beginning to think you wouldn't show," Gilberto said. "I guess I haven't been forsaken."

"I told you we'd come," Becca said as they approached his pew. "But seriously, a lot is going on tonight. Why do I get the feeling we aren't here for missionary work?"

Gilberto finally looked over at them. "If you want to call this missionary work to make yourself feel good, I won't stop you."

This was the first time Cyrus saw Gilberto with human eyes. The man who saved his life. He didn't look nervous, not the way Becca described him.

"You healed up well," Gilberto said, grinning.

"Thanks again," Cyrus said. "I appreciate it."

Cyrus sat in the pew next to Gilberto. Becca sat in the pew in front and turned to face them, one arm resting on the back of the wood.

"What happened to you?" Gilberto asked, eyeing Cyrus's blazer.

"Long night," Cyrus said.

Silence grew between them.

"What's up, Gilberto?" Becca asked. "Why are we here?"

"This is the only safe place for me," Gilberto said. "I couldn't speak in public. It was too risky. It's a miracle I'm still alive."

Pangs struck Cyrus's stomach. He didn't want to hear what came next.

"I'm being followed," Gilberto said.

"I'd ask you to call the police, but I get the feeling it isn't that simple, is it?" Becca asked.

"It's paranormals," Gilberto said. "The police couldn't help me if they wanted to."

Silence.

"Well, then, who?" Becca asked.

"That's what I want you to find out," Gilberto said, looking at Cyrus.

Cyrus shrugged. "Why me?"

"Whoever they are, they're nearby," Gilberto said. "I'm tired of running. I want to know who they are so I can figure out who else to call for a favor."

Cyrus shook his head. "Gilberto, I want to help. But when I'm a rat, I can't see very well. I'd be useless to you."

"You can't see?" Gilberto asked. "Bullshit. If you don't want to do this for me, just say so."

"If you don't believe me, look it up," Cyrus said. "Rats have terrible eyesight."

"Whoever's following you might follow us next," Becca said sharply. "You put both of us in danger."

Gilberto cursed. He stood, dug his hands in his pockets, and walked around the sanctuary.

"There has to be something you can do," he said. "I took a gamble by even calling the two of you. If my gamble is wrong, then you might be the last two people I ever speak to." He ran a hand through his hair. "Damn. I'm fucked."

"Who do you *think* is following you?" Becca asked.

"Could be anyone," Gilberto said. "If I get killed, I can't exactly heal myself, if you know what I mean. The good Lord knows I've pissed off plenty of people in this city. All I know is that they can't enter the church if they mean to harm me. This is the only place where I'm safe."

"Tell you what," Becca said. "We will try to see if we can find out anything about the person who's following you. We can't help you stop him or her, you're on your own with that, but we will do what we can to get some intel. Deal?"

"You're not the one transforming into a rat," Gilberto said. "What can you do?"

"I'm his big sister and I make the business decisions," Becca said.

"I can make my own decisions," Cyrus said.

"Cyrus, that hasn't really been working out well for you, has it?" Becca asked, talking to him like he was a three-year-old.

Cyrus smirked as his sister continued her negotiation.

"After this task, we're good and our deal is finished," Becca said. "Agree?"

"Maybe I'll decide to cash in my favor later," Gilberto said, frowning.

"Maybe I won't listen to you next time," Becca said. "You already put us in danger. That's my half of the bargain. Take it or leave it."

"Fine," Gilberto said. He pointed at Cyrus. "I want as much as you can give me. Get extra close to them if you can."

"Give us a second to talk about it," Becca said, wandering over to Cyrus.

"Do you think this is a good idea?" Cyrus whispered. Becca took him by the shoulder and led him into the lobby, where they were out of earshot.

"It's not our fault he didn't know your actual abilities," Becca said. "I'm trying to get us out of this arrangement as safely as possible, because from the way he's acting, it's going to get dangerous fast. Just turn into a rat, do some snooping, and come back with a report. Then we can go back and help Desmond and Captain Asshole."

"Fine," Cyrus said. He waved to Gilberto. "One rat shifter expedition, coming right up."

CHAPTER TWELVE

"Nine hundred and seventy-five. Nine hundred and seventy-six. Nine hundred and seventy-seven."

Kirk sat underneath a loading bay in the alley between a furniture upholstery shop and *La Iglesia del Espiritu Santo*, smoking a cigarette and counting bricks.

Gilberto had been inside the church forever, and it was getting boring in this alley. The healer would have to come out sometime, and when he did, Kirk would end this mission, get paid, and find something, anything better to do than sitting here.

He couldn't read a book in this darkness, so he counted the bricks on the side of the church. Gave him something to do.

So far, he'd reached nine hundred and seventy-seven. He squinted at a black and white mural of Jesus wearing a crown of thorns, and that was where it got complicated. He resisted the urge to walk up the wall and inspect it. Once he reached Jesus's crown, he gave up.

"Anything?" he whispered.

"It's been around fifteen minutes since the two entered," Aidan said.

He knew his brother was far more comfortable on the roof of the school across from the church. Aidan always relished the opportunity to climb something.

"The chick from the coffee shop," Aidan said. "What's her story, you think?"

"The one with purple hair?"

"Yep."

Kirk took a drag of his cigarette. "Friday night catch-up with Jesus?"

"No service tonight."

"Hmm," Kirk said. "Then I have no idea."

"Is she some kind of paranormal or what?" Aidan asked. "I don't think so. The guy with her…he definitely was. Just couldn't tell what. Must be a boyfriend, maybe."

"They're inside talking, and whatever they're talking about, it probably isn't good," Kirk said.

A gray silhouette drifted down the alley like a lazy cloud. Once it reached Aidan, it swirled around him.

"Whaddaya know, Dad?"

Kirk looked over at his father, whose mushy silhouette was like a blistering cloud.

"Absolutely nothing," Bruce MacLeod said. "This is a damned dreadful mission your brother put me on."

"Dad says you're a screwup," Kirk said, grinning. He scissored his cigarette toward the ground and stubbed it out.

"Tell him I love him too," Aidan said.

Bruce's spirit hovered next to Kirk.

"Tell me something," Kirk said, pointing at the wall. He scratched his chin. "How many bricks do you think are on that wall? That mural is throwing me off. Looks like two bricks in the first thorn, but I've been staring at it for the last few minutes, and I'm stumped."

"Only you can make staring at the wall interesting," Bruce said wanly.

"It's the little things, Dad," Kirk said. "Give me a count."

Bruce counted quietly as the breeze blew. "Sixteen hundred and two."

"I was right," Kirk said. "The paint concealed the doubles. I win."

"You're playing against yourself," Bruce said.

"Isn't that the only game worth playing?" Kirk asked.

"Ask him about the coffee shop," Aidan said, irritated. "I don't feel like listening to you counting bricks anymore."

"There are strong wards at the door," Bruce said. "They repelled me the moment I tried to enter."

"Ah, so our lady has some magical game," Kirk said.

"I couldn't follow them into the church for obvious reasons," Bruce said. "So here I am, counting bricks."

Kirk laughed.

"Did they talk while they were coming here?" Kirk asked.

"More sibling banter than the two of you," Bruce said.

"You're wrong again, brother," Kirk said. "You're on a streak tonight."

"He kept teasing her about purple hair," Bruce said. "At one point, I thought she was going to strangle him."

"Purple hair," Kirk said. "That's dramatic."

"I had no luck," Bruce said, "so I decided to sit here and spend some time with my other favorite son."

"You only have two sons," Kirk said flatly.

Kirk and Bruce shared a laugh. Then they waited.

In rat form, Cyrus crossed the flat roof of *La Iglesia del Espiritu Santo*. The gravel roof wasn't kind to his rat feet as he found the edge of the roof, which was buttressed by bricks.

His whiskers gave him the night: summer breeze, full of the humid night air, exhaust, and the almond-sweet fragrance of a nearby cluster of maples. A car horn blared in the distance, followed by a yell. Closer, a constellation of voices and laughter floated toward him—sounded like someone having a party in their backyard.

He brushed up against the brick wall and his whiskers guided him.

He made his way across the roof, his rat brain leading him toward the spot.

"East side of the building," Gilberto had said. "There's a guy in the alley. I know he's waiting for me."

It sounded simple enough: access the roof, sneak down to the alley, and investigate. Maybe the guy was just a bum. Maybe not.

Cyrus stopped, stood on his hind legs, and sniffed. He smelled rust from a nearby pond of water on the roof, and dirty rocks. He continued his journey across the roof until his whiskers sensed an opening in the brick.

He stood on his hind legs and sniffed again, his whiskers leading him to a ledge that dropped off below. The height made his rat stomach nauseous. The church was three stories —there was no way he'd survive if he fell.

Another animal scent caught his nose. Rodent.

Not a rat, but furrier. Traces of gravel in the air.

A squirrel.

Cyrus's feet carried him onto the ledge, and up the top of the brick wall, where a metallic, buzzing energy beckoned him.

He only made out a faint line tracing itself through the sky.

A power line.

His human brain asked him what the hell he was doing, but his rat brain overruled it, and the next thing Cyrus knew, he was balancing himself on the power line. The electricity ripping through the line was so powerful, it hummed and shook the wire.

Don't die, don't die, don't die, he thought as his little feet carried him over the line as it sloped downward. His tail worked over-time to keep him balanced. All the while, the electricity thrummed through the line, shaking every bone in his rat body. Below, an alley lay below, but it was as though he was looking at it through slanted, blurry glass. Being so high up in a rat's body sharpened his sense of depth, and that didn't help his rat body's intrinsic cautiousness of heights. Thank God he couldn't see very far ahead and that he couldn't see down too well. This was the only time near-blindness worked to his advantage.

The wire swayed and Cyrus hung on, flash bangs sparking on his whiskers as he remembered Gilberto's voice.

"The power line goes to the roof of the upholstery shop next door. From there, use the gutter to get yourself down into the alley. Don't use the church downspouts, or the guy might see you."

The line seemed like a bridge over water. The electricity was so loud, he couldn't think about anything else.

His whiskers perked up as they sensed the line's run coming to an end. He jumped, and he landed on another gravel roof, surrounded by the gentle whine of roof air-conditioners.

Cyrus shook himself off and instinctively looked for some-where to hide. Phantoms of the buzzing still reverberated through his bones. He found shelter under one of the huge roof air-conditioning units. A giant fan sliced above him at several hundred rotations a minute.

He waited until his body calmed and his senses told him no predators were lurking above. Then he ventured out, sniffing at first, then running to the roof's edge where the line ended. He smelled a column of metal tinged with rainwater—a downspout several inches away.

He leaped headfirst, claws outstretched. They seized on the ridged metal of the downspout, and then all four claws dug into the small surface that was barely wide enough across for his body. His nose pointed at the ground, and he was almost defying gravity now.

One claw after the other, he scurried down the downspout. The ground loomed closer, even though he couldn't see it. His rat brain telegraphed comfort as he made it further down.

Then he passed through a wave of something that almost made him fall off the spout. His heartbeat accelerated and his rat heart throbbed rapidly in his chest.

A voice. A gush of swirling energy like a freight train.

Anger. Decay.

Screaming. The voice was screaming at the top of its lungs. An old man. A mixture of pain, longing, fear, and malice. A skull appeared in Cyrus's mind's eye, cracking apart as its jaws opened into a nightmarish scream.

The sound rattled Cyrus's skull and he wanted to shriek along with it. He froze on the downspout as the energy passed through him. His rat heart beat so hard it threatened to explode inside his chest. The skull dissolved from his vision, and the quiet night returned.

What the hell?

He dashed down the metal until it sloped against the asphalt. He jumped onto solid ground and sought shelter against another brick wall, a wave of relief washing through his body.

He made it.

The alley was narrow.

Cyrus stayed against the wall, stopping and starting on his quest toward the loading bay that Gilberto described.

A few steps later, the energy passed through him again, stopping him. The scream tore through him again, and the same skull reappeared as if it had never broken. It dissolved again as the energy faded.

Every hair on Cyrus's body stood up. His rat brain yelled to him.

Turn back. Turn back. Danger.

Gilberto's voice spoke: "If I don't figure out who's following me, it'll be the last mistake I make."

Then Becca: "Just turn into a rat, do some snooping, and come back with a report. Then we can go back and help Desmond and Captain Asshole."

His rat voice.

Danger!

He stood against the brick wall, paralyzed. He didn't know what to do, and his human and rat minds argued with each other.

The screaming didn't fade this time. It grew louder and louder, and now a pink wall of skulls washed over Cyrus. Hundreds of faces swirling and screaming and melting and whining. Cyrus instantly recognized them as dead souls, and he felt their pain.

He shrieked.

The souls keened and spiraled into the sky. They were connected. To what? The skulls collapsed into a circle, and another head rose out of them like a disgusting amalgamation. A bald, elderly man with glowing runes all over his face. His face was lit up in ultraviolet, and the runes were dark freckles on his essence. He had a hooked nose, a severe countenance, and no eyes—only gray sockets. He wore the other souls' heads like a necklace, like they belonged to him. He didn't have legs—just a barrel-shaped torso. He grinned at Cyrus with stained teeth.

The wind blew, Cyrus smelled a whiff of garbage mixed with a human scent.

Footsteps scraped against the ground and Cyrus seized up.

"Well, well, I've never seen this before," the old man said.

"What is it, Dad?" a voice asked. The man in the alley, whoever he was. Cyrus couldn't see anything with all the swirling energy.

"We've got a visitor," the old man said. "And don't be fooled by its appearance."

"Is that right?"

Cyrus started to run away, but two fingers grabbed his tail. Instantly, he was dangling in the air, his legs flailing.

He met the face of a grinning black man wearing sunglasses.

"Sometimes spies come in the strangest packages, don't they?"

CHAPTER THIRTEEN

Cyrus smashed into a bed of trash bags.

A pistol clicked.

The black man stood over the dumpster, pointing a gun at him.

"If you're a shifter, turn back," the man said.

"Kirk, don't kill him yet," the old man said. "We've got an interesting one this time."

"I prefer not to investigate, Dad," Kirk said. He waved the gun at Cyrus. "Let's go, rat."

Cyrus processed the conversation. Dad? This spirit was the guy's dad? Jesus.

Reluctantly, Cyrus shifted back into a human, lying on the trash. It stunk like rotting food in the dumpster. Flies circled him.

The black man's face sharpened into higher definition. He wore a dark blue denim jacket. His eyes were obscured by thick sunglasses.

But the old man was completely gone now. No visual trace of him remained in the air, yet Cyrus sensed him, hovering just behind Kirk. The realization scared him.

"It's blazer boy!" Kirk said.

Cyrus stared angrily.

"Help me connect some dots," Kirk said. "A few minutes ago, you entered that church. Now you're here. A reasonable assumption is that you're working with Gilberto, right?"

Cyrus said nothing.

"You can tell me," Kirk said. "It's not like I'm going to let you live for much longer anyway."

"Screw you," Cyrus said.

"You're the one who looks screwed," Kirk said, inspecting Cyrus's blazer. "You get into a fight or something, man?"

Again, Cyrus said nothing.

Kirk paused as he listened to something.

"No," he said. "Be quiet." Kirk swatted around him. "You too, Dad. Knock it off!"

Then Cyrus saw an earpiece in the man's ear, and a wire running down his neck. He was talking to someone.

"Who are you?" Cyrus asked. "And who the hell is the spirit with you?"

Kirk shrugged.

"I get to ask the questions," Kirk said.

Silence.

"I hope being loyal to Gilberto was worth it," Kirk said.

"We'll see if you find out," Cyrus said. "Go ahead and pull the trigger. I'm having a shitty night and it'll just do me a favor."

Kirk smirked, then shrugged. "You got it."

Kirk paused, his face wrinkled in concentration as the voice in his earpiece spoke. It was loud this time, and almost frantic.

"What the hell do you mean?" Kirk asked.

At the end of the alley, tires screeched and headlights swept down the narrow corridor, throwing a blinding sheen across Kirk.

An engine revved and a horn honked.

"Shit!" Kirk cried.

The man was gone in a flash, followed by a whoosh of air that rocked the dumpster.

The horn blared and blared.

Cyrus climbed out of the dumpster. A white fifteen-passenger van chased Kirk down the alley at a high speed.

There was only room enough for one of them in the alley.

Kirk ran like a marathon sprinter. He tore out of the alley and took a hard left.

The van braked hard. The tires squealed. The reverse lights switched on and it backed up toward the dumpster.

Cyrus dipped back into the trash, his heart racing.

The van pulled up to the dumpster and the horn blared again.

"Are you going to keep hiding or are you going to let me save you?" Becca asked.

"Bec?"

Cyrus peeked out of the dumpster. Becca was in the driver's seat of the van, which had the name of the church along the side.

"Get in!" she cried.

Gilberto sat up from the front passenger seat, looking in the alley for any signs of Kirk.

"Hurry up, man, before he comes back!" Gilberto cried.

Cyrus leaped over the dumpster and climbed into the backseat of the van. Becca put her arm around the passenger seat and craned her neck back as she guided the van in reverse out of the alley and into the street.

"The pastor is going to kill me," Gilberto said.

"Better you than us," Becca said, cranking the gearshift into drive.

Blam! Blam! Blam!

Cyrus dove onto the floor. One of the rear windows shattered and shards rained on his head.

Becca cursed.

"Go, go go!" Gilberto cried, covering his head.

Becca stomped on the accelerator and tore down the street, ripping past a stop sign.

"Where did that gunshot come from?" Cyrus asked. Slowly, he peeked up and spotted a man on the roof of the school, staring after them.

He must have been the one Kirk was talking to.

Becca blew through another stop sign before the quiet set in. The night air whipped through the van.

Cyrus sat up and sighed. "Gilberto, I know you wanted us to find answers, but now I have more questions."

Gilberto relaxed and sat up. He ran his hands across his short hair and let out a small whimper.

"Um, hello?" Becca asked, slowing to a stop at a green light. Her eyes darted to the rearview mirror and she muttered under her breath for the light to change. "Start talking. Now."

"They were hit men," Gilberto said. "I don't know the guy we chased. Around here, when you don't know the guy that's trying to kill you, it means you screwed up."

"And you still don't know who you pissed off?" Becca asked. "You know what? Stop. Don't answer that. I don't want to know."

She shivered. "It'd be nice to have an unbroken window right now."

Cyrus opened his mouth to speak but he sensed something pass through him.

Not wind, but something stronger. Energy.

"Cy, what's wrong?" Becca asked.

"Stop talking," Cyrus said.

"What do you—"

"Bec, be quiet!"

He shifted into a rat, landing on the worn cloth seat.

He spotted the spirit immediately. The old man was swirling in the front driver's seat, passing in and out of Becca. He was laughing maniacally.

Cyrus's rat hairs raised and he shrieked.

"I'm surprised it took you this long," the old man said. "You're endlessly fascinating, rat shifter." Then he laughed, and all the souls around his neck screamed in fright.

Cyrus transformed back into a human. "There's a spirit in the car with us."

Becca arched both eyebrows as the light turned green. "What do we do?"

Gilberto clasped his hands and prayed in Spanish. He spoke quickly, softly, and forcefully.

"Ask it to leave," Gilberto said. "It can't linger if you ask it to leave."

"Get the hell out of this van, then," Cyrus said, facing the old man's direction.

"Get out!" Becca cried.

A cold wind ripped through Cyrus, knocking him back into the seat. He sensed the old man's essence drift out the broken window, and stillness passed across the van as Gilberto completed his prayer.

Cyrus transformed back into a rat and confirmed the old man was gone.

"What is going on?" Becca asked.

Cyrus changed back and stared out the shattered rear window.

"Whoever that spirit was, it wasn't good," he said.

Aidan slipped down the fire escape of the elementary school and dashed across the parking lot to the school playground, where Kirk was doubled over between two trees, next to a jungle gym.

He watched as Kirk panted and wheezed in pain.

"You're just going to stand there?" Kirk asked, looking up.

"What else do you expect me to do?"

Kirk cursed. "Valentine isn't going to be happy."

"Not with you," Aidan said, folding his arms.

"Get out of here with that," Kirk said. "We do this together."

"You hesitated," Aidan said.

"I…sensed something," Kirk said. "Dad told me to wait. There was something…unusual about that kid."

"Unusual or not, now we've got to deal with it," Aidan said.

The wind brought Bruce's laughter to them.

"You two did great!" Bruce said.

"Great?" Aidan asked. "Do words mean different things in the afterlife?"

"I told you to wait," Bruce said to Kirk. The old man swirled around him like a python. "And you delivered."

Kirk stood. "Well? Are you going to tell us what the good news is?"

"The girl," Bruce said, rocketing into the air. "You asked me to learn more about her. I glommed her spirit, and it's beautiful. Complex. She's capable of far more than the rat. She's a perfect host."

"Dad, we don't have time for that," Kirk said, frowning.

"Make time," Bruce said coldly. "Father knows best."

A sharp pain struck Kirk's chest and he dropped to his knees as a black ball of energy bubbled from inside him.

Kirk yelled as a horned silhouette tore itself out of his chest. First came a pair of cattle horns, which pierced through Kirk's sternum, then dagger-sharp, gold ring-ridden claws, which came out in a frenzy, like a mole tearing through dirt. The demon straddled its legs out one at a time, and using Kirk as leverage, it leaped into the air.

Kirk hit the ground like a pile of empty milk crates. Thank God the demon didn't actually do damage to him. It would have been a bloody mess.

The demon landed with an enormous boom, and Aidan

looked away out of respect. All he saw were the demon's cool blue ankles, which were covered in platinum anklets.

"I want her," the demon said in a snarl.

"Garamanthus," Bruce said. "I knew you'd come digging your way into this conversation."

Bruce swirled down to Kirk.

"I told you. I can sense these things in death, you know," the old man said.

"Give me the girl," the demon said in a deep growl. "When I have her, I will release you from bondage."

The demon disappeared in a flash of dim light, Kirk turned to face the bubbling ball of energy just as it smacked into his chest, knocking him down again.

Aidan helped Kirk up.

"I'm doing you a favor," Bruce said insistently. "That's one less demon you have to please later."

"Not a favor," Kirk said.

Aidan pitied his brother. How many demons lurked inside Kirk, just like Aidan? They announced themselves at the worst times, and when they asked, they had to be obeyed.

"We'll deliver," Aidan said. "But we've got to see Valentine first. He's going to want a report."

Kirk shook out the pain and straightened his sunglasses. Aidan clapped him on the back.

Together, the brothers walked away as Bruce swirled around them, laughing triumphantly.

CHAPTER FOURTEEN

"Congratulations, Gilberto," Becca said. "You're stuck with us for the foreseeable future."

Becca eased through a left turn and waited for the GPS on Cyrus's phone to tell her where to go next. They were headed toward the Lakeshore. The wind from the broken window rippled her bandanna, but she was so concentrated on driving that she didn't adjust it for once.

"Cy, is there a tarp or something in the back you can put over the window?" Becca asked.

"Negative," Cyrus said, rooting in the back of the van.

"We can't drive around with a broken window," Gilberto said. "We'll get pulled over."

"If that happens, you can explain to the police what happened," Becca said.

"Why me?" Gilberto asked.

"When I bargained with you, my only obligation was to send my brother to spy for you," Becca said. "Now you get to deal with me, and that's probably more than you wanted."

Gilberto said something in Spanish under his breath. Becca couldn't understand a single word. All those semesters of Spanish in high school didn't pay off.

"I hear ya," Cyrus said from the backseat.

Gilberto's eyes widened. "You understand Spanish, dude?"

Cyrus shook his head. "My ex spoke it. I know just enough to understand when I'm being insulted. And to know that you said that you're fucked."

Gilberto slammed his head against the seat. "Any chance I can persuade you to drive to Mexico?"

"You're a comedian tonight," Becca said. "Nope, you're stuck with us."

Gilberto cursed again.

"We have a rendezvous with Desmond," Becca said. "We're not thrilled about it, but if things go bad, you can heal us."

"What's the deal with Desmond?" Gilberto asked.

"He's investigating a bunch of dead people," Cyrus said. "You know, a normal night."

"How did they die?" Gilberto asked.

"Not sure yet," Cyrus said, "but it wouldn't surprise me if the killers were rats."

Gilberto screwed up his face. "Rats? Like you?"

"It's a long story," Cyrus said.

"Tell Desmond to remove my magical block for good and maybe I'll be useful," Gilberto said.

Becca turned onto Lakeshore Drive. The winding river road was bathed in a tungsten glow, with passing headlights in strings of white, orange, and blue. In the distance, a high-rise glass condo complex rose into the sky, its base awash in siren lights.

"The entrance is blocked off," Becca said as they approached a circular drive in front of the building. "I have no idea where to park."

"Next block over," Cyrus said, eyeing his phone. "Desmond says there's a parking lot. He and the other shifters are there."

"Shifters?" Gilberto asked. "What kind of crap are you getting me into?"

"Nothing worse than what you've gotten us into," Becca said.

The next street over, Becca found the parking lot.

Desmond, Rocco, and a group of a dozen others had gathered in the middle. Desmond saw the van first but quickly ignored it. Then Rocco saw it and pointed. Desmond frowned and put his hands on his hips as Becca put the van into park.

She handed the keys to Gilberto. "This is your problem."

"Thanks for the confidence," Gilberto said.

"You do realize there are cops nearby, don't you?" Desmond asked as Becca hopped down from the van.

"Tell that to your friend here," Becca said, thumbing at Gilberto.

Gilberto smiled wide. "Desmond, baby, aren't you happy to see me?"

"All of you better start talking now before I decide to shift into werehyena mode," Desmond said.

Becca gave him an abbreviated summary about the two men and the spirit accompanying them.

"Describe that spirit again," Desmond said.

"Weird guy with runes all over his head," Cyrus said. "He carried a bunch of screaming souls with him in the form of a necklace. Creepy doesn't truly describe it."

"That sounds like Bruce MacLeod," Desmond said. "Makes sense that his sons would bring him back."

"Who?" Cyrus asked.

A gronk distracted the group as a raven swooped down and landed near the group. It morphed into Luna. Her face was serious, but it softened when she spotted Cyrus and Becca.

"I found a way in," Luna said. "Cyrus, you're just in time."

"One second," Cyrus said, holding up a finger. He wasn't

going to let Desmond get away with interrupting the story. "Who's Bruce MacLeod?"

"It's a long story," Desmond said. "Remind me to tell you later."

"No, tell me now," Cyrus said.

Silence.

"Later," Desmond said. "In case you've forgotten, we've got a giant rat creature loose across the city, several dead bodies, and a pissed-off nephilim who's making my life hell right now."

"Don't add a pissed-off brother and sister to your list," Becca said. "Give us the summary."

Desmond pursed his lips. He glanced at the condo. A news helicopter circled it.

"He was a necromancer," Desmond said. "A powerful one."

"That explains the souls," Cyrus said.

"Bruce was a complicated guy," Desmond said. "He was an evil necromancer and never hesitated to use the dead to serve his goals. At the same time, he and his wife took in paranormal foster children who lost their parents to the underbelly of the city. Bruce was adamant about these children having a childhood that accentuated their skills."

"How…noble," Becca said.

"Two of his kids developed a penchant for the dead," Desmond said. "One was white, and the other was black. Yet they never let their skin color get in the way of their brotherhood."

"Yep, that's them," Cyrus said. "I ran into the black guy in the alley."

"That's Kirk," Desmond said. "His brother is Aidan. Since they're inseparable, we refer to them as Aidankirk."

"Okay, that's creepy," Becca said.

"You wanted the answer, didn't you?" Desmond asked.

"They were following me," Gilberto said. "They were going to kill me."

"They're contract workers," Desmond said. "Wouldn't surprise me if someone put them up to it. But really, Gilberto, what did you do to deserve this?"

Gilberto shrugged. "Right. Blame the victim."

"We all know you aren't an angel," Desmond said. His gaze lingered on Gilberto before returning to the skyscraper. "In any case, as long as you're with us, you'll be safe."

"Remove my magical block and let me defend myself," Gilberto said. "You all made me vulnerable. I deserve a way to fight back!"

A helicopter broke the conversation, circling the air above and climbing around the skyscraper.

"We blocked your magic because of necromancy," Desmond said. "And we're not removing it this time. But I'll help you if that's what you want. It won't be free."

Gilberto muttered something.

"Um, guys," Luna said. "We don't have much time."

Desmond pointed at Cyrus. "You're up. Find your way into the woman's apartment and tell us what you can find."

Cyrus rolled his eyes. "Great. More reconnaissance."

Becca grabbed Cyrus's elbow. "Be careful, Cy. I can't keep an eye on you this time."

Cyrus put a hand on hers and nodded.

Becca's big sister vibes kicked in. She wanted to protect Cyrus, but she felt helpless now.

She watched as her little brother morphed into a rat. Luna morphed into a raven and carried him high into the sky, toward the Smyrna Condominium Tower.

CHAPTER FIFTEEN

IN THE PARKING lot of a grocery store, Aurora Grant sat in her car, staring at her cell phone's screen. She had hoped that in the 15 minutes it had taken to drive from her house to the store that Becca would have responded to her texts.

It was a rare miracle that she had gotten Cyrus on the phone earlier. Her texts to Becca went unanswered. It was Saturday night, but she didn't usually take this long to respond.

A mother shouldn't have to remind her children about her birthday, but here she was. She'd felt uneasy since sundown. She didn't know why.

Clear summer night. Nice chat with her neighbors in the front yard. Her parakeets sang more than usual tonight. Zucchinis were flowering in the garden. She read on her back porch with a glass of merlot. In other words, a perfect night. Yet she had that weird pit at the bottom of her stomach, that motherly sense something was wrong.

Were her kids drifting away from her? She barely knew Cyrus anymore. Not since he disappeared for months and returned with no explanation. If Becca knew the secret, she wasn't telling with her evasive answers. She'd hoped that maybe a night out with both of them would give her a chance to see what was really going on.

She grabbed her purse and stepped out of the car into a crowded parking lot. Several people passed with twelve packs of beer and plastic bags with meat. Everyone was dressed for the weekend. Aurora was in sweats. She was enjoying every minute of summer vacation, her only break from the university and her students, and she was determined to make the most of her leisure time, even if it meant going to the grocery store in sweats. That was one of the perks of living in the suburbs—you could hop in your car, go wherever you wanted, and not have to worry about your appearance so much.

She slung her purse over her shoulder and squeezed between two trucks.

She stepped on something squishy, and it hissed at her.

She jumped a foot in the air as a brown rat bared banana-yellow incisors at her. It lunged at her, but she hopped back, screaming.

Someone nearby said, "Holy cow, look at the size of that one!"

Aurora ran until she was safely away from the rat. Her heart raced. She had never seen a rat in Wilmette. This was a tree-lined suburb, not the heart of the city.

The moon was high over the big box grocery store when she entered. The automatic sliding doors whooshed open, ushering out the smell of fried chicken and barbecue from the grocery store's restaurant. A man in a Marines hat stomped out. Aurora met his gaze, and for a split second, she wondered if he was going to explode with anger.

"Don't bother going in there," the man said. "There are so many rats in there that I wouldn't trust the food."

"I saw one just now," Aurora said, confused. "I didn't think we had a rat problem here."

"That makes two of us," the man said, not looking back.

Rats in the grocery store…

Aurora processed the thought as she grabbed a cart and pushed it into the produce section. Surely this had to be a joke. She'd lived in Chicago a long time, but despite the headlines, she'd never seen too many personally unless she was in an alley.

She passed the first end cap in the produce section. She raised a pineapple and spotted a blur in the corner of her eye on the checkered floor.

Another rat raced around her feet, and she dropped the pineapple, screaming again.

"What is going on?" she cried.

A manager with slicked black hair wearing a blue button-up shirt approached her, wringing his hands.

"We're very sorry, ma'am," the man said. "We don't know what's going on."

"You have rats," Aurora said.

"It's not just us," the manager said. "This is happening all over."

Shouts erupted all over the grocery store like a dissonant symphony.

"Attention, shoppers," a voice on the intercom system said. "We are experiencing a minor problem with pests in the store. We will be closing for the rest of the night so we can address the issue. Thank you for your understanding."

"I wouldn't buy that pineapple if I were you," the manager said.

Aurora looked at the pineapple and slowly put it back.

A teenage girl pushed her cart rapidly past, constantly looking over her shoulder. She crashed into an elderly man on a scooter.

"Watch it!" the old man cried.

The girl whimpered as she pointed back at a rat that darted across the aisle. The man flinched at the sight and gunned his scooter toward the door.

Goosebumps popped up across Aurora's arms, along with

a sense of dread. She tightened her purse around her arm and jogged to the door. A steady stream of people joined her, and she fought her way through the crowd.

"What the hell is going on?" one person asked.

"One of the rats bit me," a child cried.

"How am I supposed to make dinner now?" a third person said.

Soon, Aurora found herself in the humid night. Headlights and taillights flashed across the parking lot.

After narrowly missing a collision with a pickup, Aurora tip-toed back to her car, one eye on the ground watching for the rat that she had stepped on earlier. Could rats remember people? She didn't stand a chance if it ambushed her from underneath a car.

A rat ran by and she jumped over it and quickened her pace.

She fumbled for her keys and threw herself headfirst into her car, slamming the door behind her once she was safely in. She took a deep breath and centered herself amid screams and blaring car horns.

She backed out of her spot quickly, almost colliding with a van.

Only when she joined a line of cars exiting the lot did she relax—just a little.

She switched the radio on.

"Authorities are working extra hard tonight investigating an attack at a Bucktown restaurant, where eyewitnesses are reporting a large rat disturbing patrons. Authorities believe it may have been an elaborate costume."

"Is this a joke?" Aurora asked.

Traffic loosened somewhat and she inched forward. A brown blur darted in front of the car, and she braked.

Aurora squinted and studied the rodent. It ran in a haphazard circle. It looked confused. Another rat trampled it on its way across the lot.

Aurora almost felt sorry for the little things. They reminded her of scared dogs.

All across the lot, the rats were acting in the same erratic manner. Something had stirred them up and forced them aboveground. She didn't know what it was like to be a rat, but she empathized. At least, as long as she was safe from them.

Hunger pangs struck her stomach. She'd come here for dinner, and now she was leaving empty-handed. She thought about stopping at a sub shop for dinner, but maybe they had the rat problem too.

"I guess I'll settle for a frozen pizza for dinner," she said, pulling out of the parking lot.

CHAPTER SIXTEEN

Luna set Cyrus down gently on the roof of the tower. Cyrus dug his feet into the soft, black rubber roof membrane and instinctively looked for shelter.

He followed a flapping of wings to his left and found shelter next to a vent stack. Rust flaked off as he nestled against the cold steel.

A helicopter droned through the air, and Cyrus's rat ears told him it was near. He waited for the noise to fade before transitioning into a human.

Luna, in human form, sat next to the stack. She pointed toward a triangle-shaped structure. "Door's on the other side of that," she said. "No idea what you'll find inside. A lot of these towers have roof detection systems, so you might want to shift once you enter."

"Gotcha."

"I got you up here," Luna said. "The rest is up to you."

She tilted her head at Cyrus in concern. "Be careful. I don't like that Axel is putting you up to this."

"The sooner I do it, the sooner we'll all get rid of him," Cyrus said.

"You're a brave gent, Cyrus Grant," Luna said. "Braver than my boyfriend."

Cyrus shrugged. "I have my big sister to back me up if something goes wrong. If someone messes with me, Becca only has one setting, and that setting is nuclear."

Luna laughed and then covered her mouth at the realization that they were supposed to be hiding.

They stopped and listened.

"The helicopter is swinging back," Luna said. She kissed Cyrus on the cheek and wished him luck. She shifted and took to the sky.

Cyrus watched her trail downward for a moment, wondering if that kiss might be a final goodbye. He'd talked a good game about having courage, but now he wasn't so sure, glancing out across the beady city lights along the shore of Lake Michigan.

He centered himself and shifted back to a rat, plopping onto the rubber roof. He sniffed his way in the direction Luna pointed, across pools of water, constellations of rust and dust, and the remnants of footprints, probably from maintenance workers.

A spotlight above swept across the roof, blinding him. The helicopter's engine blew over him like a hurricane, and he sheltered in place, his heart pounding.

The light left him as quickly as it lit him up. Could the helicopter operator even see a rat from up there?

No way.

The realization of invincibility quickened his step as darkness fell across the roof like silent rain. He dashed across the rubber membrane, his whiskers orienting him toward the triangle he saw earlier.

He expected a cacophony of smells, but this high up, the city didn't smell like much, other than smog, exhaust, and occasional smells wafting in the air that he couldn't place.

Mostly, it was cold; the wind tore through his bones because there was nothing to protect him from it up here.

He sought shelter against another vent stack. He stood on his hind legs and sniffed. A cluster of metal lay just a few feet away. He knew it was the structure. He even smelled a difference in the air around it. Warmth radiated from the triangle, though he couldn't see it.

He investigated the distance between him and the structure. All clear. He paused and listened to the sky. Nothing.

He morphed into his human form and crouched against the edge of the roof. Ahead, he faced an orange door.

He looked at the sky one more time, saw the helicopter making its round over Lake Michigan. It sliced through the sky diagonally, its beacons glowing over the jewel-dark waters.

He didn't have much time. Still crouching, he rushed to the door and opened it. He didn't crawl in. Instead, he shifted into a rat again and slipped in just before the door shut.

He hoped his eyes would have adjusted to the darkness a little more, but he could hardly see a thing.

He sniffed. His whiskers led him to a small drop-off.

A stairwell.

He hopped down the first step. Then the next. Cold concrete met his feet every time. Before long, he found himself in a carpeted hallway. The carpet stank like dirt, specks of rainwater, and other unfathomable residue people tracked in from the streets below on their shoes. The lights were dim, and he could only rely on his whiskers and sense of smell to guide him.

He made his way down the hallway, hugging the wall.

A distant mechanical sound made him pause. Far, far below, he heard a ding, followed by screeching metal.

Silence.

Then clanging doors again, and metal grinding against metal as a ghostly whine rose toward him.

An elevator.

He sniffed again, searching for more metal. His nose told him that he wasn't far away from an elevator shaft.

The end of the hallway brought him to two gray doors. He couldn't tell if they were gray or if it was his colorblindness. But their smooth texture and his whiskers brushing against them told him they were elevator doors.

He waited, sure that no one was around before he shifted into a human, long enough to press the downward call button before shifting back to a rat again.

The doors opened to an empty elevator car with metal railings and mirrors on three of the walls. Cyrus rushed in, transitioned to human, hit the button for the seventeenth floor, and made the rest of the journey downward as a rat, staring at himself on his hind legs.

This was the first time he got a look at his brown rat self, though he couldn't see himself that well. The mirror was more like a funhouse distortion. Wasn't that a metaphor for his life up to this point?

He preened his ears as a mechanical voice announced the floor and snapped him from his reverie.

When the doors opened this time, several people stood in the hallway.

Cyrus slipped out of the elevator just before the doors shut and hid under the shadow of a couch in a waiting area. Thank God the hallway was dimly lit. Good ol' Chicago residences had a lot of good things—bright hallways weren't one of them.

"Hey, did you see that?" someone asked in a Chicago accent.

"What?" a female voice asked.

"I swear I'm not crazy. The elevator door just opened. And there was no one on it."

"I don't know what you're talking about."

The first voice paused. "Huh. I need more coffee."

The two bodies walked away, leaving behind a quiet soundtrack of camera shutters and murmurs.

He sniffed and detected sweat—fresh, from people nearby. Several people. Police. They were a few yards away, recessed in a condo.

The hallway was clear, so he raced to a nearby wall, where a thick carpet with an elaborate circular design started.

He started, stopped, started, stopped as he ventured closer to the condo.

The door was ajar.

"Nothing about this makes any sense," a voice said as it moved deeper into the condo.

Cyrus stopped at the doorway. He traced the voices—they were at least a room away from the door.

Quietly, he snuck in.

Though he couldn't see very much, the condo smelled swanky and clean, like the places he saw in ads but could never afford. The concrete floor was polished to a high gloss.

He found a kitchen just off the foyer and raced into it, hiding between a metal trash can and a cabinet.

"Has anybody found out what the hell this lady does for a living?" the voice asked again, returning to the kitchen. Thick boots pounded on the concrete floor, then stopped.

"From what we could find, she's some kind of computer programmer," a female voice said.

"That explains the computers," the voice said. "But not why all the wires are chewed to hell."

Cyrus ventured out from behind the trash can. The cold concrete floor was covered with dusty footsteps from police boots. He navigated around them to avoid anyone seeing rat prints.

A quick succession of photo flashes drew his ear to a room in the distance. He dashed alongside the kitchen cabinets, then into a wide-open space, hoping that no one would see him. He found shelter under a chaise lounge and rested on a thick, furry blanket. His nose pointed him toward the room, where he smelled night air and the hot buzz of camera filament.

A human shape moved out of the room and across the living room. The front door opened, then shut.

The apartment was empty.

Cyrus knew this was his chance. He raced from the chaise lounge into the room that the police were talking about.

He stopped on the threshold. A languid, coppery smell floated into his nose.

Blood. Little pools of it radiated from the center of the floor.

He tracked along the wall until he arrived at a massive bundle of wires that snaked around the room. The wires were chewed apart, their innards exposed and dangling along the baseboard of the room. The hot and metallic flash bangs of circuits assaulted his whiskers as they rubbed the wires. The little rat voice inside his head screamed at him.

Rats. Rats. Rats!

The same rotten smell from the restaurant returned to him, when the giant rat had been standing over him and rats swarmed over its body and he thought it would be the end and he saw Murgalen's face.

Had the giant rat been here? He was certain of it.

A breeze blew through the room. He sensed that the window was broken from the way the wind shook shards loose, making them fall to the floor like coins.

He reconciled the blood and the night air. The woman who lived here hadn't jumped. She had been thrown out.

But what about the wires?

Cyrus told himself that he was an idiot for what he was about to do, but he couldn't leave here without answers.

His rat sense told him that the apartment would be clear for a little while. He morphed into his human form, and the condo sharpened into view around him.

Damn. This place was nice. Easily a million-dollar condo.

He glimpsed the ultramodern kitchen that was probably worth more than the entire Wicked Cat building.

He studied the office. A desk with several computer monitors. A jagged maw in the window behind the desk. With his eyes, he followed the trail of wires that ran around the room toward a desktop computer that sat lifelessly beneath the desk. He squinted.

Why were the rats chewing on the wires in the room?

A gentle buzzing rose from the desk and he spotted a cell phone neatly inside a sandwich evidence bag. The screen illuminated and Cyrus craned his head to see who it was—the name "Letitia" flashed on the screen.

The front door opened, sending his instincts into hyperdrive.

"You hear that?"

He shifted back into a rat and zoomed under the desk as footsteps approached the room.

"Looks like we got a phone call, huh?" the female officer asked.

"Who's it from?" the male officer asked.

"A Miss Letitia," the woman said. "Could be someone we need to talk to."

"The life of law enforcement, huh?" the man asked.

Cyrus sensed his window closing. He ventured to the threshold of the office. The two officers were standing nearby, conversing. Then they turned their backs, and Cyrus rushed into the kitchen.

The front door opened again and someone called the two officers. Cyrus detected a single man in the hallway.

"Come on in," the male officer said.

A shadow passed Cyrus, shaking the ground with its footsteps.

The hinges on the door creaked. Cyrus ran as fast as he could.

The door was closing. Closing!

At the last second, he squeezed through and the door clicked shut behind him.

Panting, he dashed down the darkened hallway toward the elevator. No one saw him as he rode the elevator down to the lobby, zoomed past police barricades, slipped into the automatic revolving door, and onto the street, where Luna, who had been waiting on a car, scooped him up and carried him away.

CHAPTER SEVENTEEN

Letitia Frankland expected to die as she stared at the giant rat monster barreling down at her. Rats writhed up and down the beast's body and its energy-filled eyes hardened. It meant murder.

Her mouth wouldn't let her scream. Her feet wouldn't let her run.

She looked the beast right in the eyes and chose to face her fate. She would die standing tall.

The rat sneered.

WHOOSH!

A blue blast slammed into the beast, knocking it out of the air. It crashed onto the street in an explosion of screeching rats.

Blue magic sparkles lingered in Letitia's peripheral vision, drawing her eyes to the news van that lay crushed on the road.

Kedron hung out the passenger window. His face was bloodied. His busted glasses hung crooked on his nose.

She cried his name and ran toward him, but he held out his hands to stop.

He tried to speak, but blood sputtered across his lips and dribbled down the side of the van.

The little empath voice spoke softly to her.

Pain. Love. Sacrifice.

"Kedron," she said, tears in her eyes.

Kedron raised his hands. More blue energy bloomed from them.

The rat climbed to its feet, wobbled, and narrowed its eyes at Kedron. It roared angrily.

Letitia ran as the rat charged Kedron and a brilliant flash turned the street negative.

Her feet carried her through alleys, across busy streets, through parks, and other places of the city she had never been. The chains on her leather wallet jostled against her wrist.

She ran silently.

Every week, she and a group of friends ran together at a local park. Sometimes they'd chat as they ran down the jogging path. Other times, they'd just run in each other's company, swiftly and in unison. The world would fall away and it was as if they all had a single brain that told them where to go and where to step.

Letitia closed her eyes for a split second and imagined her girls running alongside her, drawing on their collective wisdom of the streets to tell her where to step, how fast to go, and how to pace herself.

She opened her eyes and kept going, her hands raised into furious blades. The chains on her leather wallet slapped the air as she clutched it tight.

She couldn't trust anyone. Not even the bystanders who turned as she passed, probably recognizing her from TV. She ran and ran and ran, past liquor stores and cell phone shops and pizzerias and storefront churches and brownstones and cultural murals.

She stopped at a quiet corner and caught her breath. She glanced behind her at an empty sidewalk and panted with relief.

Images of Kedron's bloody face rushed back to her. Tears poured down her cheeks for him. She wiped them away.

She wouldn't let his death be in vain.

She pulled her phone from her wallet. Should she call Kedron's girlfriend? No. Letitia needed to tell her in person. It wouldn't be any consolation but at least they could hold each other and share their grief.

All that mattered now was getting to Axel Valentine's. She'd be safe in the compound.

By foot, it'd take her all night to get there. But she couldn't take a bus. She wasn't going to trap herself like Kedron.

She called Axel.

No answer.

She called the station.

No answer.

She cursed.

She dialed the only other person she could trust—her friend, Cynthia.

"Pick up, Cynth, please," she whispered.

"You've reached the voicemail of Cynthia Longvale…"

Letitia looked up at the sky, stretching her neck. The adrenaline had distracted her from the pain of the car accident. The moon blunted the starry sky and she wondered why tonight of all nights had to be the night she encountered death.

She was no stranger to danger, but it never came when she expected, and she had never gotten used to it—not as a news anchor and definitely not as a paranormal.

Her phone vibrated. The words "Scam Likely" appeared on the screen. She answered anyway.

"Hello? Please help!"

A robotic voice replied.

"Hello! Letitia, don't let your car warranty expire— "

She disconnected.

Maybe *that* should have been her next story—scammy telemarketers and how they called even when you were running for your life. That was a story everyone in the city would get behind.

A small tremor shook the ground.

She froze.

Boom…Boom…Boom…

Every hair on her body stood on end and time slowed down.

A hundred hisses blew on the wind, carried up into a staticky screech as the shaking intensified.

Boom…Boom.

Letitia turned around as the giant rat stomped toward her, snarling.

CHAPTER EIGHTEEN

BECCA HATED TWO THINGS: awkward silence and awkward conversation. She had to endure both as she stood on the grass in the parking lot with Gilberto waiting for Cyrus to return. Gilberto had been trying to talk about the weather, and she secretly hoped he'd tell her why he was being followed. But it wasn't her business.

"What do you think he's gonna find up there?" Gilberto asked.

"Hopefully some balls," Becca said.

"That kid has a lot of balls if you ask me," Gilberto said.

"I'm pretty proud of my brother," Becca said. "But I get to make fun of him too."

Gilberto put his hands on the back of his head. "Sorry I put you guys through this. I'll make it up to you."

"I like the sound of that," Becca said, folding her arms.

She watched the moon glinting off the cold glass of the skyscraper as the helicopter circled it again, sweeping a spotlight across the building. Something wild must have been going on up there. She couldn't imagine making the same circles over and over again. It would have been so boring.

Hopefully, Cyrus didn't get caught or crushed. She didn't

even want to think about what unknown dangers a rat would encounter up there.

Her mind went back to the Wicked Cat. At least one or two patrons were probably drunk by now. Did she have enough vodka to last through the night? She couldn't remember. It irritated customers when she ran out.

She hated that she couldn't settle her mind—it kept racing in different directions. If only she could focus! Then she might figure out how she and Cyrus could get out of this mess.

Someone whistled in her direction. She turned to see Axel Valentine crossing the street toward them. He walked with his shoulders out—like a jock. He didn't even look when he crossed the street because he was too busy beelining for her. Becca felt her face grow flush at the very sight of him.

She said kind words to herself to calm her mind down. She told herself that she'd be the bigger person…unless circumstances required her fist to strike his face.

"You looking for trouble?" Axel asked, pointing.

"What's your problem?" Becca asked.

Gilberto stammered. His skin was as pale as the church van. He backed away.

"H-h-he's not talking to you," Gilberto said quietly.

"You're more allergic to him than I am," Becca said.

Gilberto didn't reply.

"If he's an enemy of yours, he's an enemy of mine," Becca said. "And he was already an enemy, so…"

"Well?" Axel asked, approaching.

"F-f-fuck off," Gilberto said, stepping back.

"Last I heard, you don't have your magic," Axel said. "If I destroy you, there's no healing yourself this time."

"That's two people now that can't stand the sight of you," Becca said, stepping in front of Gilberto.

Axel smirked, a glimmer in his eye. "There's no window to put me through here."

"Don't you have better things to be doing right now?" Becca asked. "I thought you were supposed to be important."

Axel smirked at Becca again as his hands glowed with white streams of power. He made a parting motion, and she slid out of the way. Static energy held Becca in place as if she had been Tasered. She couldn't move her arms or legs. She opened her mouth to curse Axel, but her mouth filled with violent static, keeping her quiet.

Axel pointed at Gilberto. Suddenly, Gilberto levitated in the air, his legs kicking and thrashing under him.

"Leave me alone!" Gilberto asked.

Footsteps tore across the parking lot.

"Dad, don't do it," a voice said. Axel's teenage son, Ezekiel. He grabbed his father by the shoulder, eyes widened with worry.

"Maybe you should," another voice said. Axel's short-haired secretary Johanna stood next to Axel, staring at Gilberto scornfully. "Therese would be alive if he hadn't failed."

"I did my best to save her," Gilberto said.

"Your best wasn't good enough," Axel said. "I asked you to do one fucking job."

Job? Becca couldn't follow, but whatever job it was, it must have been in the past.

"Dad, you can't let the hate destroy your heart," Ezekiel said. A tear welled in his eye.

Axel turned his head slightly to his son. "One day you'll understand."

Gilberto let out a small cry.

Becca wanted to curse, but the static washed through her skull, more painful now.

Axel turned to Gilberto and growled. Then, with an aggressive arching gesture, he hurled Gilberto across the parking lot. Gilberto screamed and crashed into the canopy of a nearby tree.

Axel laughed. "Score!"

Johanna crossed her arms and looked the other way.

Ezekiel sighed with relief. "Dad, I'm glad you didn't—"

Axel raised a hand, silencing his son. He snapped his fingers, and the static energy around Becca faded.

"What the hell," Becca said, shaking out her arms. They tingled like they had gone to sleep.

"Mind your business," Axel said, not even looking at her. He hollered to the tree and said, "Gilberto, get the fuck out of that tree and get down here. If you want to redeem yourself, I got a job for your ass. Otherwise, if I ever see you again, you won't be so lucky."

A groan emerged from the tree, and several leaves rustled as Gilberto scrambled down.

Becca started to say something snarky but stopped. If Axel could send Gilberto flying into a tree, he could probably do worse to her. Never egg on a paranormal when their magic was hot—she had already learned that the hard way tending bar.

She rushed over to Gilberto as he landed at the trunk of the tree, leaves in his hair. She helped him up.

"He's a certified organic asshole," Becca said, "but I'm glad you're all right."

Gilberto said a small prayer. "Me too."

Axel whistled and motioned for him to hurry up.

"You shouldn't listen to him," Becca said. "Even though I don't think his threat was idle, you have more dignity than that."

Gilberto groaned. "Dignity? What's that?" he asked sarcastically. "If it comes down to living or getting flattened, I'll take my chances."

"It's up to you," Becca said. "If it were me, I'd walk away."

Desmond had joined Axel when they reached him again. Desmond stared at Gilberto, shaking his head.

"The life of a healer," Desmond said.

"Any news?" Becca asked.

"Not yet," Desmond said. "We haven't heard anything on the scanners, so Cyrus must be undetected."

"Desmond, unblock Gilberto's magic," Axel said. "I need him to do something for me."

Desmond looked as if Axel had asked him to kill someone. "Mr. Valentine—"

"I need it," Axel said. He stared up at the skyscraper. "I've only got a limited amount of time for magic before they haul the body away."

"The district gave me hell last time for removing his block," Desmond said. "You have no idea how many people I had to give a report to—"

"I'll talk to whoever I need to talk to," Axel said. "I don't want to ask you again, Desmond. Do me a favor, will you?"

Desmond frowned and said, "Yes, sir, Mr. Valentine."

Becca wanted to slap Desmond. He did everything this clown asked, even addressed him by his last name. The deference sickened her.

"Gilberto, I authorize you to use your magic to assist Mr. Valentine," Desmond said.

"Got it," Gilberto said dejectedly.

The last time Desmond removed his magical block, Gilberto had been elated. He danced around his house and cranked up his music, drinking too much beer. Now, getting his block removed was more like a death sentence.

"All of this is messed up," Becca whispered to Desmond. "You're not helping."

"Tell me something I don't know," Desmond said. "I'll be glad when this night is over." He glanced at Gilberto one final time and walked away, shaking his head.

Something told Becca to go with Gilberto. She didn't know why, but she followed Gilberto, Axel, and his entourage as they crossed the street.

"I'll give you a little cover," Axel said, "but we don't have much time. Even I can get in trouble for doing what we're about to do."

What was he about to do?

Axel motioned for them to wait. He jogged across the street to the police cordons.

A police officer yelled at him to stay back.

Axel snapped his fingers, and the officer froze, his eyelids closed in a weird half-blink. He looked as if he were having a seizure.

"Let's go!" Axel said.

Becca ran with Gilberto and Axel's entourage across the street past the cordon. Becca stopped for a moment at the officer, who was convulsing just like she had been.

Ahead, Axel froze two other officers mid-blink. They barely saw him coming. Whatever they were seeing now, it was in their eyelids. She quickened her pace and joined the group as they made their way down a small alley next to the Smyrna Condominium Tower.

The alley broke into a parking lot covered with squad cars. A rack of large work lights stood in the middle of the parking lot, surrounded by caution tape.

Becca's stomach turned into a knot at the sight of a hand, curled fingers, and a splatter of blood.

"Oh my God," Becca said.

The stench of bowels and blood barreled into her and she wanted to vomit.

Death.

"You may want to stay back," Gilberto said.

But Becca couldn't stop herself. She kept walking forward, toward the dead body on the asphalt.

Several officers around the area froze, convulsing quietly.

"Let's go, healer," Axel said. "I've got about five minutes before people start asking why these officers aren't responding."

Gilberto gulped.

"Necromancy!" Axel shouted. "Since you can't take a hint!"

Becca remembered that Gilberto had gotten in trouble because of necromancy. Something about resurrecting his dead mother and robbing a bank. Was it really possible to heal the dead?

Cynthia Longvale's body was flattened against the ground. The impact had created a small crater of cracked cement. Her skull was shattered, blonde hair strewn about. Her mouth was open in agonizing pain as if she had been screaming the entire way down. Her eyes were milky. Her arms were covered with little bite marks that oozed blood.

Becca couldn't look away.

Gilberto knelt and said a prayer in Spanish. How he didn't vomit at the sight of her astonished Becca, but maybe he'd seen worse.

Gilberto touched the dead woman's arm and continued praying. Green energy suffused from his hands and flowed into her. He opened his coat and pulled out a travel kit that looked like a grooming kit. Instead of hygiene supplies, it was filled with herbs and small bottles of Florida water.

He pulled out a stick of Palo Santo and lit it. The heady smell of sweetwood wafted into Becca's nose.

"This dispels the negative energy," Gilberto said. "I want you to know that I am here for good. You don't have to return to pain."

The woman's finger made a small, almost imperceptible twitch. Becca saw it before Gilberto. Then—it reached up and grabbed his wrist.

Becca jumped and her heart raced.

Gilberto looked as if he had been expecting the gesture. He leaned in close.

"Who did this to you?"

The woman's eyes were still milky, but they moved in

Becca's direction. She opened her jaws of broken teeth and gasped.

The woman wouldn't stop staring at her. Then, she blinked and Becca almost fainted. Her legs went weak and it was a miracle she could still stand. All the dead woman was doing was staring, but she might as well be casting a spell. Why the hell was she staring?

Yet Becca didn't look away. She stared into the woman's glazed-over eyes.

Gilberto took the dead woman's hand in his.

"Please trust me," he said. "I need to know who did this to you."

Slowly, the woman's face animated to life; her broken jaw of cracked teeth hung down, a line furrowed one half of her face, one eyebrow arched, then drooped. She gripped Gilberto's hand so tight he couldn't pull away.

"Ruh…" the woman said.

"Come again," Gilberto said.

"Ruh…"

Becca mouthed the syllables with the woman, trying to say them with her.

Then the woman's head and neck snapped up from the concrete and she intensified her gaze at Becca.

"Ruh…" the woman cried. "Rats!"

The dead woman screamed at the top of her lungs, her eyes rolling up into her skull. Then her head slammed into the concrete and she died. Gilberto hung his head and said a prayer as her hand relinquished his arm. He placed her other hand over her heart.

"Fuck me," he said. He stood and turned to Axel. "She said rats. She couldn't tell me."

Axel cursed. "What did she mean, 'rats'?"

"No earthly idea," Gilberto said.

Becca glanced at the bite marks on the woman's arm. "No, she meant rats."

"Rats?" Gilberto asked. "Like, a shame?"

"No, rats!" Becca cried. "Like the rodents, idiots."

Axel's eyes widened. Then he looked up at the skyscraper.

"Looks like we've got ourselves a rodent problem, then," he said.

CHAPTER NINETEEN

"YOU BOYS DOUBTED ME, but I'm right again," Bruce said as he swirled through the moonroof of Aidan's sedan.

He circled Kirk, who watched his father's spirit wanly as it settled into the skull on the dashboard. The skull's tattooed runes glowed and swirled.

"Father knows best," Bruce said. "Hee hee ho! Old Brucey has still got it."

"Is that right?" Kirk asked, pursing his lips.

He wasn't keen on his father's recommendation to make Rebecca Grant a demon host, but he wasn't going to say no to his dad, even in death. The bastard would haunt him. Since Kirk was a necromancer, that was saying something.

"She's a hell of a girl," Bruce said. "She might even be your type, Kirk."

"Eh, Dad, how come Kirk gets all the ladies?" Aidan asked jokingly.

"He's better looking," Bruce said. "What can I say?"

"That hurts," Aidan said.

"Out of the two of you, you can handle the truth, Aidan."

Kirk's jaw dropped. "What's that supposed to mean?"

Silence.

"Dad," Kirk said after a moment, "you don't think I'm good-looking at all, do you?"

Bruce squawked, and the laugh told him everything he needed to know. Kirk didn't know whether to be offended or to laugh.

Aidan put a hand on Kirk's shoulder. "I guess that means I'm handsome and a realist and you're an optimist and ugly."

"Such is life, apparently," Kirk said, folding his arms. "But I'll have the last laugh, Dad. All the ugly guys get the ladies in the end."

Kirk spied the parking lot across the street where paranormals had gathered. He kept a lock on Desmond Lovelace, who paced the lot as if waiting for a report. The tall man's leather trench coat was a dead giveaway for a paranormal—no one wore a jacket like that in summer unless they were selling something illegal or wanted to give off a don't-fuck-with-me vibe.

"Dad?" Kirk asked. "What made you so happy that you had to come back and insult me?"

"I just witnessed an extraordinary event," Bruce said. "It looks like your mark knows necromancy."

"Gilberto?" Kirk asked. "Well, shit."

"Hold on," Aidan said. "Necromancy with a little N or big N? He doesn't look like the type who would deal with a demon."

"He can speak to the dead," Bruce said. "As for demons, it's never too late to start."

"Valentine didn't tell us about this," Aidan said.

"He brought a woman back from the dead," Bruce said.

"The one who fell from the tower?" Aidan asked.

"She even sat up," Bruce said. He let out another sinister squawk.

Aidan smacked his forehead. "You didn't do what I think you did," he said.

"Of course I talked to her," Bruce said. "Told her to

behold the lady in the camo tank top and purple hair. Come on, boys—even the dead couldn't have missed that purple hair. We freaked the girl out something terrible."

"Which one?" Kirk asked.

"Both!" Bruce exclaimed.

"You're horrible," Kirk said.

"A host must believe," Bruce said, his runes glowing more intensely. "They must feel the power of the dead. Only then can they be opened up to the possibilities of a demon host. And then, there's just the final matter of a blood swap."

The skull did a quarter turn, and the spirit pinpoints stared right at Kirk.

"It's one less demon you two have to carry," Bruce said. "Your mother would advise you to unload a few."

Kirk puffed and wished he had something to reply to the utter absurdity that Mom cared at all when it was she who made them *believe* in the first place. Mom, with her candlelit séances and stories about the dead she'd tell the kids at the kitchen table, and the way she'd hold their bodies as the demons entered them and they screamed and screamed as the darkness ravaged their insides. All so she and Bruce could complete a shadow deal. How screwed up did you have to be to do that to your kids in the name of love? How screwed up did you have to be to follow the same path?

Outside, Desmond was gone. Kirk lost his lock.

"Where'd Desmond go?" Kirk asked.

All the paranormals were gone.

"Shall I?" Bruce asked.

"You've done enough for tonight," Kirk said, slipping on sunglasses. He nodded to Aidan and gave him a fist bump.

"I'll report back," Kirk said.

He slipped from the car into the hot summer night.

~

Aidan watched Kirk's back as he slunk into the shadows of a hedgerow along the street. Kirk broke into a crouch and disappeared under the foliage.

"I'll keep you posted," Kirk said through the earpiece.

"Gotcha, brother."

Aidan settled and glanced across the parking lot. It was still empty. He cracked his window. The crickets were loud as hell tonight.

"Now that I can dispense some truth," Bruce said after a while, "I don't trust that Axel Valentine. I never did. You really should have called me before you did a deal with him. I could have counseled you."

Aidan watched Kirk disappear around a corner. His brother never wasted time on a mission.

"I hear you, Dad," Aidan said. "But we don't choose who we go to bed with. We just care about the money."

"I taught you to be mercenary," Bruce said. "But not stupid."

"Not many can do what we do," Aidan said. "You made sure of that."

"I suppose," Bruce said. "I'm going to keep an eye on Valentine for you."

"You sure that's a good idea?" Aidan asked.

The skull's eye points wiggled as Bruce laughed. "I'm dead and can do whatever I—"

Bruce stopped.

"What is it?" Aidan asked.

"Son, check your six."

Bruce's spirit shot out of the skull like a Roman candle and through the moonroof.

"What the?"

A glance in the rearview mirror showed several people approaching. Paranormals.

Were they coming after him?

Aidan turned the key in the ignition and inched the car forward, but he was too late.

An impact rocked the car and Aidan flew forward, hitting his head on the steering wheel. His earpiece fell into the cup holder.

His world slanted as the car lifted upward like a bad carnival ride.

"Son of a— "

Gravity brought him tumbling onto the dashboard, with his face smashed against the windshield. Then he came face-to-face with a giant, salivating werehyena in a trench coat with a gold chain.

Desmond Lovelace growled as he held the car up, and when he met Aidan's eyes, he shook the car.

Aidan bounced off the walls like a pinball.

Kirk turned a corner, making his way toward the crime scene.

How crazy he was, heading directly into the heart of the problem.

But if he didn't track Desmond, he'd lose Valentine. They had to give him a status update; it couldn't wait.

He found an apartment building diagonally across from the tower with a dimly lit doorway. It had tall hedges, and there was an alcove by the front door adorned with vines and flowers on the wall.

He stood in the shadowed doorway with his hands in his pockets.

He listened. The night bustled around him, full of sirens and hushed whispers and helicopter blades.

A beet-red SUV passed by slowly, its driver rubbernecking to see the incident.

What the hell was going on over here?

Part of him said he didn't care. The other part of him was morbidly curious.

The helicopter droned past, toward the lake.

"Any news?" Kirk asked quietly.

His brother didn't respond.

Kirk puffed. Aidan usually responded.

"Come at me when it's safe," Kirk said. "I'll be here. I'm at…"

He looked behind him at the address on the door. There was no number.

"Never mind," he said.

The helicopter droned past again, toward the lake. Was it circling?

Maybe he needed to move.

Across the street, several officers were talking next to a barricade.

A beet-red SUV passed by again, the same driver craning to get a good look at the scene.

Kirk's gut dropped when the helicopter blazed overhead a third time toward the lake.

"Tell me you're free now," he said quietly.

Silence.

"Brother?"

An electric shock ripped through his ear. He tore his earpiece out. The small black unit burned as it fell to the ground. The wire vanished in smoke.

Behind him, the glass door to the apartment complex creaked open. A strong gust of wind nudged him toward the threshold.

He slanted his eyes at the apartment lobby awaiting him, a beautiful, Italian-style room with marble floors and chandeliers. On the other end of the lobby was a courtyard with a fountain of a naked woman holding a sword.

Kirk put his hand over his heart and shifted his mind to dark thoughts. Blood. Death. Suffering. The darker the thoughts became, the more vividly he saw them against his mind's eye. Skulls and bones and screams and bloody wounds and people crying and stained-glass windows shattering and candles being snuffed and everything that signaled the death of hope.

He muttered an incantation his father had taught him when he was a teenager.

A fullness of energy bloomed in his chest, a mixture of pride and hatred.

Hard, bony fingers took hold of his ribs, pushed them aside, and clawed their way out of his chest.

Kirk suppressed a scream as the demon birthed itself from him—first sharp claws, then curved cattle horns, and a blob-like body of shadows and twinkling fire that smashed to the ground. The impact shook Kirk to one knee.

Emptiness settled into his chest, and he felt lighter. His chest pounded and his heart raced. He centered his thoughts on the mission.

A warm sweat had broken on his brow, and he wiped it off with his arm.

He'd done this enough times to still be coherent when the demon exited after a summoning. The first time a demon crawled out of him, it almost killed him. He'd lost conscious-ness and awoke to a face that haunted him. He learned the hard way to never make eye contact.

The demon turned. Kirk dropped to his knees and beheld a pair of bony feet adorned in golden rings and swirling shadows that moved like a furious pencil was scribbling them in real-time. He didn't dare look up.

"I ask for your protection," Kirk said, hand on his heart.

The demon's voice came out in a stentorian growl.

"From whom?"

"Whoever's in there," Kirk said, pointing into the lobby. "Name your price."

The demon laughed.

"I told you my price."

Kirk sighed. "The girl, right?"

"I will do this job for you free of charge."

"No, no, no," Kirk said. "I don't accept free jobs. I won't be one of your favor boys five years from now."

Kirk had been here before. The last time a demon did something for him for free, it showed up several years later with a favor he couldn't refuse. He'd had to murder someone. Kirk wasn't above murder, but not for free.

"No favors needed," the demon said.

"Bullshit."

The demon laughed. "Very well. If you're stupid enough to ask for a price, I will now put a timeframe on the girl," the demon said. "You will deliver her before sunrise."

"Or?"

"I will take two months of your brother's life."

"Take five of mine instead," Kirk said.

"I do not do direct deals," the demon said. "It makes for more efficient transactions. Ensures we both have…souls in the game, so to speak."

Shit. This demon wasn't negotiating.

"I'd have to ask my brother's permission," Kirk said. "And he's unavailable right now."

"That's not my problem, human."

"Five months of my life and a blood tribute," Kirk said. "If you disagree, return to whence you came."

"Give me six months and you have a deal."

"Fine."

The demon stepped aside. "Your protection is granted. You may now proceed."

The gust blew harder this time, pushing Kirk over the threshold. As he passed the demon, he looked down and away to avoid its gaze. The demon followed him in.

The door slammed behind them, shutting off the loud night.

Kirk walked slowly through the lobby, which was empty and smelled like a flower shop.

The demon trailed swiftly behind him.

His footsteps echoed on the marble floor that looked like a universe of brown and gray. The gentle burbling of the fountain grew louder, and a fine mist drifted into his nose.

A wall of humidity hit him again as he emerged into the courtyard. Hedges stretched high into the air, almost as tall as the building itself. He couldn't see over them.

He stopped at the fountain and stared it up and down. The female warrior looked as if she could swing her sword at him any minute. She wore a crown of orange daisies.

"Kirk," a voice said.

He thought the voice came from the fountain, but it was a male.

Axel.

An oak tree rested behind the fountain. A television hung from one of the branches. Axel Valentine waited on the screen. He ran his hands over his face and down his long beard, sighing impatiently. He stood against a brick background.

"That's one hell of an entrance," Kirk said, approaching reluctantly.

Axel smirked and nodded to the demon. "Thank you for the respect."

"Respect?"

A pit opened up in his stomach as the demon laughed quietly. Kirk looked behind his shoulder and down. The damned demon was kneeling. Kneeling for Valentine!

That motherfucker…The realization that he screwed up hit him, making it hard to think clearly. The demon cheated him. He was never in any danger, and the hell spawn knew it.

"Status," Axel said. His stare on screen was as intense as it was in person—Axel was making a quick read of him. This guy wasn't one to make small talk, but Kirk didn't care.

Kirk tilted his head toward the lobby. "What happened across the street?"

"Mind your business, necromancer."

"I could," Kirk said, "but it's impacting my work, and it's going to make things more difficult to finish this job. Am I right?"

Axel smirked. "Maybe."

"Then *maybe* you ought to say more words."

"It was a cleansing," Axel said.

"So that's what you nephilim call death now."

"It's the beginning of a new realignment," Axel said. "It need not involve you unless you desire it."

Kirk frowned. Something wasn't right, but he didn't even know if he could trust his instincts anymore.

"I didn't know you knew how to use the word *desire* in a sentence," Kirk said.

"First time for everything, asshole."

Kirk puffed. "That sounds like the Axel I know."

"As I said, you'd best mind your business," Axel said. "It doesn't involve you. Give me a status. Now."

"Sanchez got away," Kirk said. "We almost had him, but it appears he's working with a rat shifter."

"Shifter?" Axel asked. "I know of Cyrus Grant. And his sister, Rebecca."

"If you know them, how about you tell me how to remove them from the picture?"

Axel's face went long. "So you're telling me you don't know how to do your job?" he asked.

"If I don't, then fire me."

"How hard is it to kill a rat, Aidankirk?" Axel asked.

"That rat is trouble, and you know it," Kirk said. "I don't even have to counsel with the dead to tell you that. But in the future, I'd appreciate a proper heads up on the obstacles that will be in my way."

Kirk balled his fists. He didn't know why, but he imagined

the gesture giving more power to his words.

Silence. Axel stared him down, thinking.

"Your feedback is noted, necromancer," he said. "I'll give you more time to produce Sanchez's body. I want him dead."

"Or what?" Kirk asked.

"Or else."

Axel disappeared from the television with a final, menacing frown.

Kirk hated conversations that ended with more questions than he entered with.

He got more time to finish the job, but now he had to contend with a meddling rat.

"Our transaction is complete," the demon said.

The fullness of rage in Kirk's chest blossomed back, evolving into hate. He wanted to rip the demon apart, starting with its horns.

He looked down at the ground and behind him. "I'm not done with you yet."

If he had a sword, he would have slashed it at the demon's face.

"What other business do you have?" the demon asked, irritated. "This wasn't in the bargain."

"You cheated me," Kirk said. "You knew there was no danger."

The demon paused. Then laughed.

"That's why you offered to do it for free," Kirk said.

"I would have indeed asked you for a favor in the future, so your instinct was correct," the demon said. "What did you expect me to do? Act like an angel?"

"Maybe I shouldn't have expected anything at all," Kirk said. "And for that, maybe I should renege on my offer."

"Renege!" the demon bellowed. A shadowy fist crashed into the ground. "You wouldn't dare."

"You want the girl, don't you?" Kirk asked. He tried to keep his cool, but the demon was going to explode in about five seconds. Despite how many bad demon encounters he'd weathered, he never got used to it.

"Do you wish to forfeit your life?" the demon asked.

"I have a lot of demons within me," Kirk said. "Kill me and you'll kill them. And you won't get your girl."

"You stupid bastard!" the demon roared.

"Fine, no contract cancellation since you're being a baby about it," Kirk said. "Instead, consider yourself charged. You will not be released until you complete a final task for me. I'll give you the girl in exchange for its completion."

The demon roared so loud, the ground shook. The fountain toppled, sending a geyser of water into the air. Kirk didn't move.

"Your reply," he said calmly. "Screw me and I'll screw you."

"Name your terms," the demon said.

"Answer me one question truthfully," Kirk said. "Tell me who I just spoke with and where they broadcasted from."

"You don't know your enemy?" the demon asked. "You doubt your conversation with the nephilim? Was my bow to his power not enough, human?"

"I'm not getting the answers I want from him…and I don't like the vibes," Kirk said. "Accept, or let's see how this ends."

The demon screamed and stomped toward him. Smoky, putrid breath rolled down Kirk's neck. But still, he didn't move.

After a long growl with smoky, fecal undertones, the demon grunted.

"Fine, I accept," the demon said finally. "But you're going to regret this, necromancer," the demon said.

"I'll be the judge of that."

"Close your eyes."

Kirk obliged. A hand grabbed him by the waist, lifted him

up, and set him down on a soft, moist surface. The demon's shoulder.

"Keep your eyes closed until I say so," the demon said. "Understood?"

"Only with your assurance that you won't attack."

"Your assurance is granted."

Kirk closed his eyes. The demon jumped into the air and Kirk instinctively reached out, feeling his hands on one of the demon's horns.

He held on tight and the demon bounded into the sky, then plunged downward, disappearing from the mortal world with a pop.

CHAPTER TWENTY

Luna carried Cyrus around the Smyrna Condominiums, over Lake Michigan, and around the back toward the parking lot. As she climbed, Cyrus expected a gorgeous panorama of city and lake, and that was exactly what he got—albeit in muted colors. The city lights circled by his rat's bubble field of vision in muted greens, grays, and yellows. To the tune of roaring lake waves, the blurry jewels winked at him and the breeze calmed him as Luna wheeled over the water. Luna let out a hearty gronk as she turned back to the city.

Cyrus replayed the apartment scene in his mind—the clean decor, jagged circle in the window where the woman had been thrown out, chewed-up wires all over her office, the ringing cell phone in the bag, his heart pounding at almost getting caught, and his narrow escape from the police.

Who had called the woman? It couldn't have been a coincidence. And it probably wasn't the woman's mom. He felt sorry for her, suffering a fate like that. What would it be like to die that way, to fly out a window and see the city like he was seeing it now but on a one-way trip down to the concrete? What would his final thoughts have been?

Even though he didn't know the woman, he wanted justice for her.

Soon they were upon the swirling siren lights and beads of slowed traffic in front of the tower.

A man's voice drifted up toward them.

"Son!"

Cyrus recognized the voice and it chilled him.

Bruce MacLeod.

Luna tightened her grip on Cyrus.

"Where the devil are you, Kirk?"

The dead man rocketed past them like they didn't exist. His voice was frantic.

"Kirk! Son, we need you!"

Bruce whistled by like a Roman candle, twirling across the parking lot and surrounding buildings, calling for Kirk. The souls on his necklace screamed in agony.

Bruce doubled back and zoomed toward them. Luna fanned away as the dead man blew by, his voice growing even more desperate.

Luna flapped faster and steered for the parking lot. They touched down near a group of people. Cyrus immediately shifted to a human and spotted Desmond standing over a white guy lying unconscious on the asphalt, arms and legs bound. He wore sweatpants and a blue nylon training jacket. Cyrus recognized him as the man on the school roof. The man who had shot out the back window of the church van. Cyrus hardened when he saw a glint of cold steel lying next to him—the very gun he'd tried to kill Cyrus and Becca with.

Desmond pursed his lips and had his hands on his hips.

Rocco stood next to him and waved at Cyrus.

"Bud, you've got impeccable timing," he said, clapping Cyrus on the back. He kissed Luna on the cheek.

"What happened?" Cyrus asked.

"We were followed," Desmond said.

Cyrus glanced up at the rooftops. He couldn't see Bruce,

but he knew the dead man was still there, streaming through the sky.

Desmond started to speak, but Cyrus put a finger to his lips. Desmond cocked his head at him.

"Don't say anything," he said, mouthing Bruce's name and pointing up.

Desmond's eyes widened.

Someone whistled to them from across the street. Axel, Becca, and Gilberto came jogging over.

"Mission accomplished!" Axel said.

Desmond waved to get Axel's attention and gave him a quiet signal.

Axel shrugged, then noticed Aidan on the ground. One of his eyes shifted to red as he scanned the sky.

"Wandering spirit, huh?" he said.

Cyrus felt a soft punch on his shoulder. Becca stood next to him.

"What's up?" she whispered.

He shook his head.

Axel held out a hand. "Bruce MacLeod," he said. "It isn't every day that I have the unfortunate displeasure of running into your evil ass."

Axel held out both hands and motioned as if he were pulling a giant rope. He strained and groaned.

"Come on!" he cried like a jock at the gym. "Whoo!"

He made a hard pull that brought him to his knees. Every muscle in his arm flexed as he gave a gargantuan pull.

"Fine. You want to play tough. I'll play, old dead man!"

He snapped his fingers. Ezekiel ran to his side. Johanna also joined him. Each put a hand on his shoulder and began speaking in Latin.

Desmond called Cyrus and Becca. He had backed up to the street.

"I recommend that you back up," Desmond said. "And shield your eyes."

Cyrus and Becca exchanged a "what the hell" look as they hurried to join Desmond.

Cyrus covered his eyes with his arm just as a blinding white flash ripped through the parking lot. Even though he closed his eyes, the hot light seared against his eyelids.

The gentle sound of wind chimes filled the air, followed by a cooling sensation.

Then the white light dissipated, followed by pure blackness that was so dark, it drowned out the city lights.

The blackness blocked out the city sounds. The car horns and roaring lake shore waves disappeared, replaced with zen-like stillness.

Cyrus made the mistake of opening his eyes.

A seven-foot-tall winged beast hovered over the parking lot. It was covered in black feathers. White chains covered its torso and ran down its left leg. The chains glowed as if they were heavenly. A long, curly brown horn extended from its forehead. In one hand, it held a sword; the other, a book. Though it had a human face, it lacked a mouth. Its wings had a mind of their own, flapping to keep it afloat. Specks of golden dust emanated from the wings, sprinkling down and disintegrating on the pavement.

Underneath the creature, Axel's assistant, Johanna, held a white chain attached to one of Axel's legs. His son, Ezekiel, was glowing inside a column of golden light. Ezekiel held another chain attached to Axel's other leg.

The beast held Aidan with both arms. Hanging from the unconscious necromancer was Bruce Macleod's spirit, connected by a shining thread. His spirit wailed incessantly, and for once, the blue souls hanging from the old man's neck were silent and resting.

Axel opened his eyes—like oval eggs with no pupils. His gaze met Cyrus's. Axel winked, and white light exploded from his body again, making Cyrus cover his eyes.

The light faded, and the sound of the city returned. Cyrus opened his eyes.

Axel knelt in the parking lot, holding Aidan. Though Bruce wasn't visible anymore, Cyrus sensed the dead man hanging from Aidan.

Axel staggered up. His son and assistant steadied him.

"Let's go," Axel said. "We've got some interrogation to do."

"Cy," Becca said quietly, staring at Axel. "Did you see—"

"Axel turn into a giant monstrosity?" Cyrus asked. "Yeah."

"I threatened to kick his ass," Becca said incredulously. "And put him through a window."

"Not your finest moment," Cyrus said.

Becca still stared. "If I have to take him, you've got my back, right?"

"How about we *not* put ourselves in that situation?" Cyrus asked.

Becca extended a fist. "Deal."

CHAPTER TWENTY-ONE

"You may now open your eyes."

Kirk opened his eyes to a twilit glade with swaying tall grass. An endless orange sky spread over the rolling hills, and golden cumulus clouds scooted across the sky.

An overwhelming scent of flowers, honeysuckle, and fresh-cut grass overwhelmed him. Pollen danced on his tongue. He stumbled backward into a soft surface—the demon.

A clawed hand pushed him forward.

"I don't have all day," the demon said.

"You have as long as I damn well want," Kirk said.

He took in the place. It might have been beautiful if he had been here for other reasons. But in the paranormal world, beauty was always code for death. Show him a dark, dusty space, and he'd take it every time over a world like this.

A rock path appeared under his feet. The grass parted as new stones flashed into the dirt. They wound their way across a hill to an oak tree whose leaves rustled in a gentle breeze.

"Your answer lies ahead," the demon said.

"I hope so," Kirk said.

Kirk knew he had to walk. He stepped on the stones, following them across the glade, listening to birdsong.

As he approached the oak tree, he knew immediately that it was not an oak tree. The branches in the canopy moved like the hands of an opera singer—in long, sweeping gestures across the burning dusk sky.

Then he heard singing.

The oak tree shifted toward him and the singing grew louder.

He stopped at the base of the tree and looked up at its canopy, and a giant maw of triangular bark teeth moving up and down.

The singing stopped. The leaves crinkled and the maw slid down to the ground level. Two slits in the bark parted, revealing two giant eyes with brilliant brown irises that sparkled like brown diamonds.

The nymph grinned at Kirk, bark cracking loudly.

"Hello, necromancer," the tree said in Axel Valentine's voice.

"So you're not Axel?" Kirk asked. He glanced behind at the demon in the corner of his eye—it wasn't kneeling. Maybe it was smart enough not to betray its allegiance this time.

"I am your puppeteer," the tree said. "I am called Oleandra, and I am a sacred nymph. I'll allow your disrespect in not worshipping me due to your ignorance."

"What do you want with Sanchez?" Kirk asked.

"He is a healer," Oleandra said. "I can't afford to have healers stop the flow of fate."

"Fate?"

"The will of one of our deceased," Oleandra said. "This is an experiment."

"Last I checked, I'm not a test tube," Kirk said. "Find some other puppet."

"No, you're the one."

"I'm inches away from making another shadow deal, so no, you're not," Kirk said. "I'm a free agent. I didn't sign up for deception."

"What do you care so long as you get your money?" Oleandra asked.

"Maybe I've had a change of heart," Kirk snapped.

The demon approached. "Name your terms," it said.

Kirk waited.

The tree woman shifted uncomfortably as a barky frown gnarled across her face.

"Wait," she said.

"Ah," Kirk said, grinning. "I'm listening, my lady. Sing me a song I want to hear."

"Perhaps we can…sweeten this deal," the tree said.

A gust blew a jumble of leaves across the field. They cast shadows across the grass as they fell, and Kirk told himself that this place would be beautiful again if he weren't in mortal danger—a beautiful place to rest, place his head on the dirt, and enjoy the fading day.

"You need to procure the body of that girl to fulfill your bargain," Oleandra said.

"How did you know that?" Kirk asked.

"The flowers are my ears," Oleandra said as a vine with wildflowers hung in front of one eye.

Kirk remembered the flowers in the lobby of the apartment and puffed, disappointed with himself. He was stuck between two supernatural beings he couldn't trust…just another day in the life of a necromancer.

He looked down and behind his shoulder, keeping an eye on Oleandra.

"Time to deal," he said.

"Deal!" the nymph cried.

"Once a liar, always a liar," Kirk said.

"What is your wish, human?" the demon asked.

"I wish to transfer my deal with this nymph to you," he said. "You will complete the work in exchange for my and my brother's freedom."

Even the demon gasped.

"You ignorant fool!" Oleandra cried. "This wasn't in our deal."

"And the collateral?" the demon asked.

The nymph screamed at him. The ground shook.

He had to get out of here. The demon would at least grant him safe passage. He'd make an eternal enemy of Oleandra, but at least he'd live to make more shadow deals. He could figure out how to fight a nymph if needed. His dad would know what to do. Back in the human world, he'd have the advantage.

"I will give you one additional year of my life," Kirk said, "but it sounds like the nymph can't argue with me, so let's be honest, okay?"

"That is not sufficient," the demon said.

"Why not?" Kirk asked. "You have a guaranteed offer. We shouldn't even be discussing collateral. Just get me home and we'll both be on our way."

"This job warrants new stakes," the demon said. "I desire the right of possession."

Possession. The most dangerous of deals. Once a demon occupied a human body, it could hop from host to host and wreak untold havoc.

Kirk laughed. "You want to deal like that?"

"Possession of your body if this deal falls through," the demon said. "I have killed a nymph before. I can handle her if needed."

"We'll see about that," Oleandra said.

"Now," the demon said.

As soon as the deal was done, he'd be back in the human world within seconds. He had to move fast.

His brother could help. Bruce could help. Better to trust a demon than a secretive nymph.

A brother's gotta do what a brother's gotta do.

"Deal," Kirk said. "I amend our previous agreement."

"Foolish necromancer," Oleandra said. "You will regret this day forever."

"I'll take my chances," Kirk said as the demon faded and materialized in front of him. He saluted her. "Good luck killing your healer, lady."

Oleandra scowled at him.

In a flash, a tree branch lashed at Kirk.

The demon grabbed it and broke it off.

Another branch lashed from above, but the demon blew a fireball and sent a vein of fire sizzling into Oleandra's canopy.

The nymph shook the flames out.

"Just making sure you got a good deal," she said, smirking.

"Deliver me from here and finish your business with her," Kirk said.

The demon knelt and Kirk walked up its back and sat on one of its massive horns. Holding on, he closed his eyes as the demon leaped into the sky.

The last thing he saw as he zoomed upward was the intense vermilion horizon meeting the treetops, and the sun sinking behind a cloud.

CHAPTER TWENTY-TWO

As Cyrus tied knots around Aidan MacLeod's wrists, he mused how the Wicked Cat had seen many things: drunks, habitual drunks, violent drunks, wedding parties, bike nights, hipster gatherings, and even birthday parties. Now Becca could add interrogations to the list. Yay her.

The necromancer was still unconscious, and he was drooling all over his chin. A puddle had formed on his training jacket. His head lay tilted, and Cyrus wondered if he'd get whiplash when he woke up and realized he wasn't in his car anymore. He didn't exactly feel sorry for the guy, though.

He wiped sweat from his brow; the fans overhead were spinning hard, but it was crazy hot. They were just blowing around hot air. This would have been a great time to open up the bar's loading doors and let air in from the patio, but it wouldn't have been a good idea to advertise the upcoming interrogation session to passersby.

"You deserve a Keystone Ice for that rope job," Becca said. She was behind the bar, fixing drinks for everyone.

"Pour me one and you die," Cyrus said.

"Challenge accepted," Becca said. "You tie knots like a failed Boy Scout."

The joke triggered him, even though Becca probably didn't mean to. So what if he'd dropped out of the Boy Scouts because he hated camping? He called his mom during the first night because a daddy long legs crawled on his face and across his eyeball. Becca never let him hear the end of it—and that was in the first grade.

"It's better than you could have done!" he said angrily. "I don't see you over here tying anything."

"It did take you six times to get it right," Rocco said. He sat at the bar, nursing a glass of straight scotch. Luna sat next to him with her legs across his lap. "Just getting the facts on the record, bud."

"It's been a long night," Luna said. "Why don't we all just enjoy our drinks and stop the jokes for a while, okay?"

"Yeah, let's all kick Cyrus while he's ensuring we pump this clown for information," Cyrus said. "It's my honor to serve as your punching bag tonight." Gritting his teeth, he pulled both of the ropes on Aidan's wrists and tightened them further.

It *had* been a long night. He loosened up a little and took a deep breath.

The front door opened and the bell chimed as Desmond strode in. He was battle-worn, his eyes tired, and seemed more irritable than usual.

Desmond took one look at Cyrus's knot-work and shook his head.

"Stick to rat-shifting," he said. "Next time I need a knot, don't volunteer."

Cyrus shrugged. Becca slapped an ice cold lager on the counter and motioned for him to get it.

"We'll wake up Aidan shortly," Desmond said. "But first, I'd like to go over a few things."

The door opened again and Axel walked into the bar in

human form, followed by his assistant, who carried a metal case with her—it contained a skull that had been in Aidan's car. Axel had sealed Bruce's spirit inside. Axel's son trailed in behind them, his eyes wild with worry.

It was weird seeing Axel in human form now—Cyrus would never forget his awe-striking nephilim transformation, a scene from a hellscape movie. He didn't want to see it again.

"You're up, Mr. Sanchez," Desmond said.

Gilberto sat at a nearby table, nursing a glass of beer. He stared into the brown liquid with sad eyes and gulped.

"If you want to attack me or make jokes at my expense, go ahead," he said. "I don't care anymore."

Cyrus straddled a chair next to Gilberto. "Don't worry. I'm pretty sure you did us all a favor by resurrecting that woman."

"Sure doesn't feel like it," Gilberto said.

"What else can you tell us about Cynthia's resurrection?" Desmond asked.

"She kept talking about rats," Gilberto said.

"It was the only word she could say," Becca said.

"Rats?" Cyrus asked.

Gilberto nodded and took a swill of beer. Cyrus thought Gilberto would burst into tears any minute. His face wrinkled like he was going to cry.

"Her body was covered with little bite marks," Gilberto said. "She was terrified."

"It lines up with what I saw," Cyrus said. "I could definitely smell rats in the apartment. All of her computer wiring was chewed. If I had to guess, I'd say the giant creature threw her out the window after the rats bit her."

"Cyrus is right," Gilberto said. He slammed a fist on the table and shook his head. "I didn't sign up for this."

"Unless you're completely daft, you know the city is in danger," Axel said. "Quit being a baby about seeing a dead person, and feel good that you did us all a favor. I thought you liked necromancy anyway."

"Screw you!" Gilberto said, flipping Axel off.

Axel held up his hands. "I was paying you a compliment, but if you don't want it, fine."

"When I connect with the dead, I connect with their emotions too," Gilberto said, rising. "So unless you want to know what it's like to die, maybe you ought to have more respect for the dead." Gilberto stomped toward Axel and the nephilim's eyes widened.

"We can talk all night about the dead, can't we?" Axel asked, smirking. "Why don't we talk about how you're a failed healer? I'd have one more team member who'd be with us tonight if you hadn't failed to save her."

Gilberto let out a cry and lunged for Axel.

"Let's have some respect among the living," Desmond said, squeezing between the two.

Cyrus jumped up and grabbed Gilberto by the collar, dragging him back. "Come on, Gilberto. It's not worth it," he said. "Shake it out and let's avoid more trouble."

Gilberto lingered at Axel with an angry gaze before returning to his table.

Axel let out a small chuckle.

Fucking asshole, Cyrus thought, but he didn't dare say it.

"Cyrus," Desmond said, "when you were in Cynthia's apartment, you said the phone rang. Did you see who called?"

"The name said Letitia," Cyrus said.

"She's one of my suppressors," Axel said. He snapped his fingers, and his assistant whipped out her phone and dialed. "She's a news reporter."

"Wait—Letitia Frankland?" Becca asked. "From the evening news?"

Axel winked. "My network of suppressors controls everything. Hope I'm not shattering your faith in anything."

"You already did that," Becca said under her breath. Cyrus shot a "shut up" look at her.

"No answer from Letitia," Axel's secretary said.

"Can someone trace her?" Axel asked. "If she's still alive, we need to find her." Axel nodded to Cyrus. "Good job, kid. I was beginning to doubt you."

Cyrus folded his arms and let the comment go. He didn't want to trigger Axel into his nephilim form.

He remembered his ultimatum from Oleandra. He didn't exactly have much time, and the nymph would love nothing more than to tell him he failed to meet her ultimatum.

"We need to hunt the rat," Cyrus said. "Desmond, the clock is ticking."

"We'll see if we can find Letitia," Desmond said. "Given our luck tonight, we may not find her alive. Luna, Rocco—fly out to Letitia's apartment as well as the bistro where she was last seen reporting. See what you can find out."

Luna and Rocco saluted, downed the rest of their drinks, and walked out of the bar. Seconds later, they took to the sky as ravens.

Cyrus's phone buzzed in his pocket. He pulled it out.

His mom. He cursed and declined the call.

Another phone buzzed on the bar. Becca's.

Becca gave the phone a quick look and did the same thing. He and his sister shared an "oh shit" look. If both of them declined Mom's calls, she was going to ask some hard questions later.

His phone buzzed again. Mom. Cyrus quickly silenced it again, and Becca silenced her phone too.

"Let's wake our necromancer up," Desmond said, grinning. "Mr. Sanchez, any recommendations on how to wake him up safely?"

"Lemon," Gilberto said.

Desmond motioned to Becca, who opened up a tray on

the bar, pulled up a lemon wedge, and tossed it to him along with a rag.

Axel kicked over a chair, caught it with his foot, and flipped it up into his hands. He slid in front of Aidan, who was still incapacitated and drooling more than before.

"Everyone, stay quiet," Desmond warned, looking back across the bar.

Desmond extended the lemon toward Aidan's nose.

"Tilt his head forward," Gilberto said sharply. "I don't like the guy any more than you do, but you don't want to give him whiplash."

Desmond grunted at Cyrus, who reluctantly took the man's head and positioned it so that it hung down on his chest.

Desmond held the lemon in front of the necromancer's nose, varying the angle and making circles with it.

Aidan snorted. Desmond kept the lemon under his nose.

"Is it going to work?" Becca asked.

Aidan snorted again and his eyes fluttered. When they opened a final time, he jerked in the chair, moving his arms. His eyes went down to the ropes and a fan of drool exploded from his mouth as he cried out. Then he looked around wildly, first at Cyrus, Becca, Desmond, Axel's secretary who stood smirking with the skeleton case in her hand, at Gilberto who looked at him with a mixture of anger, sadness, and curiosity, and finally, at Axel, who propped his head on his fists, smiling.

Aidan's eyes might as well have bulged out of his head upon seeing Axel—the shocked expression on his face reminded Cyrus of a cartoon character. He struggled against the ropes.

"You don't like being tied up?" Axel asked. "I thought you were into kinky shit since you were a necromancer. "

Desmond wiped the drool from Aidan's face.

"Mr. MacLeod, we meet again," Desmond said.

Aidan glanced up at Desmond and scowled. He didn't say a word.

"I've got urgent questions, and you're going to give me urgent answers," Desmond said. "Why don't we start with why you were following me?"

Aidan puffed, sat up straight, and stared straight ahead.

"I won't take your answer personally," Desmond said. "Let's try another one: why were you following Gilberto Sanchez?"

A sly smirk spread across Aidan's lips.

"A little better, but it's not an answer," Desmond said.

"Why don't you go ahead and answer?" Axel asked. "My assistant back there has your dad trapped in a skull."

Aidan said nothing.

"I thought we might send him back to hell where he belongs," Axel said. "Unless you had other plans?"

Aidan didn't respond.

"Oh, so you're the mute one," Axel said. "Maybe we ought to ask your brother the same questions. He's in the backroom, you know."

Cyrus raised an eyebrow. Kirk Macleod most definitely was *not* at the Wicked Cat. Axel Valentine was scum. Nothing was beneath him.

"Prove it," Aidan said.

"He speaks!" Axel said, laughing. "It's not every day you catch necromancers snooping around and spying on people. What's your story? Tell the truth and maybe we'll let you off without kicking your ass."

Aidan locked on the nephilim. "Truth?" he asked coldly.

"Want me to define the word for you?" Axel asked.

"Truth?" Aidan asked again.

"Yeah, the fucking truth!" Axel asked, rocketing to his feet.

"Okay, since you want the truth," Aidan said. "I was tailing Gilberto Sanchez because you asked us to do it, Valentine."

CHAPTER TWENTY-THREE

MARISOL BANGED her fists on the front desk of Channel 64.

The front desk attendant, a young Caucasian male with unruly black hair, stared at her blankly.

The lobby's fluorescent bulbs buzzed gently overhead.

"Listen to me," she said in a half growl. "I know what I saw. I have been halfway across this city tonight and I am begging you to let me tell my story."

"Like I said, miss, there's no staff here tonight. At least not the ones you want to talk to."

"Then call them!" Marisol said. A tear formed in her eye. "Isn't that what reporters are supposed to do? Get the scoop? Why won't you *listen* to me?"

"It's nothing personal, ma'am," the attendant said.

"You're not a reporter," Marisol said. "You don't get to make that decision."

The attendant rose. "Please leave, or I will call security."

Marisol wasn't going to leave without giving her hardest try. This was the third news station she'd visited tonight upon taking Letitia's advice. Even that wasn't working. The police turned her away too, since there was no threat of bodily harm. She felt alone. Desperate. Hungry. Angry. Scared.

She slung a laptop out of her purse and set it on the desk.

"I know I seem like a crazy woman," she said. "But if you think I'm crazy after I show this to you, I'll leave and you won't have to kick me out."

The attendant shrugged.

"This evening, I got attacked by a monster," Marisol said. "It was a giant rat."

She paused for effect. The attendant's face didn't change.

"I spoke to a reporter," Marisol said. "I even recorded an interview, but it didn't air."

"Go figure," the attendant said quietly.

"I'm not the only one who was attacked," Marisol said. She swiped on her trackpad, bringing up a map of the city. Several glowing red dots pulsed across the metro.

"If you don't believe me, I have a legion of others who were with me during the attack."

She pointed to one of the dots. "I created a bot that crawled all over the posts on social media in the last few hours."

"You created a what?"

"A bot," Marisol said. "It's a robot that performs a special task. I use them all the time in my day job. Anyway, I made a post about the event and someone edited it. I have no idea how they did it, but somehow they must have hacked my account. I scraped every post from city residents that were also edited during the same timeframe earlier tonight. I put them on a spreadsheet, where it was much easier to spot the posts that were doctored. Many of them have misspellings just like mine."

"So?" the attendant asked, yawning. "People have clumsy fingers."

"Someone doesn't want the public to know about the rat," she said. "They're covering it up, trying to silence dozens of people. Well, guess what? No one is going to silence me. If you won't respect my story, I'll make sure everyone in the city hears it."

"Oh?" the attendant asked.

"I already have," she said, grinning. "But I'm not telling. Maybe you ought to call your people now? Because if you don't, I'm going to list the names of all the stations and people who ignored me. And I would love, love, LOVE to see how you bend yourselves into knots trying to explain why you dismissed me."

She had no idea how to make everyone in the world hear her story, but the threat sounded awesome. For once, her anger felt good, like she was healing part of herself after all the trouble she had been through.

"So what are you gonna do?" she asked.

The attendant frowned. "Give me a moment."

He picked up the phone and said a few words to someone on the other end.

She folded her arms.

"Someone will be down shortly to talk to you," the attendant said.

"You made the right decision," she said. "Thank you. Thank you so much."

A silver door with frosted glass behind the desk opened. A lanky security guard walked out.

"Good evening, ma'am," the guard said.

"Who will you be escorting me to see?" Marisol asked, grinning.

The guard clapped a hand around her wrist and dragged her to the door.

"I'm escorting you out of the building," the guard said. "That's enough crazy for one night."

Marisol resisted, but the guard's grip was iron tight.

"Let me go!" she cried.

"Ma'am, please don't make me call the police," he said.

"It's late and I'd hate to press charges against a nice lady like you."

"I'll show you nice," she said, swatting him.

The guard ushered her into the hot night and let her go.

"Don't come back," he said. "Or we will call the police."

"Screw you!" Marisol yelled at the top of her lungs. "You're complicit in this coverup! I will never forget this!"

The guard tipped his head down the street.

"Please leave."

Marisol stared at him incredulously for a few moments. Then she gave him the middle finger, called him something in Spanish that would have shocked her mother, and stomped down the street.

How could they do this to her? Why wouldn't anyone listen?

She was so upset, she couldn't even cry.

She rounded a corner, lost in her thoughts.

No one would help her.

No one would listen.

No one would support her and tell her she *wasn't* crazy.

A car horn yanked her from her thoughts.

Headlights lit up her face and blinded her. She jumped back as a car flew by.

She had entered an intersection without a pedestrian walk signal.

"Wake up, Marisol," she told herself.

Halfway across the intersection, she froze.

Her laptop.

She left it on the counter at the front desk.

She ran back to the glass skyscraper that held the news studio, pushing through the revolving door. She didn't care if they arrested her.

The attendant jumped to his feet.

"We told you to leave!" he said.

Marisol scanned the desk. Her laptop was gone.

"I came back for my computer," she said. "Where is it?"

The attendant shrugged. "I don't know what you're talking about."

"You stole my computer," Marisol said. "Give it back to me now or I'll sue."

The silver door with the frosted window opened again. The security guard rushed out.

"You didn't learn your lesson, did you?" he asked.

Marisol screamed as he grabbed her and ushered her out of the building again.

"Call the cops," she said. "I'll prove you stole my laptop."

"And how will you do that?" the guard asked. "Lady, we didn't steal anything."

"I'll have my lawyers grab your security footage," she said.

"With what cameras?" the guard asked.

Marisol glanced across the ceilings. No security cameras. What kind of building didn't have cameras?

Marisol watched as he locked the revolving door and stood with his hands on his hips.

They stood, staring each other down for at least a minute. The lanky guard meant business, and he didn't avert his gaze. She studied every nook and cranny of his face, swearing to remember it for the rest of her life.

She called the police on her cell phone, still staring him in the eye.

"You called a few hours ago, right?" the operator asked.

"Yes," Marisol said, letting out a sigh.

"Ma'am, please stop calling this department," the operator said. "Unless you've got evidence of a crime, I suggest you solve your own problems."

Marisol hung up and cursed.

Then she sighed and walked away.

~

The attendant and security guard huddled over Marisol's laptop and scrolled through her evidence.

"That was one damned resourceful woman," the guard said. "Masterful, if I do say so myself."

"Yeah, she definitely knew what was going on," the attendant said. "Too bad Cynthia died tonight. If our best technomancer had finished the job, this lady wouldn't have had a clue where to dig."

"Yep, there's a technomancer in Seattle working overtime," the guard said, "but he's not as good as Cynthia. There are lots of gaps he can't address."

"Should we tell Axel about the lady?"

The guard paused. "He's under enough pressure tonight. I trust you to take care of it, right?"

The attendant slid the computer closer. "Yep. Good ol' fashioned computer wiping. We'll have someone drop it off at her doorstep before she gets home."

The guard watched as the attendant started typing on the computer.

"Do you ever wonder what it would be like to be one of them?" he asked.

"Them?"

"Humans," the guard said. "The lady probably thinks she's going nuts."

The attendant shrugged. "Would you rather her go nuts or start digging, expose herself to the paranormal, and then die a miserable death at the hands of a demon, or worse, a monster?"

The guard paused, regarding the comment. "You make a good point. I still feel for the lady. Maybe when this is all said and done and we're all drinking coffee in heaven, she'll thank us."

"If we go to heaven," the attendant said, not looking back.

"Another good point," the guard said. "Ah well. Have a good night, buddy."

The guard slipped out of the room and into the lobby. Seconds later, the attendant emerged from the door with golden wings fluttering behind him, laptop under one arm.

The guard waved and watched as the boy flew into the glass and disappeared in a flash.

Sighing, the guard snapped his fingers. His body dissolved into a silhouette. The room shifted left with a loud crack. In the corners of the walls, security cameras reappeared.

The guard snapped again and the room shifted again like it received a chiropractic adjustment. The ceiling lights blinked out, the floor became the ceiling, and new lights appeared, faded to half brightness.

With one final crack, the room adjusted into the true lobby of Channel 64, one that looked nothing like the one that had existed a moment ago—concrete walls and floors, and an empty mahogany front desk.

In silhouette form, the guard floated toward the front door, which was not a revolving door, but a double glass door with gold lettering on the glass that said the building was closed until Monday.

"Job well done," he said, spiraling into a column of smoke and away from this place.

~

"One, two, three!"

Marisol counted off as she ran around the corner with a death grip on a shovel.

She had found the shovel lying near a construction site as she walked away.

One hit and the guard would go down. Then, she'd reclaim her computer from his room and run like hell.

At least that was what she told herself as she wobbled around the corner.

"I'm not crazy," she told herself. "I won't let them stop me."

The shovel was light as a baseball bat. Not even the guard would try to fight her. He didn't have a gun either. It wouldn't even be a contest.

Ha. Ha! She was going to get her computer back and then she was going to add this incident to her data.

She slid to a stop at the front door of the Channel 64 building and almost lost her balance as she stared at the building's facade.

She dropped the shovel.

Where was the revolving door?

Inside, the lobby was lit by dim lights recessed in the ceiling—they were nothing like the can lights she had seen earlier. And the front desk—it wasn't the same, and it wasn't even in the same place.

She looked up at the building—it too was different. The glass exterior was replaced with a twentieth-century granite face. Not a single light was on.

She stepped back, shaking her head.

When she realized that she was truly powerless, Marisol Garza dropped to her knees and wept.

CHAPTER TWENTY-FOUR

BECCA TOOK a mental tally as Axel roared and slammed a chair into a table.

Fifty dollars.

One hundred dollars.

There go four glasses. Fourteen dollars.

Despite the fact that Aidan just revealed the fact of a lifetime, she couldn't stop counting how much damage Axel was doing to the Wicked Cat. The bastard had earned every bit of his lifetime ban. She shouldn't have let him back in, but she couldn't stop the group from debriefing.

"Cy, am I living in the twilight zone?" Becca asked. She refreshed her brother's lager and slid a bowl of bar pretzels to him. Together, they munched as Axel smashed the chair into pieces on the floor while Aidan laughed hysterically. Axel raised a glass over his head with both hands. His enormous biceps flexed before he threw the glass to pieces on the floor.

"You think Axel wanted to kill Gilberto?" Cyrus whispered.

"In the parking lot at that skyscraper, Gilberto and Axel got into a fight," Becca said. "Something about Gilberto not saving Axel's friend. He mentioned it again just a minute ago. Axel can't seem to let it go."

"Welp," Cyrus said. "Maybe you and I ought to get out of here. I think Axel is going to torch this place."

"If he does, he's paying for everything," Becca said. "Nephilim or not, he's gonna pay."

Becca took a swig of her beer. It went down hard. Axel kicked out a leg from the chair that held Aidan. All the while, the necromancer kept laughing.

Fifty dollars…

"If you think I put you up to this shit, prove it!" Axel said. He pointed at Aidan, the cords in his neck extended. "You idiot!"

Everyone in the Wicked Cat stared slack-jawed at Aidan.

"Go on," Aidan said, shifting his weight on the broken chair, orienting his body toward Axel. "Tell them how you hired me and my brother."

Axel's face hardened. "I didn't hire you."

"Oh?" Aidan asked. "You didn't send a black car after us?"

Axel snapped to Johanna. "Check the records."

"You didn't meet us at Montrose Beach a few nights ago?" Aidan asked. "Late evening, just before dark."

"Fuck that," Aidan said. "I was never there."

"It sure looked like you," Aidan said. "Acted like you. Talked like you. Or maybe you didn't want me to tell. Maybe Gilberto should step outside so we can talk facts, and you can finish him yourself."

Gilberto, who had been listening with wide eyes, stepped forward.

"Is it true?" Gilberto asked.

"You heard me," Axel said quietly. "Stay out of this if you know what's good for you."

Gilberto took another step forward.

"You put a hit on me, Valentine," he said. "You wanted me dead."

He screwed up his face and shook his head.

"I didn't do it," Axel said. "I hate you, but not that much."

"What was it you told us?" Aidan asked. "Ah, yes. I remember. The healer has to go. If you tell him it was me, I'll deny it."

Gilberto balled a fist.

Aidan glanced at Gilberto. "Guess how much your head was worth, amigo?"

"I'm not your fucking amigo," Gilberto said, not taking his eyes off Axel.

"Seventy-five thousand dollars," Aidan said. "That's my lucky number. Seventy-five thousand to put you out of commission forever. Isn't that right, Axel? Or are you going to keep denying it?"

Silence.

Becca cursed under her breath as Axel breathed heavily. The nephilim was going to explode.

"Cy, I suggest you hop behind the bar," she said.

Cyrus gave her a confused glance.

"You tried to kill me!" Gilberto shouted, charging at Axel.

Axel didn't evade him. Gilberto landed a hard punch on the side of his jaw, and the nephilim recoiled.

"You want to kill me, go ahead and do it," Gilberto said. He reached for a chair, but Axel tackled him by the legs.

Becca grabbed Cyrus's shirt and pulled him over the bar as Axel grabbed Gilberto by the legs and swung him, narrowly missing Cyrus.

Axel circled several times and launched Gilberto out the window. Glass rained down on the floor.

Someone outside screamed.

Axel panted as he walked outside, hopped over the windowsill, and stood over Gilberto, who lay bloodied in a wave of glass.

"So it's true," Gilberto said, grimacing.

"It's not true," Axel said.

"Prove it," Gilberto said, straining.

"Fine," Axel said. "I'll prove it. Get out of here. Go heal yourself and stay out of my sight. If I wanted you gone, I could have done it just now. Unless you want me to—"

Becca flew over the counter and threw herself between Axel and Gilberto.

"Leave him alone!" she cried. "You've caused enough trouble for one night."

Desmond grabbed Axel by the shoulder and pulled him back. "That's enough."

Axel pushed Desmond away and walked down the street, beating his chest and letting out angry grunts. Then he rested against the wall, his head against his shoulder. Ezekiel comforted him.

"Why so sad?" Aidan taunted.

"Mr. MacLeod," Desmond said, "unless you want to go flying out a window, I'd advise you to shut up until I'm ready for you to speak again."

Aidan rocked back and forth, laughing.

Becca tried to help Gilberto up. His face was bloodied and he was covered in glass.

He pushed her away.

"Don't touch me," he said.

Becca shook her head. "We need to get you medical attention."

"I'll be fine by morning," Gilberto said. "I'm a healer, remember?"

Gilberto staggered away from her and she tried to catch him, but he pushed her away harder. For a second, her eyes locked on his, and she saw a Gilberto she'd never seen— diminished, fearful, and hurt. The intensity of despair in his gaze scared her.

Then she fell onto the broken glass as Gilberto stumbled away.

"Gilberto," she said quietly. "Don't go."

He ignored her and limped away.

Cyrus pulled her up and brushed glass from her back.

"I did this," Becca said.

"Did what?" Cyrus asked.

"I got Gilberto into this mess," she said.

"Bec, you didn't do this," he said.

If she hadn't sent her brother on that death errand to the church roof, then they would have never encountered the necromancer brothers. She and Cyrus would have never been embroiled in this mess. If only she had refused and offered to help Gilberto another time…but then she would have broken her word, and her word was important.

Or maybe her decision saved his life. Maybe Aidan might have killed Gilberto in the shadows, and she would have felt even more remorse for *not* helping him.

She didn't know. A lump formed in her throat as she stared after Gilberto. She remembered the pain in his eyes just a few moments ago. It weighed down every cell in her body, and she felt so sorry for him.

"Helluva night, eh?" Cyrus whispered.

Becca stared at the carnage left behind—a broken window, Axel cooling off near the front door, Desmond with his hands on his hips, and Aidan rocking in his three-legged chair, laughing.

"I need another drink," she said.

CHAPTER TWENTY-FIVE

LETITIA RAN FASTER and longer than she ever thought she could.

How long had the rat been chasing her?

The giant rat stomped after her, hissing and knocking over streetlights.

She wouldn't stop.

She ran, not just for herself, but for Kedron. For all the other people this damn rat killed.

A dark, expansive green space stretched out ahead—a park.

She steered toward it. The rat followed, and a car horn blared.

Soon she was running on grass toward a baseball field.

This rat was going to make her run until she dropped dead.

Fine. Better to drop dead than be mauled. She wasn't going to give the beast that pleasure. Dropping dead of a heart attack would be a victory for her.

A black mass flew overhead, followed by a throaty gronk.

A raven.

Another raven flew over, crisscrossing with the first.

Maybe it was true that ravens could sense when something was about die. Her dad told her that once. Her heart sank at the revelation.

One of the ravens gronked, wheeled in a circle, and dove toward her.

She ducked, and the bird swooped over her hair, narrowly missing it.

The rat hissed and roared.

Letitia looked behind her. The ravens were flying around the rat, and it swatted at them.

Letitia grinned with relief. Paranormals.

One of the ravens distracted the rat and forced it to turn its back to Letitia. It stomped off after the bird, who flapped its wings and gronked loudly.

The other raven morphed into a beautiful white woman with long blonde hair, a flannel shirt, and ripped jeans.

"Hell of a scoop you've got here, Letitia," the woman said. She grabbed Letitia's hand and they ran together.

"I'm Luna," the woman said.

"Thanks," Letitia said.

"Don't thank me yet," Luna said, "but I have an idea."

They ran onto the outfield, past third base, and toward a backstop surrounded by tall, thick steel pillars—stadium lights.

"What's your plan, Luna?" Letitia asked.

"One part prayer, another part girl power," Luna said.

They stopped at one of the lights. A control box was clamped to the column, but it was locked.

"That was what I feared," Luna said, trying the lock.

Behind them, the rat roared and the other raven took to the sky.

The rat sniffed, looked around, and spotted the two women. The raven swooped down to distract it, but it ignored the bird.

"Our rat friend isn't taking the bait anymore," Luna said. "Fortunately for you, we know a few things about rats."

Letitia eyed the giant rat, who was quickly approaching, rats scurrying all over its body.

Luna looked around quickly. "Where's a Louisville Slugger when you need one? Oh well. I guess we'll settle for the next best thing."

Luna grabbed a nearby plastic trash can and shook out a waterfall of soda cans, pizza boxes, and candy wrappers.

"One," Luna said, lifting the can over her head. "Two, three!"

Wham!

Luna got a good running head start and smashed the control box with the trash can. The impact knocked the box loose.

"Here we go again!" Luna cried, slamming the trash can into the box.

The rat dropped down to all fours as it cruised into the outfield.

"Come on!" Luna cried, hitting the box again.

The metal casing flew off with a hard snap and landed on the gravel.

Luna smashed a few buttons on the control panel.

In a flash, the lights in the stadium lit up, temporarily blinding Letitia.

"Let it burn," Luna said. "Let it burn, baby!"

The giant rat recoiled at the light, falling into the dirt. Several of the rats clambered off its body and back toward the shaded green space. But there was nowhere to hide.

The second raven landed next to them and morphed into a hunky white guy wearing a t-shirt and jeans.

"Home run!" the man said.

"You can thank me later, babe," Luna said.

The giant rat screeched and hissed, rats falling off its body. The rats screamed and scampered into a black wave that rushed to the shadows.

Together, Luna, Rocco, and Letitia ran.

CHAPTER TWENTY-SIX

Cyrus never thought he'd get any sleep.

The sleepiness hit him as he helped Becca clean up the mess that Axel caused. Every act took twice as much energy, like his entire body was weighted with cement blocks. His eyelids slid down of their own accord and he had to blink to keep himself awake as he swept broken glass off the floor.

The warm air in the alley was so inviting, he could have shifted into a rat and slept under the stars. He threw a broken chair in the dumpster and seriously thought about it.

He yawned and told himself he had to keep pushing, when a loud cheer erupted from the bar.

He stumbled back into the Wicked Cat as if sleepwalking when Desmond told him that Rocco and Luna had found Letitia Frankland alive and were on the way to Axel's compound. Letitia would be safe. He was so tired, he couldn't even celebrate.

"Cool," he said to no one in particular.

As he wandered around the bar looking for something to clean, Becca complained about Aidan and asked that he be moved somewhere else. Desmond said something about having to report Axel because of Aidan's claim. If Axel intended to commit murder, there would be a commission formed to investigate. As such, Aidan and Bruce would have to remain at the Wicked Cat until further notice. Desmond and a few Regulators would camp out downstairs to make sure nothing happened.

At that point, Cyrus must have been falling asleep in one of the booths because Becca prodded him awake and said, "Cy, go to bed."

He trudged upstairs to Becca's apartment and threw himself on the couch in her living room.

He couldn't even take his wine-stained blazer off.

He fell asleep staring at the ceiling and thinking of nothing at all.

A dream shaded over his mind like a sudden summer thunderstorm accompanied by the sound of whipping wind, wind chimes, and a languishing howl. Cyrus spun off the couch and onto his feet.

The floor jolted and carried him forward. Becca's chic apartment with exposed brick walls and tasteful furniture was mixed with restaurant tables and chairs with white linen cloths. Diners with blurry faces ate and talked in quiet murmurs.

A rash of fear rose in Cyrus's breast as he thought about the giant rat. He knew what was next. A tree would crash through one of the windows and all of these people would run screaming. Just like last time, he wouldn't be able to protect them.

He wanted to run, but his feet wouldn't move.

He was standing on a conveyor belt made of Becca's hardwood floors, and his shoes had melted into the floor.

"Come on," he said, struggling to lift his feet.

The fear rose, clouded his thinking. The rat was going to

crash in and crush him on this conveyor belt and then he'd be a goner.

An accordion played and he passed a burly man with a blurry face sitting at Becca's dining room table and squeezing a blue accordion. Another man sat next to him playing a piano, but the piano keys were embedded in the table. The piano player nodded at Cyrus, and Cyrus nodded back.

"Why don't you fine folks relax while we play a classic chanson?" the accordion player announced to the room.

A waiter in a black vest hopped over the conveyor belt carrying a haphazard tray with cloches that rumbled and rocked. He set the cloches down at a nearby table, uncovered them, and rats popped out.

But the people at the table didn't scream. Instead, they speared the rats with their forks and ate them.

All around the restaurant/apartment, the people ate the rats joyfully as the piano and accordion played a French classic.

Cyrus tried to run again, but he was still stuck. The fear in his breast kept rising and rising until it entered his throat. He wanted to vomit.

A swirl of wind rushed through him, paralyzing him.

"Oh, Kirk," a strained voice asked. "Kirk! Where are you? Kirk!"

Cyrus recognized the voice.

Bruce MacLeod.

The dead man cried out in a painful howl mixed with bells, and then his voice was gone and Cyrus could move his arms and body again.

His feet were still stuck to the conveyor and now it was leading him in a circle.

Since he couldn't go anywhere, he stopped fighting and let the belt carry him.

He listened. And observed.

No one was afraid. They ate the rats with joy. One table

even asked for more. Cyrus shook his head as a couple gobbled them down.

Somehow, the fact that no one else was afraid calmed him down a little.

Something crawled across his feet.

A brown rat.

Cyrus startled and the rat jumped back. It stood on its hind legs and tilted its head at him.

"Get out of here," he said. "They're going to eat you."

The rat dropped on all fours and crawled on his feet again and chewed Cyrus's shoes.

"Hey, stop!" he said.

More rats spawned out of the hardwood conveyor floor and covered his feet.

He felt the fear rising again but centered himself.

Sharp incisors gnawed at his shoes, pinching him.

"Ow!"

Soon, one of the rats crawled up his leg, hopped on an arm, and clambered up to his shoulder. It screeched.

He lifted a foot out of a shoe and planted it on the belt. Then the other.

Thank God.

The rat on his shoulder purred. Cyrus stepped off the conveyor belt.

Becca's brick wall busted open, exposing a gray void that sucked everything up like a vacuum, and the conveyor belt ramped up speed. Cyrus's shoes flew out of the apartment and into the void, forever gone.

One by one, the patrons in the restaurant zipped into the void, still eating their rats. Did they even know what the hell was happening?

Cyrus ran. His dress socks slipped on the hardwood floor, but he ran as fast as he could toward the apartment door.

Bruce's voice returned.

"Oh, my son! What are they doing to you, my boy? Kirk! We need you…"

Bruce's voice paralyzed Cyrus in mid-stride.

"God…damn…it…" he said. His lips moved, but his body froze. The vacuum pulled him back and the rat jumped up and down on his shoulder.

A chilling wind ripped through him again and his ears filled with the sound of out-of-tune bells.

"Oh, Kirk! Your brother is suffering. I have been through too much for you to abandon me!"

Then Bruce was gone again and Cyrus could move.

Cyrus broke forward, trying to regain lost ground.

He was only a few feet from the door now.

Bruce's voice again. And the wind and bells.

"Kirk!"

"Shut…up…"

Cyrus broke free again and fell on his knees. He pulled himself up but lost his balance. He was halfway toward the door when Bruce's voice cried again, this time in a unintelligible keen that broke all the remaining windows in the apartment.

Tiny little hands sank into Cyrus's blazer, pulling him against the vacuum in a game of tug-of-war. No, not hands —mouths.

A wave of brown rats had hold of him and they pulled him hard. A wave of rats behind them pulled the first wave's tails.

Bruce's howl disappeared. Cyrus broke free, but it was too late. The two waves of rats lifted into the air as if they were in space. They screamed as they zipped past Cyrus.

Cyrus could only wave his hands and hope for the best as Becca's apartment collapsed around him and he was sucked into the ravenous void.

～

Becca shook her head at the sight of Cyrus sprawled on her couch. He hadn't even taken his shoes off.

She threw her keys on the counter and slipped quietly into the living room. She untied her brother's god-awful-looking brown dress shoes that he had bought from the thrift store and tossed them on the floor.

Cyrus turned, nudging his face into the couch cushion.

Becca stood, yawned, and shut off the lights. She was so tired, she could barely walk. Her brother did such a crappy job sweeping the floor that she had to do it again while enduring Aidan's taunts.

"You're even prettier than you looked in my binoculars," he said.

Then she hit him in the face with her broom.

"Aaaagh!"

"Next time, you'll join your dad in that metal box," she said.

Aidan frowned and spent the rest of the night scowling at her. His eyes didn't leave her as she swept the floor, organized the glasses in the bar, and got the bad news from Desmond that both Aidan and Bruce had to stay at the Wicked Cat for the night. Something about a conflict of interest if they stayed at Axel's compound.

Sigh. Another weird day awaited her. And her restaurant was in shambles.

She staggered down her hallway and into her room, where her spongy full-size bed was waiting for her. She kicked off her tennis shoes and face-planted into bed. She rolled over, staring up at the ceiling, thinking of Gilberto.

Where was he right now?

She couldn't shake the image of his hurt face from her mind. There had to be something she could do to make things right for him.

Despite how tired she was, her mind wouldn't shut off. She

tossed and turned for an hour thinking of solutions until she finally closed her eyes to sleep.

"Beer is the best antidote to every problem, you know," Becca said, pouring a tall stout into a glass.

Her mom sat at a table near the bar, eating a bowl of snack pretzels. The Wicked Cat was packed with customers, drinking and laughing in the middle of a sunny day. Cristián rolled open the front loading doors of the bar, exposing the patio, which was covered with tables and chairs and bright red umbrellas that Becca had gotten for cheap at a wholesaler blowout. The umbrellas rippled in the wind, and more patrons funneled into the building, sending the door chime into a frenzy.

"Be right with you!" Becca said.

She carried the beer carefully to her mother, set it down, and sat across from her.

"Where is your brother?" Aurora asked.

A pang of guilt struck Becca as she shrugged. "Probably chasing another girl."

"Maybe you should drink that beer," Aurora said. "You need it more than me."

Suddenly, Becca was drinking her mom's beer. It tasted like shit.

Aurora nodded with encouragement. "Go on," she said. "Drink it all up, honey."

Becca wrinkled her face. "But it tastes horrible!"

"You're even prettier when you drink beer," a male voice said. Aidan was tied in a chair next to their table.

Becca wished she had her broom. "Shut up."

Aurora didn't notice Aidan. The necromancer opened his mouth, but Becca threw the rest of her beer at him.

"I said be quiet!" Becca said.

Aidan sputtered as beer poured down his face.

Becca turned to her mom. "So, I think I need something else."

"You mean, I need something else," Aurora said. "It was my beer."

"Right," Becca said, slipping out of the chair. She grabbed Aidan's chair and dragged him across the busy bar and into the kitchen.

"Don't want to scare Mommy, eh?" Aidan asked.

Becca stared daggers at him before walking into the bar again. A line of people had gathered at the bar. She primped her bandanna, apologized, and started taking orders.

She was making a Manhattan when the front door to the bar opened again and a speckle of prismed sunlight caught her eye. A rush of love and nostalgia tore through her, and she finished the drink and handed it to a customer with a smile.

Even though she couldn't see him, she knew that her father had just walked into the Wicked Cat.

A hand tapped her shoulder. Cristián was waiting behind her.

"Get out of the bar," he said with a grin.

Becca took off her apron and made her way through a crowd, toward the front door, where sunlight was spinning in the glass.

"Dad?" she asked.

She sensed him but couldn't see him.

A pained voice swelled in the air around her.

"Kirk! Son, where are you? You can't do this to us."

Becca whipped around. All the patrons at the bar were enjoying each other's company. No one's face matched the one that was screaming now.

"Kirk! Oh, Kirk, you're failing us, and failing us fast!"

The man's voice mixed in with the sound of bells. A harsh wind ripped through the bar, knocking over one of the patio tables outside. Someone yelled as glass shattered. A waiter helped a woman pick up a broken glass.

Then the man's voice was gone.

A hand waved at Becca, catching her peripheral vision.

"Go on," Aurora said. "He's waiting for you."

Becca smiled again and turned to find her father. She spotted the prism of sunlight across the bar next to the stereo. She pushed through another crowd of people.

"Dad!" she cried.

She saw his bushy blonde hair through another party of people. Thick Coke-bottle glasses and a short-sleeved button-up shirt. He looked around the bar as if he were confused.

"Cyrus?" he called.

"Dad," Becca said.

"David, I don't know where Cyrus is," Aurora called across the bar. Her voice turned sour. "I honestly don't know who he is anymore. But Becca wants to talk to you."

Becca shoved a stubborn party of patrons away.

The man's voice came back again.

"Aaaaaaaaaah…..Kirk…..Noooooo…..Son!"

The voice stopped Becca in her tracks and she looked around again.

"Have fun playing with Mommy and Daddy, sweetie!" another voice cried. Aidan.

Becca gritted her teeth and screamed for her dad.

The entire bar stopped and stared at her. She became self-conscious of everyone's eyes.

Aurora folded her arms. "Now that wasn't necessary, honey."

The swinging doors to the kitchen swung open and then flapped shut.

Becca ran through the doors, calling her dad again.

David Grant had stopped to look at Aidan, who puffed and stared him down.

"Nice feet, buddy," Aidan said.

And then Becca looked at her father's feet and realized that he had none.

Her father said nothing to Aidan and continued walking toward the back door.

"Dad," she said. "You came all this way to see me and then you're just going to leave? That's really sweet of you."

Her dad stopped at the back door and didn't turn back.

"Becca, don't follow," he said. He pushed open the doors and bright white light enveloped his body as he walked out.

Becca stood, stunned.

"You heard him, sweetie," Aidan said. "What'll it be?"

The strange man's voice echoed across the kitchen, reverberating off the pots and pans.

"Oh, Kirk, my Kirk!"

"Quit your cryin', Dad," Aidan said. "He abandoned us."

"No! Kirk…"

"He's not your dad," Becca said.

"Yes, he is."

"Leave my dad out of this!" Becca cried, pushing him over.

"Ha. Wrong dad," Aidan said, laughing.

Becca's face hardened and she tore toward the front door, pushing the center bar.

Brilliant white light blinded her as she burst into the alley.

Cyrus woke up on his back in a puddle of water. His clothes were soggy.

He snapped upright. He was in a dark tunnel that smelled like mold and river water.

Dozens of eyes stared at him in the darkness.

The rats. Were they the ones that tried to save him? Their energy was calm and he did not fear them.

Cyrus shifted into a rat and landed in the puddle he woke

up in. The tunnel was completely dark now, but he sensed the rats.

The rats surrounded him, and he walked with them in a train down the long tunnel that seemed to stretch into noth- ingness.

They walked and walked until the tunnel ceiling opened. Cyrus shifted back into a human.

He couldn't discern anything in the shadows. It was hope- lessly dark, squalid, and smelly.

The rats squabbled beneath him, nipping at each other and hissing

All he could do was shift back into a rat and keep walking in solidarity with the rats. Wherever they were going, they were all in it together.

Becca floated in an endless sea of milky white light.

She was awake, but her body was asleep.

She watched her own body as it floated in a fetal position, so serene and peaceful.

Becca settled in her own thoughts as her body drifted in a quiet stasis.

Had she ever heard her true inner voice before? It babbled and babbled, and she couldn't understand it. But whatever it was saying must have been important. Her voice said the muddled words with such intensity and conviction.

The sound of a distant toilet flushed, then the sprinkle of a shower. She lost sight of her body. One second it was there, and then it was gone.

Fear struck her as she scanned the endless nothingness for herself.

She felt her consciousness zoom forward with its own energy, and the milky world burbled and swirled as she searched for herself.

It might take forever, but she told herself she had forever and a day.

She calmed down, listening to her inner voice speak as her mind sped forward, spinning and swirling and gyrating toward the unknown place where her body had gone.

~

Cyrus woke slowly to bright morning light. The sun shining through Becca's bay window hurt his eyes. He covered his eyes and turned his head away.

He smacked his lips and yawned, stretching his legs and arms.

Crazy dreams.

His phone rang. The words *Lorenzo Fontanelli* appeared.

His new boss. Owner of Fontanelli & Son Pest Control. The burly exterminator who had a brusque personality but a kind heart. Cyrus was training. Becca gave him hell about being an exterminator of the very species he shifted into, but he took the job because it would teach him how not to get killed as a rat.

"This is Cyrus," he said.

"Hey, champ," Fontanelli said. "You awake?"

"No, I'm still in dreamland," Cyrus said.

Fontanelli paused.

"Listen, uh, I hate to do this to you on a Sunday and all, but I'm getting calls out the wazoo and I need some help."

"Seriously, Leo?" Cyrus asked. "I'm supposed to go to Sunday school."

"You're young, but you ain't that young," Fontanelli said. "You wouldn't believe how many rat sightings there were last night. My voicemail box was full this morning and that *never* happens. This'll be good trainin' for you. I'm missing out on mass myself, so I'm making sacrifices too, know what I mean?"

Fontanelli gave him an address in Bucktown. Cyrus said

he'd be there in an hour. He glanced at the clock. Five after nine.

He stretched again and hopped to his feet. A dream about rats followed by unexpected rat work nearby…was this why he had the dream? Something told him he needed to go.

On his way to the bathroom, he passed Becca's room. The door was open. Becca lay tangled in her sheets, her pillows strewn all over the bed. Her sheets hung off the side of the bed like dramatic theater curtains. Becca snored loudly.

He could have totally taken a picture for future blackmail, but she had been through a lot. Just as much as him.

He shut her door quietly, showered, and went to the kitchen to make breakfast.

~

Becca jolted awake with a gasp.

Seconds ago, she had been searching for herself in an endless world.

She rubbed her head as she lay staring at her ceiling again. A needling sadness fell upon her. A heaviness in her heart she couldn't shake. She didn't even want to get out of bed. But she didn't want to go to sleep either.

The smell of bacon, sausage, and potatoes drifted into her nose. A sizzle came from the kitchen.

Yawning, she rolled out of bed. Her hardwood floor was cold on her feet.

Cyrus was at the kitchen table, eating a steaming plate of bacon, sausage links, and potatoes O'Brien. His hair was still wet from a fresh shower, and he wore a red ringer t-shirt and khaki shorts. He had put a plate in Becca's spot and covered it with a napkin. A steaming coffee mug sat next to the food.

Becca stretched and slid into her chair. She said a quiet thanks before eating.

Cyrus watched her.

"Tough sleep?" he asked.

"That's an understatement."

"Me too," Cyrus said. "I slept like a storm. I'm pretty sure it was because Bruce is down there. He's pretty restless."

Becca cut into a sausage link and said nothing. As she ate it, it reminded her of her dad. He had taught Cyrus how to make sausage. Then she remembered the dream and got lost replaying it in her mind.

"Bec?"

She looked up.

"You all right?" Cyrus asked.

"I just woke up weird, that's all," Becca said. After a short silence, she said, "I dreamed about Dad again."

"Again?" Cyrus asked mid-chew. "Geez. I mean—don't take the wrong way. It's just strange."

Becca shrugged. "Grief never goes away, I guess."

Cyrus scooped up the rest of his food. "I gotta run. I told old Font that I'd give him a couple of hours this morning. I'll be back before you open the bar. Maybe then we can figure out what to do about Aidan, and Desmond will have an Axel update."

He grabbed his black backpack off a hook and he unplugged his electric skateboard near the door.

"Cheer up, Bec," he said. "Today's a new day and hopefully a good day. Can't get any worse, at least."

Becca regarded her coffee cup. "Yeah. You're right," she said flatly.

The front door opened and shut. Cyrus left her at the table, staring at the ripples that flowed across the surface of her coffee from the door shutting.

CHAPTER TWENTY-SEVEN

CYRUS CLIPPED ON HIS HELMET, threw his electric skateboard down, and palmed his remote control as he rolled down the alley behind the Wicked Cat.

He leaped onto his skateboard and soon he was cruising at half speed as he turned left out of the alley onto a residential road.

Man, after all he'd been through, it felt so good to be back on his board. For the first time in twenty-four hours, he was back in control. Wheels rolling on asphalt, fresh summer air hitting his face, hints of coffee grounds and croissants from the Wicked Cat's morning rush, distant car horns, and nothing but endless city streets, brownstones, shops, and waving trees ahead—this was his kind of morning.

He wove between two cars and ran a red light at an empty intersection before he hit full speed and the skateboard's motor whined. For a while, the only thing that mattered was the ride: the closed storefronts, people walking down the street in their Sunday best, hungover twenty-somethings eating breakfast on patios, sleepy shoebox condos that he swore weren't there two months ago, and cars that weren't in a hurry for a change. He crossed under the riveted L tracks of the

Blue Line just as a train bolted across in a metallic, creaky rush.

If only he had had time for a ride last night. He did some of his best thinking on the board. Surely he could have come up with an idea that might have changed his fortune. He would have gladly switched the church van for his electric skateboard any time.

He had been so busy reacting that he didn't have much time to think. This is exactly how Murgalen wanted it. If she could have watched, the tree nymph would probably have a sadistic grin on her face.

The bitter taste of iron jumped into his mouth at the thought of Murgalen succeeding at her plot.

He slowed to a stop at a red light. Two tall glass buildings framed a huge vertical cloud in the sky. It reminded him of the cloud of rats. He stared at it, reminiscing about that night: the thunderstorms, the screeching rats, Murgalen's murderous laughter.

A horn honked at him and he realized the light had turned green. He waved an apology at the car behind him and hit the acceleration button on his remote. He crouched down to get wind, and soon he was at full speed again.

He whisked by a sign for a local community college advertising a certificate in data and analytics. A beautiful woman in a business suit with her arms folded smiled. The sign said, "We'll make data your business."

As he coasted through a right turn, he thought of Marisol.

Oh boy, what a date that had been. At least she was okay.

Crap. He told her he'd call her to check in. If he didn't do it now, there was no telling when he'd get around to it.

He crossed into a bike lane, slipped his earbuds out of his pocket, stuck them in, and told the smart assistant on his phone to call Marisol.

After a few rings, she answered. Cyrus expected to wake her up, but she sounded awake.

"Hey, Marisol, it's Cyrus."

"Oh. Hi."

Cyrus merged lanes. "I was just calling to check in. Last night was pretty crazy, huh?"

"I've been better," Marisol said quickly.

Silence.

"Are you sore?" Cyrus asked. "I remember lying on top of you. I didn't hurt you, did I?"

"It's not that," she said. "I'll be okay. How are you?"

Cyrus narrowed his eyes with suspicion.

As one of Desmond's Regulators, he had to keep in contact with her for a while to monitor her. The paranormal was known to make people crazy.

"I didn't sleep much," Cyrus said, laughing in an attempt to get her talking. "I kept dreaming about rats."

"At least you slept," Marisol said, her voice brightening a little.

"I'm…sorry," Cyrus said.

"I think I'll spend the rest of my day with a bottle of wine," Marisol said. "Several bottles of wine, actually."

"That bad, huh?" Cyrus asked. He needed to switch lanes to the left, but a flower delivery van wouldn't let him over. He motioned to the driver to get her attention, but she stared ahead, ignoring him. He wanted to curse her out.

Marisol didn't say anything at first. She started to speak, but then stopped. From the tone in her start, Cyrus knew she was thinking something.

"What we saw last night was…out of the ordinary, to say the least," Cyrus said. "Just know that if you want to talk, I'm here."

"Thanks. You're so sweet."

"This whole thing is my fault," Cyrus said, grinning. "If I hadn't spilled wine on my blazer, calamity wouldn't have ensued."

Marisol let out a small laugh.

"Can I make it up to you tonight over ice cream? If I spill anything on myself this time, it might be the end of the world, but hey, we only live once, right?"

"Sure," she said. "I'd like that."

"Cool," Cyrus said. He gave her a name of an ice cream shop.

Marisol agreed and they hung up.

Cyrus shot an angry look at the delivery van.

"Hey, lady, do you see me over here, or what?"

The driver kept her gaze ahead and slowed to a stop at the light. He officially missed his turn. He flipped her off as he wheeled through the intersection.

Freaking people.

His earbuds buzzed and an electronic voice said, "Incoming call from Mom."

Cyrus tapped his buds as he finally merged into the left lane a little too late. He'd catch the next light and loop around.

"Hey, Mom."

"Cyrus Alexander Grant," Aurora said sternly.

"What did I do this time?" he asked, eyeing the next intersection. He had a few hundred feet before he needed to slow down.

"You better give me one good reason why you can't return a phone call," Aurora said.

Cyrus made an eek face. His mom had called him last night in the middle of all the hustle.

"Aaaah, yeah, sorry, Mom," he said. "I got carried away."

"I called you two times in a row, which might have meant it was an emergency," Aurora said. "I'm the only parent you have left. When I'm gone, you and your sister are on your own, buster."

Cyrus paused. "Mom, are you okay?"

"I was attacked by a bunch of rats last night," she said. "And I had a four-hour commute to go two miles from the grocery store to the house. And I was up sick, worried about you and Becca, but you wouldn't return my calls. But otherwise, I'm fine."

Every word hit him like a bullet.

"Rats?" he asked, gulping. He slowed down as he approached a red light, flanked by a truck on his right. "I didn't think your part of town had them."

"It was horrible, Cy," Aurora said, venting. "I went to the grocery store and the place was overrun with rats. They were running around as if they were scared. On my entire drive home, I kept seeing waves of them in the street."

Cyrus didn't know what to say. It was just another confirmation that his dream meant something.

"Is it so hard to pick up your phone and send a text message that asks if everything is okay?" Aurora asked. "If something had happened to me, I wouldn't have been able to count on your *or* your sister, and frankly, that pisses me off."

"I'm sorry, Mom," Cyrus said. "Lesson learned."

"You're on your skateboard again, aren't you?" Aurora asked.

"I prefer not to answer that since I'm already in trouble," Cyrus said.

"Double trouble," Aurora said. "You are going to give me a heart attack."

"Public transit is going to give *me* a heart attack, Mom."

The light turned green and he got a left turn arrow.

Aurora's line went silent as he arced through the turn.

"Mom?" Cyrus asked.

Aurora's line crackled.

Cyrus slipped his phone out of his pocket. The screen still showed that he was connected with his mom, but the call timer was stuck at one minute, twenty-three seconds.

Cyrus slipped his phone in his pocket and accidentally crossed into the right lane. Thank God there was no one there.

A flower delivery van passed him on the left. The smell of fresh cut flowers assaulted his nose.

He sighed as he saw the same female driver. He passed the same buildings and came to the same intersection where he couldn't pass on the left.

"Here we go again," he muttered.

He veered to the right and between two parked cars and flipped his board onto the sidewalk. He stopped and slung his board on his backpack as he stared at a dimly lit alley with a pergola covered with hanging vines.

A cool breeze blew as he passed under the pergola toward a cobblestone square where two trees waited for him.

The trees shifted into female shapes as he approached. Oleandra and Rue waited for him. They looked exactly the same as the last time he saw them—stylish. Oleandra wore the same business blouse and skirt, and Rue wore the same leopard print dress. Cyrus wondered what the hell they had been doing since he last saw them, and if nymphs ever bathed.

"You are failing us, Cyrus," Oleandra said.

"Screw you," Cyrus said.

"Have you forgotten our ultimatum?" Rue asked.

"No, it's etched into my brain," Cyrus said. "Kill the giant rat or you'll destroy my loved ones. How could I forget?"

"Why haven't you produced results?" Oleandra asked.

"Maybe you both have had your heads up your trunks, but I've been busy working on it," Cyrus said. "Criticize me all you want, but I don't see you lifting a tree branch to help me."

"Ah, so it's help you desire?" Oleandra asked. A sly grin spread across her lips as she circled him.

"No deals," Cyrus said, not taking his eyes off the nymph. "I'm not that stupid."

"Pity," Oleandra said. "We're just reminding you of your obligation."

"Can I go now?" Cyrus asked, folding his arms.

"Perhaps we should give him a *little* help," Rue said, giggling.

Cyrus raised an eyebrow.

"Go ahead and attach some strings to me while you're at it," he said.

"How do vines sound?" Rue asked.

Cyrus puffed.

"It has come to our attention that there are two necromancers who desire to make your life hell," Oleandra said.

"Wow, you're super late," Cyrus said. "If that's the help you're giving me, then piss off."

"But there is something else you should know," Oleandra said. "One in particular—the dark-skinned one—is rumored to be particularly powerful. He is not who he appears to be. Perhaps that will be useful to you."

"Cryptic much?" Cyrus asked.

Both of the women had transformed into trees again. A gust blew him back, telling him his time was up.

He glanced at them angrily and threw his skateboard down, bulleted into traffic and back to the street where he needed to make his left turn. Ironically, the flower delivery van was gone.

A shimmer rippled across the street as he leaned into the turn.

"Cyrus?" Aurora asked. "Are you there?"

Cyrus sighed with relief as he continued down the street.

"Sorry. Some jerk cut me off."

"I'm leaving in about two hours," Aurora said. "You have the address of the restaurant, right?"

"Leaving?" Cyrus asked, confused. "Restaurant?"

"You didn't seriously forget—"

Cyrus remembered in a flash and he finished her sentence.

"Your birthday—no way," he said as quickly and convincingly as he could.

"I have the theater tickets already, remember," Aurora

said. "You can make it all up to me by being present for once."

Crap. His mom's birthday celebration.

"Yep. See you soon," he said.

They hung up, and he gulped.

CHAPTER TWENTY-EIGHT

Kirk landed in an alley with a sickening pop, a sizzle of bright light, and a thud.

He landed face-first on asphalt and grimaced.

Traveling to wherever the hell he just went took a lot of energy from him. He wanted to lie there with his eyes closed and just rest, but he couldn't.

Well, maybe he could. He took in a few deep breaths, taking in the odor of rotting trash and humid air.

The air…It smelled different.

He opened his eyes and bright sunlight made him squint. He rolled over and looked up at the bright blue sky.

"What the hell?"

Slowly, he rolled to his knees, panting. He stood.

When he left to speak with the nymph, it was late at night. He couldn't have been talking to her for more than five minutes. He put a hand in front of his face as his eyes adjusted to the sun.

Sun.

Was it…morning?

He swallowed as a low-pitched, frenzied laugh started on the wind, quiet at first. The laughter carried over to him.

Then he sensed a large mass standing behind him. His peripheral vision caught a long cattle horn.

"What's going on?" Kirk asked.

"I delivered you from the faerie world," the demon said. "Just like you asked."

"No, not like I asked," Kirk said. "When we left, it was dark."

The demon laughed again. Pangs of fear struck Kirk. A little voice told him to run, but he knew he could never outrun a demon.

"Time moves differently in their world," the demon said. "It is morning. That means you failed to deliver the girl to me as promised. Therefore, I'll have to secure my collateral to achieve the goal myself."

Kirk repeated the sentence, unable to believe what he was hearing.

"We had a deal, human," the demon said, taking a step toward Kirk.

Kirk stepped away. "You son of a bitch."

"I'm a demon, remember?" the demon asked. "Son of a devil is more accurate."

"We'll make another deal," Kirk said, trying to think of a solution. His mind raced and for the first time, he didn't know what else to say. "What do you want? More years of my life? More—"

"No more deals," the demon said. "Your desperation is frustrating."

"You will give me an extension," Kirk said.

"No more extensions," the demon said, snarling. Every word of the demon's deep voice boomed in Kirk's chest. "You made me take the nymph's assignment, remember? It will be much easier to accomplish with a human host."

"No," Kirk said frantically. "No!"

He ran, but after just a few steps, something slammed into him hard and he was on the ground. He pulled himself into a crawl, but the demon leaned on him with all of its weight. Its toe rings pressed on Kirk's jacket.

"I'll make another deal with another demon," Kirk said. "I will destroy you."

"Good luck," the demon said. "If I don't destroy you first."

Every cell in Kirk's body hummed.

"You son of a bitch!" Kirk cried again.

The demon laughed again as it descended into Kirk's body, filling him with humming.

Kirk screamed but his mouth didn't move—yet he heard the scream all the same inside of his head.

His arm moved of its own accord. Then his legs. His eyes watched as he brought himself to his feet and dusted gravel off his denim jacket.

Then he was walking. Walking. Walking!

He didn't command his feet to move, yet they were moving.

"I like this body," his mouth said. "It is a dark temple of skin, bone, and brimming potential. Though it's only a temporary arrangement, I promise to treat it right, human."

Kirk's spirit shrank inside of him and he stopped trying to fight it. He could only watch as the demon cracked his neck, buttoned his denim jacket, and strutted out of the alley and into the sunshine.

CHAPTER TWENTY-NINE

BECCA WALKED into the Wicked Cat, her hair still damp from a shower. Instead of the shambles the bar had been in last night even after she cleaned up, the scene this morning was shockingly normal.

People sat drinking coffee and reading newspapers. One woman in the corner was sipping a latte and working on a script.

Cristián was working the espresso machine. He waved.

Becca couldn't believe that a fight had happened here last night. Save for a few missing tables and chairs, not a single element was out of place. Even the glass window with the Wicked Cat logo was repaired as if Axel never threw Gilberto through it. Becca and Desmond both spent an hour tarping up the gaping hole after Cyrus went to bed. Relief washed over her at seeing her shop the way it was supposed to be.

"You're looking awfully purple today," Cristián said.

Becca took a loop of purple hair, wrapped it around her wrist, and tied it up.

"Nice to see a normal scene for a change," she said, sitting at a chair in front of the espresso machine.

"Desmond told me to come in," Cristián said. "He said you wouldn't mind."

"Not at all," she said.

"Want an espresso?" Cristián asked.

"Cyrus made me breakfast," she said.

"He is getting more mature every day," Cristián said. "I'm speechless."

"I am too sometimes," Becca said. "Thanks for opening."

Cristián finished the espresso and delivered it to a man reading a magazine.

A waiter exited the kitchen. The swinging doors flapped a few times behind him. Becca spotted a flash of leather, which seemed strange. Nothing in the kitchen had a leather texture.

She got up and pushed through the kitchen doors.

Desmond was napping in a chair next to her office, resting his head against the wall. His trench coat ran down to the floor like a leather waterfall.

The windows to her office, usually clear, were frosted over. The door was padlocked, and the lock glowed purple.

Desmond jolted awake and wiped his face.

"Morning, sleeping beauty," he said, yawning.

"You cleaned the place up nice," Becca said.

"Least I could do," Desmond said. "I put you through a lot last night. I called in a few favors—all magical, of course. Hopefully saved you some money on that front window."

"Thanks."

Becca inspected the frosted glass to her office. She'd accidentally left her phone in there. She could do without it for a while. "How'd Aidan and Bruce do last night?"

"Bruce wouldn't shut up," Desmond said. "I had to gag Aidan."

"He wouldn't shut up either, huh?" Becca asked. "Shocker."

"I don't mind *him* talking, even if he talks trash," Desmond said. "The problem is he might talk up a demon."

"Oh," Becca said. "Good idea."

She pulled her bandanna out of her back pocket and tied it on her head.

"Get some more rest," she said. "I know you're tired."

"We'll get them moved tonight," Desmond said. "I've got a location lined up. Had to call in more favors."

Out of habit, Becca checked herself in the frosted glass. She couldn't see how well she tied her bandanna. "I trust you, even though I get cranky sometimes. I'm headed out. I should be back in a little while."

Desmond nodded, folded his arms, and closed his eyes.

Becca made her way through the kitchen.

Sadness struck her.

In her dream, she'd been in the kitchen too. It was the last time she saw her dad before he disappeared.

"Don't follow," she mumbled to herself as if it would teach her what he meant.

She said it again as she pushed open the back door.

She took a bus to Hermosa, Gilberto's neighborhood. It dropped her off a few blocks from *La Iglesia del Espiritu Santo*.

She enjoyed the quiet Sunday walk. When was the last time she ever took a stroll by herself, taking in the summer day and just *being*? Not since she established the Wicked Cat. As much as she loved her baby, it took a lot out of her.

She forgot what it was like to be out from behind espresso machines and kegs and underneath the open sky. She told herself she ought to walk more often. The Wicked Cat practically ran itself without her. Couldn't she take fifteen minutes to take care of herself?

Hermosa was her home for six months before she founded the Wicked Cat. She lived in an old lady's crusty basement on a short-term lease while she used her dad's life insurance money to get the restaurant going. She didn't miss that basement, didn't miss the old lady who watched her every move and coming and going, and she didn't miss the neighborhood. Parts of it were a little too seedy for her. She had never been happier to give a landlord notice.

She passed a white house that reminded her of milk, of the universe she had explored in her dream. She still had no idea what it meant, if it meant anything at all. How many times in her life had she woken up with intense feelings of anxiety in her chest for no reason at all? With time, the impact of dreams faded. She hoped that would happen with this one.

She tried to shake the dream off again, but it wouldn't go away. It was still there just beneath the surface, ready to rise any time, and she hated it.

She turned a corner. The church rose through the trees. She recognized and appreciated its beautiful brickwork. The van they'd driven yesterday was there too, in all its broken-windowed glory. Gilberto must have returned it. This time, the tiny parking lot was full of cars. The distant echo of a rock song pulsated through the air.

She couldn't help but glance at the roof of the school across the street. Last night, Aidan tried to snipe them from there. Fortunately, the roof was empty, and two Chicago flags rippled in the wind.

She stood at the front doors of the church. The cedar doors were propped open. The music she'd heard before was louder, coming from the sanctuary.

She entered. The quiet church last night was completely transformed. Up the small set of stairs, people sang and clapped in the barrel-vaulted sanctuary. A tidy band of drums, piano, guitar, bass, and three singers played an intense song in Spanish that reminded her of a Rolling Stones tune—super old school.

Becca entered, and the same musty odor hit her hard.

An elderly Latino man in a button-down shirt and slacks

waved and said hello in broken English. She shook his hand. He smiled, revealing a gold tooth, and handed her a program for the morning's sermon. It was in Spanish and she couldn't read any of it.

The man helped her up the stairs and motioned for her to enter the sanctuary.

Becca entered reluctantly. The band wrapped up its song and everyone broke into applause and sat down.

A pastor in a blue suit spoke in Spanish, walking across the pulpit. The piano player, a teenager who looked like he was barely out of high school, played a slow, quiet song on the piano. The fans in the ceiling were spinning on overdrive, circulating hot air around the room.

Becca found an empty seat in a pew next to a Latino family with a baby. The mother saw her, smiled, and offered her hand. Becca shook it and nodded respectfully. The little baby girl on her shoulder lifted its head and stared at Becca with big black eyes. Becca wiggled her fingers at the baby and smiled. The baby girl let out a happy coo, revealing a single tooth on its bottom gum, and turned away to fixate on her mother.

The pastor raised his voice and said something about Jesus. Someone in the pew in front of her said "Amen."

Becca scanned the sanctuary and the tops of people's heads until she saw the jet black, slightly balding head she was looking for.

Gilberto sat a few pews in front of her on the opposite side. He wore a Chicago Bears jacket, and he was watching the pastor with an empty look. An open Bible lay in his lap. He had cuts on his face, but he looked much better than the bloodied version he had been yesterday. Knowing Gilberto, he probably healed himself from anything serious.

Was he even paying attention? She told herself that someone's worship was none of her business, and she waited as the piano player articulated a beautiful solo that reminded her of an open sky filled with clouds and sun rays and God's grace.

The pastor ended with a prayer, and the band picked up with another happy song as the congregation rose and headed for the exits.

Becca politely negotiated her way toward Gilberto, but the crowd was moving too slow and families were stopping to socialize. The healer dug his hands in his pockets and streamed into the lobby with the crowd.

She caught up with him on the sidewalk. She was almost out of breath.

"Hey," she said, tapping him on the shoulder. "You walk fast."

Gilberto frowned. "What do you want?"

"Can we please talk?" Becca asked.

"Leave me alone," Gilberto said, walking away.

"I'm not leaving," Becca said.

Gilberto waved her away.

"Fine," Becca said. "I'll be the world's craziest stalker until you talk to me."

He still ignored her, skipping across the street.

"You're seriously going to be like that, huh?" she asked, following.

Gilberto quickened his pace, and Becca did the same. Soon they were away from the hustle and bustle of the church and on a quiet residential street.

She mirrored his pace, folding her arms as she walked.

After two blocks, Gilberto stopped at a stop sign, whipped around, and yelled, "What is your problem? Why won't you leave me alone?"

"Because I want to talk," Becca said. "I had hoped we could talk normally."

"Normal?" Gilberto asked, fuming. "Since you haven't been paying attention, there's nothing normal about me!"

Silence.

"I ought to be dead right now," Gilberto said. "Then everyone's problems would be solved. So why don't you go back and try to convince Axel to change his mind?"

"I'm not talking to Axel," Becca said quietly and staring him in the eyes. He was frightened, angry, and bitter. "I'm here to talk to you."

"We talked. Happy now?"

Gilberto crossed the street. Becca hesitated, but then she hardened and jogged to catch up.

"I'm still here, you know," she said.

"Do you want a cookie?" he asked sarcastically, as if she deserved a prize for following him so long. She wasn't going to let him get away with a remark like that.

"Oatmeal raisin cookies would be awesome, but I didn't think you knew how to bake," she said.

They walked in silence.

"Okay, I'm sorry if I insulted your cooking skills," Becca said. "Maybe you make the best cookies in the world. Want to show me otherwise?"

Four blocks later, the sun slipped out from behind a cloud and the temperature rose. Becca took off her bandanna, let her hair down, and wiped her face with her bandanna.

She was still following Gilberto, announcing her presence every few hundred feet.

"I told you I'm not leaving," Becca said.

"And I told you I'm not turning around," Gilberto said. "The sooner you leave, the sooner you'll make us both happy."

"No, the sooner you'll make yourself happy, which is to say not at all."

Gilberto stopped again.

"I've had it with you," he said.

"Then let's talk and you can get rid of me forever."

He paused and regarded her words. "You really aren't going to leave, are you?"

"You really haven't been listening to a word I've been saying, have you?"

Gilberto sighed angrily, stomped over to a wrought-iron gate, and pushed it open.

Becca had been so busy trailing him that she forgot what his house looked like: an ugly, mustard-yellow house with a lawn overgrown with weeds. The siding was falling off and some planks were missing. The dormer window on the top floor was covered with a 2016 Cubs World Series W white flag, and a neon sign in the front window flashed the word "Curandero" in Spanish. In her limited language skills, she remembered that the word meant "healer."

Gilberto left the gate open and Becca squeezed through and shut it behind her.

A black cat mewed at them from the porch. Gilberto said something in Spanish to it and caressed it for a moment. He plopped down on his concrete steps and stared.

"You got five minutes," he said.

He had calmed down somewhat. He wasn't in the calmest state, but it was as good as it was going to get.

Becca stuck her bandanna in her back pocket, self-conscious about her bright purple hair. But that didn't matter.

"Gilberto, I'm so sorry for everything that happened to you," she said.

"Me too," he said.

"None of this is your fault," Becca said. "I feel responsible. If I hadn't sent Cyrus onto the church roof as a rat, maybe none of this would have happened. That was my crazy idea."

She paced around the yard. "I just wanted this to be over. You were so…annoying, and I thought if we could take a shortcut then you'd get what you needed and be gone."

Gilberto looked down.

"But the more I got to know you, the more I liked having you around," Becca said. "And the more I felt sorry for what Axel did to you."

"He should have just killed me like he planned," Gilberto said. He looked up at her angrily. "Do you have any idea what it's like to live like this? Knowing that every moment might be your last? To have to keep apologizing to Axel for a mistake I made years ago? I made my repentance. I've suffered long enough."

"What happened between you and Axel?" Becca asked.

"It's a long story," Gilberto said, and Becca imagined herself in his place as he told it.

"Axel sought me out..."

Because he had a job for me.

It was a few years ago. I was a full healer back then, taking care of my mom because she had dementia. I was working with gangs, healing gangbangers at night and taking care of her during the day.

I keep a garden in the backyard because that's how I grow my herbs to do what I do. One night, I was picking some rosemary and a voice called me. I turned around and didn't see anybody. It was right around the time we had a turf war here in Hermosa, so I couldn't be too careful.

The voice called me again and I put my hand on a little Glock I used to carry in those times.

A boy was standing at the gate to my backyard with his fingers on the mesh. He was probably ten or eleven. He was white too, which wasn't unusual but a little rare around here.

"Gilberto, sir, I'd like to talk to you."

"Where are your parents?" I asked. Kids being out so late at night always made me a little scared because I knew the horrors of the dark.

"My father would like to speak with you," the boy said. "Will you come with me to meet him?"

I looked behind him, and in my little alley was a black Mercedes sedan. A car like that on my street was liable to get jacked, if you know what I mean.

"Is your dad in the car?" I asked.

"No, that's my chauffeur," the boy said.

"Chauffeur," I said. I didn't believe him. Maybe it was some trick to get me in the car so some guy could pop out of the back and put me out of commission.

"Your dad ain't with *Los tiburones*, is he?"

"I don't…know what that is."

He definitely wasn't with the shark gang, then.

"He police?"

The boy's face brightened. "My dad said no, he's not police."

"*Dios mio*," I said. "He's even feeding you answers. Look, kid. I don't know who your dad is, but I'm busy. If he wants to talk, give him my number."

I pulled out a scrap of paper and a pen and wrote my number.

The boy didn't take it.

"If you don't come, Mr. Sanchez, I'm going to be in trouble."

Now he was trying to guilt me. It was bath time for my mom and she was going to start calling for me soon.

"Why won't you believe me?" the boy asked.

"Sure, I believe you," I said. "But I'm busy."

"No, you should *believe* me," the boy said. The next thing I knew, a crazy white light turned night into day and almost blinded me. When my eyes adjusted, an angel hovered in my backyard. A feather floated down and landed in my bucket of rosemary leaves.

I stared up at the boy's face in awe. He said, "You won't be harmed, and your mother will be safe. You must trust me."

I had never seen an angel before. At least, not this kind. But I'm a religious guy and I have faith, so I set my bucket down and got in the car.

To my surprise, a woman was driving. Short hair, sunglasses, and a butch vibe. I sat in the back, and as the car pulled away, I watched as night returned, and the boy stood in the backyard, waving.

The lady didn't say much. She had a constant snarl on her face. I felt like I could talk to that kid, but not her. Every time I tried to ask her something, she interrupted me mid-sentence. There was irritation in her voice, even when she asked me if I wanted more cool air.

She took me to Axel's compound. I had never met him before. I had heard of a guy named Valentine who was so powerful that you didn't want to cross him, but I was just a guy in Hermosa, and I kept to myself.

Valentine's mansion was nuts. There was a fountain with a gargoyle and an angel hugging each other in his front yard. The foyer was all marble.

The lady led me through one lavish room after another until we came to a gym. Axel was in a muscle shirt bench-pressing a giant weight without any help.

The lady introduced me and he didn't even stop benching to talk to me.

"I'm not going to waste any time," he said.

He offered me thirty thousand dollars and a free favor on the spot. Then he told me that he and his crew were in some trouble with a goddess and that he needed help.

"She thinks this city belongs to her," he said, gritting his teeth. "And I'm going to show her just how much the world has changed."

He threw the barbell on the floor. "That's all you need to know. Got it?"

I gulped. This guy looked like he could rip me apart.

"Here's what you're gonna do," he said.

Next thing I know, the lady drove me to a marina and told me to wait for a phone call or a text message. If I received a phone call, I had to be ready to heal because it meant one of Axel's crew was hurt. If I received a text message, it would thank me for my time and my help wasn't needed. I just had to find my way home.

I waited at the marina on a dock, watching the stars over the Chicago River. The place was so beautiful that I didn't want to leave. I prayed and prayed to God that I got a text message. It would be the easiest money I ever made. I prayed hard, man, harder than I ever prayed in my life. That kind of money was enough to pay for in-home nurses for my mom. It was a blessing—at least that was what I thought at the time.

Then I got the phone call. Someone was screaming at me.

"Hurry up and get over here! Don't waste a second or I'll fucking kill you!"

Raaah, raaah, raaah!

I could hardly keep the phone on my ear.

I followed the instructions that the lady told me. Dock seventeen, white speedboat. I took it east up the river and out into the lake, hugged the shore, and looked for the flashing lights.

There were flashing lights, all right. Lightning. The clouds were dark near the shore and lightning was pulsing like a strobe light.

There wasn't a dock, but there was a small gravel beach, so I parked the boat.

A black guy came running. He was just as muscular as Axel and I wondered what kind of paranormal he was. At first, I thought he was trying to escape, but I saw that he was holding a woman, and she had a giant gash across her stomach. Her eyes were closed and she was grimacing.

"You the healer?" he asked.

From the look in his eyes, I knew the woman's situation wasn't good.

He set her on one of the seats in the boat. Within seconds, blood was everywhere.

In those days before Desmond banned me from magic use, I used to carry a few herb kits with me.

Herbs have many restorative properties, but regular people don't get the full benefits of the plant. Grind up some herbs into a paste and you might feel a little better. But if I use herbs, I can unlock their true power. I can speed up the restorative benefits in addition to doing a little healing magic.

I went to work on the woman. Only then did I pay attention to her appearance. She had hair the color of dark cola, and passionate sage eyes. She was moaning. She was in so much pain that she couldn't even cry.

I pulled out my pouch and went to work, mixing up a concoction of lavender, lemon verbena, and foxtail. I cut it with a spell I learned on the streets when guys were dying in my arms and bullets were flying and sirens were on the way.

Green magic flowed into her body, but it wasn't enough. She needed just a little more to get out of critical condition. Then, a hospital could take over. I'm a healer but I'm not a full healer. I can stop you from dying and bring you back if you're freshly dead. I sling herbs. That's what I'm good at, and the only thing I'm good at.

I blew through the contents of my kit in just a few minutes. There wasn't enough healing magic in my first kit, so I grabbed another, but it wasn't there.

It wasn't there!

I searched my clothes frantically.

I never left home without at least two kits. It was a habit— I never knew when I would need them.

But when the phone rang back at the marina, I think the second kit fell in the water. I was dangling my legs over the dock and the ring surprised me. The kit was in the bottom of my coat, and I snagged it on the wood, see. I didn't think anything of it at the time, but now I was paying the price.

Without the kit, the woman was going to die.

I did the only thing I knew how to do—performed CPR, prayed, and tried to talk to her and bring her comfort. Dying is a bitch, and I've seen my fair share of it.

She died in my arms. Eyes wide open, mouth in an ugly position.

"I'm sorry," I told her.

I set her down on the seat. Death always takes your heart and stomps on it.

The black guy didn't say a word. He jumped off the boat and wandered into the field next to the beach.

Someone yelled in grief, and lightning struck again, shaking the ground.

Axel came running to the boat. He grabbed me, gritted his teeth, and threw me in the water.

Turns out the woman was his wife. Well, one of his many wives throughout history. I let her die.

I only heard a man cry like that a few times in my life.

I treaded water and swam to the beach. A boot landed on my back and I landed face-first in the gravel. It was Axel.

I told him I was sorry, but he didn't listen.

He beat the living shit out of me, and I thought for sure he was going to kill me. But just before he gave the last blow, a giant tree exploded out of nowhere and slammed into him.

He was fighting a nymph. Those damn things are horrifying in their real form.

Axel lost his mind. He turned into his nephilim form. A tornado formed and the wind blew so hard, I had to run for shelter. I threw myself on an old parking lot made of asphalt and covered my head.

Axel screamed with rage and I'll never forget how powerful he was. The nymph wasn't a weakling either. They traded blows, probably dozens of times.

Then, a loud crack ripped across the area, like a giant tree had fallen.

Well, a tree had fallen. The nymph. The thunder and wind stopped and I peeked my head up and saw Axel ripping the nymph apart limb from limb. When he was done, that nymph looked like she had been thrown in a woodchipper.

A hand grabbed me and pulled me. The black guy. He told me to get a head start and to hide.

I knew if I didn't run, Axel would kill me next.

The last thing I saw before I escaped was Axel rising into the air, his angel wings flapping furiously.

I returned home. The boy was waiting for me in my living room. My mom was sleeping, fully bathed and all of her needs were taken care of. She slept with a smile on her face.

I told the boy to go home. He must have known what had happened because my hands were still covered in blood.

He wept as he left, and I'll never forget him standing on my porch, tears falling and glinting in the moonlight before he flashed away.

For the next few months, I thought maybe Axel would come and finish me.

I wrote him a letter and asked for forgiveness. I offered to bring his wife back for a few minutes so he could say goodbye. My letter went unanswered because…

"Axel had a mental breakdown," Gilberto said sadly. "No one in his crew could force him to turn off his nephilim form."

Becca sat next to him on the steps.

"Jesus," Becca said. Then she thought the better of saying that. "I mean, wow."

A lone car passed by, the first one since Gilberto started his tale.

"The reason he didn't kill me was because a bunch of paranormals in the city had to band together to contain him," Gilberto said.

"How many?" Becca asked.

"A lot," Gilberto said. "And they punished Axel, who felt remorse for the damage he caused. The Regulators made a deal with him—he had to have two governors who controlled him if he ever morphed again."

"Governors?"

"One for the light within him and one for the darkness, since he is the son of an angel and a demon."

Becca gasped. "That explains the son and the weird lady."

"His son, Ezekiel, and his assistant Johanna. The only two people he could trust. One of the light and one of the dark."

"But if Axel is half, how is it that his son is a full-blown angel?" Becca asked.

Gilberto pointed to the sky. "The big guy up there is funny like that. I guess Axel was forgiven. His son is tender. Not like him at all."

Becca didn't know what to say.

"Someone close to me told me years later that Axel regretted not being able to ask me to reunite him with her for a final goodbye. I thought maybe that meant forgiveness, but I guess not."

Gilberto shrugged. "The night everything happened, I went back to the dock. Sure enough, my kit was there. It was caught on one of the piers. I'll always carry that guilt. Heaviness like that never goes away, Becca."

"I understand."

Gilberto slapped his knees. "Time's up, kid."

Becca's soul felt heavy after that story. She wanted to give him a hug. But the healer smiled now.

"Man, I've been holding that story in for a long time," he said.

Becca laughed. "You can talk to me anytime. How do they say it? We're *simpatico*, right?"

"Gotta brush up on your Spanish, *amiga*," Gilberto said, rising. "But yeah, we're all right."

He helped her up.

"Thanks," he said. "I feel like a weight was taken off my chest."

"Breakfast on me at the Wicked Cat," she said, tapping him on the shoulder.

"Consider it done," Gilberto said as they walked down the street toward Logan Square.

Kirk slid down a tree and landed quietly on the sidewalk a few houses down from Gilberto's. He waited until Becca and Gilberto crossed the street, and then he stalked after them.

CHAPTER THIRTY

Cyrus rolled up to a duplex apartment in Bucktown. The building was a classic Chicago style—two stories, historic brickwork with red lintels over the windows, and an exterior of tortilla-colored bricks. There was a front door on the first floor and a balcony on the second floor.

Fontanelli's van was parked on the corner. Lorenzo had the doors open and the burly man was digging around in the back.

"What's up, Font?" Cyrus asked.

Fontanelli pulled a bucket of turquoise pellets out of truck.

"Champ, it's like Christmas out here," he said, grinning. His mustache was extra bushy today and he'd forgotten to button the top button on his white jumpsuit, exposing a tuft of chest hair and a gold chain with a cross. "I ain't never seen so many rats in my life."

A brown blur ran out from under the van. A rat stopped on the sidewalk, regarded them, then darted into the front lawn of the duplex.

"They're just walking around in the daytime without a care in the world," Fontanelli said.

Cyrus wrapped a utility belt around his waist—it had a

flashlight, screwdriver, gloves, and compressed air. He kept his backpack on.

"What are the residents reporting?" Cyrus asked, adjusting the belt.

Fontanelli set the bucket down on the sidewalk. "They're all saying the same thing. They were minding their business last night, and suddenly, rats were everywhere. This street doesn't normally have a rat problem. Usually, it's confined to the restaurant areas. Rats go where the food is, you know. It's unusual to see them around here among well-kept homes."

Fontanelli tilted his head at the duplex to get Cyrus's attention. "The lady up there on the porch ain't so happy. Just be professional."

A middle-aged white woman stood on the porch in a bathrobe watching them warily. Her body language projected trouble. She had a perpetual look of frustration on her face. A rat darted underfoot and she jumped into the air and yelled.

"Why don't you follow that one," Fontanelli said. "Do some Sherlock Holmesin' for me, will ya? Don't worry about going into people's yards. Everyone knows we're supposed to be here. You run into any trouble, just tell 'em you're with me. Half the block owes me a service call anyway."

Cyrus watched as the rat that hassled the woman hopped down the steps and into the grass. He waited a few moments as it scurried through the grass and then down a narrow gangway between the duplex and the next house. He followed it into the shadows.

Since he had become a rat shifter, he'd learned how to think like a rat.

Rats didn't like coming out during the day unless they had a good reason to. That reason was almost always food. You could put a giant dumpster of food in the middle of the cleanest street in the city, and within minutes, you'd see them coming up from the catch basins. But mostly, they came out at dusk.

Some nights, Cyrus would shift and run through sewers and alleys just to get a sense of his fellow rats. During his last adventure, he experienced the brutal world of rats the hard way. They didn't take kindly to strangers encroaching on their territory, but he learned how to spot nests and avoided those as much as possible. Wild rats tolerated him as long as he kept moving.

Fontanelli taught him human ways, and how pest control professionals dealt with rat problems. The last thing he needed was dying in a rat trap on a shifter mission, so learning how and where to set them was a matter of life and death.

The rat hugged the wall and stopped momentarily next to a basement window. Then it ran into the open, made several circles, and let out a cry of distress before continuing forward.

Strange.

Another rat jumped out of the grass and ran in the opposite direction.

Cyrus kept following the original rat. A sound of hissing crescendoed to a loud grating in his ears.

He stepped into the backyard, which was a small asphalt lot with a few parked cars.

The asphalt was moving. It was covered with rats.

Even Cyrus jumped back upon seeing them.

"Holy crap," he said.

Rats covered the asphalt like carpet. Hundreds of brown rats squabbled and fought each other. The wave moved back and forth, left and right. Parts of it dispersed and ran through the yard.

Cyrus looked around. A few people stood in the alley, watching the rats.

He retreated into the shadows of the gangway and crouched to the ground, out of view. Quickly, he shifted into a rat and landed in the grass.

Instinct drove him to the wall of the house. An ultraviolet

splatter of rat urine glowed on the wall. Rat urine was normally invisible to human eyes without a special tool.

He sniffed and took in the message of the rat he had been following.

It was a mature female. Her urine smelled strongly of distress and a frantic mindset.

Normally, rats used urine to send messages about food and threats. Rats traveled in groups and warned each other of trouble. But this rat's urine was rambling. It said nothing of food and nothing of predators—only fear.

Cyrus ventured into the backyard toward the carpet of rats. The squabbling was so loud to his rat's ears that he could hardly think.

All the while, he smelled the odors of fear and distress. The rats were squabbling, but they might as well have been screaming at him, screaming out of their minds in fright.

What were they afraid of?

He caught a whiff of something different, but even his rat nose couldn't place it. Something sickly-sweet and rancid, and viciously rotten.

Cyrus dashed into the throng of crazy rats. The throng pushed him and pulled him, but he followed his nose.

He zigzagged through the pack, letting his nose guide him. One rat smashed into him and knocked him down. Instead of attacking, it kept running on its way to the edge of the fringe. Cyrus jumped up and kept running. He leaped over a rat that was grooming itself in the middle of the madness.

For a while, the carpet adjusted and moved in the direction he needed to go. He ran with the rats swiftly as if he were one with them. Then, the carpet changed directions and slammed into him, forcing him to zigzag again.

Left. Right. He ran.

Right. He stopped.

The carpet shifted quickly toward the smell and he flowed with it. Then it zigged against him, knocking him backward.

The sickly smell intensified as he reached the edge of the carpet. His whiskers swept across rusted metal, and he made out a blurry catch basin. The gentle sound of trickling water echoed off the walls below.

He stood on his hind legs and sniffed.

The smell was coming from the basin.

He inched toward it with his nose to the ground.

Soft cries also carried on the water.

People crying.

Men and women. They didn't speak—they cried long, plaintive wails of grief and sniffles.

The sounds made him sad, made him want to cry himself.

He didn't know why, but he knew he had to go down there.

He started to climb down, when someone called him.

"Hey, champ! Where are ya?"

Fontanelli. Cyrus couldn't see where he was because his vision was poor, but his voice sounded like it was coming from the gangway.

Cyrus hopped over the catch basin and onto the sidewalk. He made out the tall silhouette of an oak tree a few yards away. There were still people in the alley, and he needed cover to shift without being seen.

"Champ?"

Cyrus's anxiety increased every time Fontanelli called his name.

He sensed something behind him.

He whipped around. Several rats followed him. They stopped, staring at him. Were they going to attack?

No. Their backs weren't arched like the usual rat attack stance. Whenever a rat was going to attack, you knew it. They followed a predictable pattern.

Cyrus turned and kept running for the tree. The footsteps behind him continued.

More rats were following him now.

What the hell?

He took cover behind the tree as Fontanelli called his name.

He shifted back to a human. He glanced around to make sure no one saw him. He had gotten lucky. The rats who had followed him stared up at him and scattered. He watched as they disappeared again into the moving carpet.

"Champ, come on!" Fontanelli said. "When I told you to investigate, I didn't tell you to disapp—holy shit!"

He must have seen the carpet of rats.

Cyrus slid from behind the tree. "I'm over here," he said.

Fontanelli motioned for him to hurry up. The old Italian was covered in sweat. For an experienced exterminator, these rats were freaking even him out.

"You found the motherlode," Fontanelli said.

Cyrus shrugged. "What do you need?"

"I was checking on you," Fontanelli said, rubbing the back of his head. "I was gonna ask if you found anything, but uh…"

Cyrus shrugged. "I found it, but I don't have a clue about how to solve it."

"That's another reason I came to getcha," Fontanelli said. "If the lady who lives here sees this, she's gonna freak."

An ear-splitting scream ripped across the backyard.

"Too late, hehe," Fontanelli said. He crossed himself, unable to take his eyes off the rats.

"Oh my God!" the woman screamed. She stood on her back porch with her hands on her head.

Fontanelli held up his hands to calm her.

"Miss, we're working on getting this under control."

"You better!" she cried.

"This is my assistant," Fontanelli said, pointing at Cyrus. "We're on it."

The woman didn't even look at Cyrus.

"When will they go away?" she asked.

"I don't think they're going away any time soon," Cyrus said.

Fontanelli elbowed him. "Come on, now, champ. Don't make us sound weak."

Cyrus sighed.

"I called my peeps at the Department of Public Health," Fontanelli said, waving at the woman and putting on a big smile. "They aren't open 'til tomorrow. Best case scenario is that they'll send a snowplow down the street to scoop some of them up. The head of the department is friends with a rat expert in New York City. I bet this is so bad, they'll fly the guy in."

"I can't believe this," she said.

"We're just as shocked as you," Fontanelli said. "I've been doing this for thirty-seven years. I've never seen anything like it."

The carpet of rats streamed toward them like an ocean tide. Cyrus and Fontanelli crept back until they were on the porch with the woman.

A lighter flicked behind Cyrus followed by a cloud of cigarette smoke wafting around him. The woman was smoking a cigarette and pacing around the porch. Cyrus and Fontanelli watched the rats move in irregular patterns across her back lot.

"I got people coming over," she said. "I'm supposed to have a birthday party for my nephew this afternoon. He's eight. The kids will be terrified."

"You told me five times already," Fontanelli said.

"My mother has a condition too," the woman said.

"Between you and me," Fontanelli said, "maybe you ought to call the party off. Or have it somewhere else. These rats are gonna trigger people with *conditions*, if you know what I mean."

"I wouldn't recommend having a party here," Cyrus said. "Too much food will ensure the rats stay around."

"Can't you take them away or something?" the woman asked.

"Yeah, that's exactly it," Fontanelli said. "I'll get my translation whatsamadoozle and tell 'em all to come with me."

The woman let out a nervous cry. Cyrus remembered a technique that Becca often used with waiters at the Wicked Cat.

"You sound frustrated, ma'am," he said.

"Of course I'm frustrated!" she shouted. She took another drag of her cigarette. "I'm sorry. I'm not mad at you. I'm mad at the situation. I don't need this today."

"We'll put some bait and traps down," Fontanelli said. "But to be honest, ma'am, that's all we can do."

"From what I can tell, you take good care of your property," Cyrus said, peering into the house through the back door. The kitchen, with neon green cabinets and dingy linoleum floors, was clean. No dishes in the sink. There wasn't a single piece of trash in the yard. "Rats prefer the path of least resistance."

The woman brightened. "Well, thank you, young man."

"Trust me, I've been doing this job for a little while, and the houses we see have rats for a reason," Cyrus said. Fontanelli nodded in approval. "As long as you keep your house closed, you're in no danger."

"Yeah," Fontanelli said quickly. "I fortified your place. If they want to come in, then they're gonna wish they hadn't."

"Poison?" the woman asked.

"And traps," Fontanelli said, clapping Cyrus on the shoulder. "We may not speak rat, but we know how to think like 'em. Ain't that right, champ?"

If only Font knew how true that statement was. Cyrus's mind went back to the catch basin and the cries.

"Yep," Cyrus said. "We're the best."

The woman sighed, handed Fontanelli a check, and disappeared into her house.

Cyrus and Fontanelli watched the rats again, took in their screeching.

"What's the plan, champ?" Fontanelli asked.

Cyrus rubbed his head again. "You don't pay me enough to formulate plans."

"Ha ha," Fontanelli said.

They watched the rats some more.

"You don't have a plan, either, huh, Font?" Cyrus asked after a while.

"I got nothin'," he said.

Someone called them.

"Hey, you guys setting traps and bait?"

A black woman on a porch next door waved at them.

"One oh nine plus tax," Fontanelli said. "We got a deal?"

"Yeah, come on over. I ain't got time for this shit today."

"Ka ching ka ching," Fontanelli said, tiptoeing over the rats. "You know what to do, champ."

Cyrus glanced at the rats. The catch basin couldn't wait.

"You go ahead, Font," Cyrus said. "I saw something in the yard that gave me an idea."

"Suit yourself," Fontanelli said. "Meet me over there in a few minutes."

Cyrus pretended to watch the rats, watching Fontanelli in the corner of his eye. Once he was out of sight, Cyrus dashed behind the tree and transformed into a rat again.

He scurried across the sidewalk and onto the catch basin.

He listened.

The cries still carried on the water. He waited, trying to discern something, anything that might tell him what he was about to see, but every passing second only made him more confused.

He squeezed between the grates and down into the darkness.

CHAPTER THIRTY-ONE

THE WICKED CAT was in full late Sunday morning brunch when Becca and Gilberto arrived. Gilberto grabbed a table in the corner facing the door—the same table he'd sat at when he first sought Becca out last night. The act reminded her of something she saw in Mafia movies.

She joked about him being paranoid and he laughed and said that one could never be paranoid enough.

The patron at the next table grabbed Becca's arm and said hello. She patted it and told him thank you for coming. She took Gilberto's order—a ham and egg croissant and a coffee—and she wandered to the kitchen, making a semi-circle around the floor making sure everything was in order. She swiped a water pitcher off the bar and topped off a few people's waters.

As usual, the customers were smiling, chatting, and enjoying their drinks. Cristián never disappointed.

In the kitchen, Desmond was awake this time, reading something on his phone. He raised his eyes at her and his jaw dropped.

"What?" Becca asked.

"So this is what you look like when you relax, eh?"

"What's that supposed to mean?"

Desmond gestured to her hair.

Her bandanna. She had taken it off to wipe her face earlier because it was so hot.

"Ha. Ha. If I wasn't feeling generous today, I'd clap back with a snarky remark."

"I appreciate your benevolence," Desmond said, tucking his phone away "Back already?"

"I'm making some breakfast for Gilberto," Becca said.

"You brought him back from the dark side," Desmond said. "Your persuasive skills are impressive."

Becca grabbed a frozen croissant out of the freezer next to her office, unwrapped it from tin foil, and stuck it in an oven.

"Any word on when I'll have my office back?" she asked.

"Tonight," Desmond said. "I've got a place picked out, but I prefer not to transfer Aidan during the day. Once the dining floor clears out in the afternoon, I'll get him out."

"Good."

"You should probably know this," Desmond said, "but I have some news about Axel. It's not good."

Becca's heart sank. "I'm having a great morning, Des. Do I need to hear it right now?"

Desmond stared at her for a few moments. "Fine. I'll tell you later that he's suspected of conspiracy and has twenty-four hours to clear his name or face supernatural imprisonment."

"Thank you," Becca said, sliding the sandwich out of the oven and onto a plate, "for not telling me that."

She carried the plate to the front and mixed a *café con leche* for Gilberto and an americano for herself. She put the food on a tray and balanced it on one hand, sliding between two waiters at the bar who said hello to her.

She turned out of the bar, delivered the food to Gilberto, and slid into her place at the table.

Suddenly, a warm body slid next to her. Becca got a whiff of familiar Kate Spade perfume.

"Well, aren't you a sight today?" a female voice said.

"Mom!"

Becca spilled her coffee.

Aurora Grant was what Becca would look like in twenty years, but more prim and proper. Cyrus always joked that her mom was what Becca would look like when she gave up her hipster ways. She had warm brown eyes and long brown hair down to her shoulders. She wore a white and navy-blue striped blouse with a terra cotta-colored necklace with small beads. The outfit was finished off with white capris and sandals. She was dressed to go out.

Aurora leaned in and kissed her on the cheek.

"What are you—?" Becca asked. She stopped herself. Crap. They were supposed to celebrate her birthday today…

Aurora's eyes narrowed.

"You didn't—"

"No, I didn't forget," Becca said. "I was just having coffee with a friend. You're early."

"I thought I might see what you do when you don't expect me," Aurora said, smiling. "We are in for a wonderful day."

Gilberto passed a napkin to Becca and she cleaned up her spilled coffee.

"Mom, this is my friend Gilberto," Becca said.

Aurora shook his hand. "How do you know Becca?"

Gilberto started to say something.

"He's a regular here at the Wicked Cat," Becca said.

"Best coffee in Logan Square," Gilberto said, not skipping a beat.

"Well, that's nice," Aurora said.

Becca loved her mom, but with everything going on, she didn't have time for a leisurely day celebrating her birthday. Becca wanted to punch Cyrus for not reminding her. She instinctively reached for her phone but remembered it was in her office. Why didn't he remind her at breakfast? Yep, her little brother might be departing from this earth after she was done with him…if the giant rat didn't kill him first. She was definitely *not* dressed and *not* prepared to go out with her mom. She felt guilty, but she didn't have the heart to refuse her mom. She'd never forgive herself for that, and she didn't want to cause a rift. And she was self-conscious about her camo tank, purple hair, and ripped shorts.

"Your daughter has built a heck of a place here," Gilberto said, munching his croissant. Becca hadn't noticed, but he was almost done with the sandwich. He must have scarfed it down while she was busy reacting to her mom. "You should be very proud."

"I am," Aurora said. "I'm especially proud that they treat me on my birthday. Did you know it's my birthday today? Becca and Cyrus are taking me out."

That wasn't completely accurate. Last year, Becca planned everything. This year, she'd forgotten, and her mom did the planning. She only forgot because her brother was turned into a rat and nearly got them both killed and her bar became a regular watering hole for paranormals. Minor details.

"Happy birthday, Mrs. Grant," Gilberto said. "Let me guess: it's the big four oh?"

Aurora blushed and laughed and Gilberto laughed with her. He flashed a knowing look at Becca.

"You're off by about ten years," Aurora said. "But you made me feel so young for a moment."

"It's really nice to meet you," Gilberto said. "I'll let you both go."

He turned to Becca. "Thanks for the conversation today. And breakfast."

Becca nodded. They watched him as he offered his plate to Cristián at the bar. He waved at Desmond through the swinging doors, and walked out into the sunshine.

Aurora slid into Gilberto's spot. She tilted her head at Becca.

"So, what was so important last night that you couldn't return my phone call?"

And then Becca remembered that her mom had called her last night. Cyrus too. She didn't let the surprise show on her face—her mom was a keen lie detector.

"Last night was crazy," she said. "I'm sorry."

"I'll tell you the same thing I told your brother," Aurora said, frowning. Her voice was hurt. "I'm the only parent you have left. What if something had happened to me? I have two kids in the city and I can't count on either of you to pick up a phone, let alone send me a text message."

Becca was supposed to be her mom's advocate. This was a conversation they were supposed to be having to gang up on Cyrus. Now she found herself on the receiving end of it, and she felt ashamed. How many kids had she grown up with who never got close to their parents? Her mom was her best friend, even though Becca had been understandably distant lately.

When Aurora told her about her encounter with rats in the supermarket, Becca felt even worse.

"Oh my God, Mom. Are you okay?" Becca asked.

"It was horrible," Aurora said, throwing up her hands. "And you know what your brother said when I told him?"

"Probably something egg-headed," Becca said.

"Talking to him is like talking to a brick wall sometimes," Aurora said. "He's just like his father."

Becca took her mom's hands in hers. "I'm glad you're all right. Next time, I won't let the bar take me away from you. Do you want something to drink? Beer is the best antidote to every problem, you know."

As she said the last sentence, an intense feeling of déjà vu hit Becca, like she had been here before. Here, in this booth, staring at her mom as she smiled warmly, simultaneously feeling guilt in her heart, and sibling anger at her brother.

"We'll see about that," Aurora said. "But sure. It's early to drink, but I'll take a soda."

"Sure," Becca said. "I'll…be right back."

"Where's your brother?" Aurora asked. "We really need to leave soon if we're going to make the show."

"Would it surprise you that I don't know?" Becca asked.

"No," Aurora said, frowning. "Not at all."

Becca slid out of the table and poured her mom a cola in a to-go cup at the bar, saying the words from the dream to herself again.

"Becca, don't follow."

She screwed up her face at the words again, more confused than before.

Then, the front door to the Wicked Cat opened. A silhouette entered, but Becca couldn't make it out because the sun was in her eyes. Once the light faded, she saw it was just a regular patron.

CHAPTER THIRTY-TWO

Cyrus landed in a sewer channel. The familiar smell of dirty water, rotten garbage, and dirt washed over his nose, undercut with the sickly-sweet smell he detected earlier.

It was completely dark down here and he had to navigate with his whiskers. He brushed up against the nearest wall and listened.

The cries were louder down here. Painfully human, and grieving.

He followed his ears and started toward the noise.

A small river ran through the channel carrying a parade of trash whose smells sizzled against his nose as they passed—sweet, salty, moldy, rotten, ungodly smells that were all delicious to a rat.

He kept his nose focused on the smell. He was always amazed at how his nose could discriminate so well—nothing escaped him.

A rivulet of water ran down the wall and sprayed him. The water was cold and a shock to his skin. His feet splashed through the puddle it created.

The channel curved to the left and he followed it, staying close to the wall.

He stopped at a mound of mud. His whiskers detected a drug needle. A trace of cocaine sent an explosion of *oh shit* to his brain. He recoiled.

He hopped over the needle, and his tail narrowly missed its point, dragging a trail of mud behind him.

Something smacked along the side of the channel as it flowed by. He had no idea what the hell it was, but it smelled like an animal corpse. It definitely wasn't a rat.

He finished winding around the channel. A brick collapsed underneath him and he jumped as the water carried its pieces away.

He paused near an enclave teeming with roaches. They clicked angrily. Though he couldn't see them, he knew they were fighting over a peach pit lodged against the wall.

The cries were just ahead. The sounds drew him forward.

Suddenly, the cries stopped.

Cyrus continued along the wall.

He heard footsteps behind him, followed by a familiar odor—rats.

A crowd of rats gathered behind him. They sniffed, and their beady eyes glowed in the shadows.

He froze. Rats weren't down here before. If they were, he would have smelled and heard them.

They were the rats from above.

They were following him again.

He ignored them and kept charging forward. A few paces later, he stopped and turned.

Even more rats were lined up in the darkness after him. Not attacking, not squabbling, but completely quiet.

Why were they following him? Wild rats weren't lemmings. They minded their territories. What was so special about him that they wanted to follow him?

Something brushed against his tail and made him whip around.

Ahead, a rat trudged through the mud. But this rat was

different. It wobbled. Every step seemed like the most difficult and arduous thing in the world. It looked over the sewer channel, licked the water, and shambled forward, leaving a haphazard spray of urine behind it.

Cyrus knew that walk. They called it "dead rat walking." He'd done it himself when he was fed rat poison on his last adventure, and he'd seen it in the homes where Fontanelli placed rat poison. The rats ate the poison, but it took several days to kick in. They died a slow, agonizing death that often ended with lying down, staring at nothing for hours, and taking their last breath quietly.

Cyrus licked the air and tasted dull smoke and decay.

The rat was dead. Yet it was alive again and walking. It smelled of musk, rotten flesh, and grass.

The rat bumped into another rat that was also wobbling down the channel. He could only see their eyes, but the sound of the claws scratching against the bricks was unsteady and uneven—not like the rats behind him.

The moaning resumed.

A thin sheet of light flew overhead, blinding him with colorless light. The light coincided with the loudest cry Cyrus had ever heard.

The light dissipated and the moan faded.

The shambling rats were gone.

Cyrus's little rat heart beat quickly as he kept charging ahead.

Another pair of glowing eyes appeared in the distance and Cyrus quickened toward them. He came face-to-face with another dead rat who stared at him blankly.

Cyrus blocked the rat's path. The rat opened its mouth, baring long incisors. Its mouth kept extending until its jaws broke apart and the animal turned into a translucent human silhouette, who let out a horrible cry of pain.

Another human silhouette flashed overhead and landed on the concrete, forming into a shambling rat.

No wonder the living rats down here were terrified. The smells, sounds, and constant light show probably confused them and drove them crazy.

Then Cyrus stepped in a spray of urine on the ground. The ground ahead was covered in it.

The messages hit him hard.

Males. Females. All mature. Unlike the living rats, however, Cyrus heard intelligible voices now.

Don't make me do this.

No…

I just want to rest.

I didn't ask to become this monstrosity!

Rats didn't think that way. Their needs were more basic, like food and water. They didn't talk about monstrosities.

His heart froze at the realization that these rats weren't rats at all.

The voices intensified as he tracked forward.

The ground shook, stopping Cyrus.

Ahead, more glowing eyes popped into human silhouettes, and a heart-rending scream gathered in the distance. The ground rumbled as the screams intensified.

The souls were traveling. But where?

Cyrus paused, sensing the ever-growing colony of living rats behind him.

He nodded to them, then they trekked into the darkness together.

CHAPTER THIRTY-THREE

Kirk tightened his elbow grip around Gilberto's neck.

"Let me go!" Gilberto cried.

"You're a hell of a runner, aren't you?" the demon asked.

In his mind, the real Kirk had stopped fighting the demon's hold on him. It was pointless. He could only watch as the demon used his body for whatever it wanted.

"Let me go!" Gilberto cried again, struggling.

"You think I'm going to chase you for five blocks just to let you go?" the demon asked. "I'm on a bounty hunt, not a fishing expedition."

He slammed Gilberto against the wall. Gilberto fell down on his back.

The demon drop-kicked him, and Gilberto yelled in pain. He grinned as Gilberto gasped for air.

CRACK!

Another blow landed on Gilberto's side. He asked for mercy.

"Mercy?" the demon asked. "Tell me what that is."

Gilberto said a prayer in Spanish. The demon grabbed him by the collar, lifted him in the air, and threw him against the wall. Gilberto landed with a crunch.

Kirk winced with every blow. This wasn't how he would have done it. A gunshot execution-style was the only way to end missions like this. Only amateurs made messes. Yet, this demon didn't strike him as a newbie.

The demon grabbed Gilberto again and pushed him up against the wall.

"Here's what we're gonna do," the demon said. "Let's say, for the sake of argument, that I have a gun in my pocket. If I did, would you run?"

Gilberto stared at him, eyes half open.

"No, you wouldn't," the demon said. "Because you're not stupid, that's why. On the count of three, you're going to walk out of this alley and into the sunshine like nothing ever happened. I'm going to follow behind you a few paces. Then, you're going to walk to the Wicked Cat and take me around the back. Got it?"

Gilberto nodded.

"Three," the demon said letting Gilberto go. He patted his chest and flashed a black pistol. Upon seeing it, Gilberto gulped.

The healer staggered into the street. The demon waited a few seconds, adjusted Kirk's sunglasses, and then followed.

Gilberto was limping toward the next stoplight.

The demon's voice surged in Kirk's head as it walked down the street in his body. The demon spoke, but Kirk's lips didn't move.

"How did you like my handiwork?" the demon asked.

"You're sick," Kirk said, his voice echoing in his mind.

"You're a necromancer," the demon said. "Who's sick again?"

Gilberto crossed the street. The demon waited a moment and then jogged across the street, slowing his pace as Gilberto passed a guitar shop. The healer looked back to make sure he was still there, then he kept limping forward.

Kirk didn't think it was possible to feel compassion any

more, but he felt just a little sorry for Gilberto and wished the healer would be put out of his misery already.

"I'm doing what you should have done in the first place," the demon said. "If you had been more effective, you wouldn't have needed me."

"You better destroy my body when you leave it," Kirk said. "Because I'm going to come after you."

"You humans can't see the bigger game we're playing," the demon said. "You can't even tell that I'm about to do you the ultimate favor. We can be kind sometimes."

The demon laughed for the length of two buildings, then its voice faded, leaving Kirk with his thoughts again.

The demon whistled with Kirk's lips, and it jammed a hand in a pocket, putting a strut in its step.

Kirk's mind raced again. He willed all of his energy into his hands, but the demon had an iron grip on them. He concentrated, his mind expanding ever outward, but soon he was back to floating in his skull, as helpless as he was before.

Gilberto staggered across a block toward Logan Square Park.

The demon strolled through the sunny, peaceful park and Kirk remembered the last time he was here, just as self-assured as the demon, surveilling Gilberto at the Wicked Cat. Kirk wished he had never taken this job.

The demon whistled.

Gilberto had stopped. He stared at the Wicked Cat.

"Keep walking," the demon said loud enough that Gilberto could hear.

Gilberto wouldn't move.

Becca was standing on the sidewalk with another woman who looked like an older version of her—must have been her mother.

A gray car slowed down in front of the bar and both women got in. Only when the car had turned the block did Gilberto start walking again.

The demon's voice surged in Kirk's head.

"Inconvenient. I was hoping to accomplish both tasks here. Looks like you're stuck with me a little longer."

Gilberto took the long way around the Wicked Cat and into the alley.

The demon ran his fingers along the pistol in Kirk's inside jacket pocket.

In an instant, the demon was behind Gilberto with the gun pointed at the small of his back. It took one of Gilberto's arms and held it behind his back for leverage.

The alley was remarkably clean for a restaurant. Not a speck of trash anywhere. The Wicked Cat ran a clean operation. Might have been the kind of place Kirk would have gotten a coffee…in other circumstances. The smell of coffee grounds and nondescript cooking food hung in the alley.

The back door to the Wicked Cat opened and a young man carrying a stack of crates walked out back-first. His hair was thickly pomaded. Gilberto recognized him as the assistant manager at the bar.

The demon fired the gun in a flash and the man toppled, hit on the torso. The crates toppled onto him.

"No," Gilberto said.

"He was innocent," Kirk said angrily.

"Let's not pretend like you have a conscience," the demon's voice said. "This boy will be my calling card."

The demon whispered to Gilberto, "I know you've got one of those nice healing kits hidden somewhere. Take out some herbs and heal him. Keep him alive."

Gilberto struggled with a confused look on his face.

"Now," the demon said. It let go, and Gilberto ran to the young man.

The back door pushed open and Desmond Lovelace ran out.

The demon pointed the gun at Gilberto's head.

"Shift and he dies," the demon said.

Desmond put his hands up.

"I believe you're holding my brother and father hostage," the demon said. "Let them free and send them back here."

This bastard demon was impersonating him.

Desmond backed up slowly and disappeared through the back door. Meanwhile, Gilberto was pressing on the man's wounds, and green magic pulsated from his fingers.

Soon, the back door opened. Aidan walked out reluctantly. When he saw Kirk, he stared. Bruce's spirit flowed out. Bruce was notoriously silent too.

"They're free now," Desmond said, walking out. "Now be gone from here."

"There's my brother," the demon said, grinning.

Aidan walked down the stairs slowly, not taking his eyes off the demon. His blue training jacket was a wrinkled mess, and he had several stains on his gray sweatpants.

The demon surged into Kirk's mind again. "Ah, your brother is a smart one. He knows that I'm inside of you."

"So does my dad," Kirk said.

"It's fine." The demon laughed as it popped out of Kirk's mind. "All of you will do my bidding, and it will be a family affair. Get us out of here."

He offered an arm to hug Aidan and he brought him in close. Aidan resisted.

"Tell one of your demons to do it," the demon said. "It'll be on the house, no blood deals needed."

Reluctantly, Aidan spoke a curse.

Shadows swirled around the brothers and Kirk's world went black as a giant hand grabbed him and yanked him out of the alley.

CHAPTER THIRTY-FOUR

Cyrus walked for several miles through the sewer channel. The barrage of translucent souls continued the same pattern —crying and flying. Cyrus could even time it. Were these what human souls looked like? Would his soul look like that one day?

The living rats remained behind him, steadfast followers. He couldn't tell how many were with him, but it had to be thousands. Maybe more.

Suddenly, the souls flowed upward until they were gone.

Cyrus stopped. True, comforting silence spread across the sewers again. He had grown so used to the souls' constant moaning that he didn't know how to handle the quiet.

A duo of light rays shone on his back, warming him up. He hadn't realized how cold it was down here.

He stood on his hind legs and looked up into a slanted well that led up to another catch basin. Two pipes crisscrossed underneath a grate that cut the sunlight into slats.

Cyrus ran up the slanted wall and jumped onto the first pipe, using it to springboard himself onto the second pipe. He grabbed the grate and squeezed himself through, poking his head out first into fresh, warm air.

A car blew over him and his heart rate jumped.

He couldn't see the street he was on very well, but he listened, and when the street was empty, he pulled the rest of his body through and dashed to safety. He navigated with his whiskers, which led him to two parked cars on the side of the street. He hid between them and shifted into human form.

He didn't know the street he was on. It wasn't in Bucktown, though. There weren't any trees and the buildings were more industrial. He stood across from a credit union with an empty parking lot.

Further down the street, he spotted the giant rat. It was walking slowly, the dead rats gathering into it like a steady stream of water. It growled as it walked and the dead rats squabbled among each other.

Cyrus balled his fists.

"Hey!" he cried.

The giant rat stopped.

"I'm over here!" Cyrus called.

The beast turned, its rats casting their faces on Cyrus. It roared.

"There aren't any trees to throw at me this time," he said, walking toward it. "But you don't want to throw anything at me."

The giant rat screamed at Cyrus, but he kept walking toward it.

"You're not a rat," he said quietly. "You're not a monster. You're human."

The rat roared at him again. A few of the dead rats fell off and shambled toward Cyrus, but the giant rat scooped them up and pasted them to its body.

"You're losing control," Cyrus said, "because you never wanted to do this in the first place."

The giant rat jumped into the air and aimed a fist at Cyrus. He jumped away and the beast landed, several rats flying off its body.

This time, the beast ignored the defecting rats and charged Cyrus, grabbing him by the throat and slamming him on the asphalt.

A hundred rats bared their incisors at him.

"You won't kill me," Cyrus said, "because that's not what she wanted. She didn't want you to kill me."

Cyrus imagined Murgalen's tree face in his mind's eye.

"You came to me because you wanted my help," Cyrus said. "You wanted my help in ending your suffering."

In an instant, the giant rat fell apart into hundreds of rats. Cyrus rolled to his knees, watching a wave of them land on the street.

Behind him, the living rats were climbing out of the catch basin and gathering on the street.

"Be gone," Cyrus said. "Go and rest, and leave the city alone. You've caused enough suffering. And you've suffered enough."

Several of the dead rats stood on their hind legs and shattered into white balls of light that morphed into human silhouettes who hovered over Cyrus, waving.

Rat shifters. Victims of Murgalen. Countless innocent people turned into shifters against their will. Cyrus was the only survivor.

Cyrus waved at the shifters as they darted into the sky.

"Get out of here!" Cyrus said, swatting at the rest of the dead rats. "There's nothing for you here!"

More of the dead rats flashed into human silhouettes that flew high into the sky before disappearing over rooftops.

Soon, they were all gone.

A wave of relief washed across Cyrus as he watched the souls fly away.

"It's done," he said, sighing. He pumped his fist and uppercut the sky. "That was easy!"

The clear blue sky above reminded him of crystal blue water. Maybe he could enjoy the day now and get some sleep.

He imagined himself relaxing on the couch, cracking jokes with Becca and reminiscing how, just a day ago, their lives were hell but now all was good again. He just wished he could have found the giant rat sooner. If he did, more people would be alive.

He turned. The living rats were still pouring out of the catch basin. The frontmost rats stared at him curiously.

"You can go back home now," Cyrus said.

The rats didn't move.

"Get out of here," he said. "The threat is gone!"

It wasn't like he could talk to them, even in rat form. But the sewers were safe now. They'd be in no more danger.

Still, the rats stared. Then, Cyrus became aware of other eyes on him.

Several people had gathered on the street, pointing at him and the rats.

"Where are Axel's suppressors when you need them?" he whispered to himself.

His phone buzzed in his pocket. A text message from his mom.

You're late. Show starts in 20.

He cursed. Thank God he'd kept his backpack on. It went with him when he shifted. He slung his electric skateboard off his backpack, and rolled away. Soon, he was at top speed, and he left the rats far behind him.

The souls of the rat shifters rocketed high into the clear blue sky, forming a white mass in the sky.

The souls were calm, their energy whistling as they sailed through the sky.

They aimed for the horizon and broke apart from each other and scattered on the wind.

Then, a gentle singing filled the air.

La la la laaaaaa…

The souls began to moan again.

The singing intensified as the souls bound together tightly and plummeted toward the ground.

They crashed into the street, morphing again into dead rats.

Slowly, they gathered again into the giant rat, who stood tall as several cars darted around it.

Then the giant rat stumbled, the little rats on it screaming in protest.

The beast roared, cowing all of its constituents into submission, and the feelings of freedom and peace subsided.

All they could think about was the young man who had promised them freedom.

What was freedom when they could not rest? What was death if they kept on living?

The giant rat growled as it stomped down the street, all of the rats holding an image of Cyrus in their heads.

CHAPTER THIRTY-FIVE

AIDAN POPPED into existence on a roof somewhere in the city. He landed with a hard thud and rolled. His nylon jacket crinkled as he came to a stop.

Bruce popped into the air next to him. The old man wailed.

Two Timberland boots landed in front of Aidan's eyes. He tracked the boots up over black jeans, a denim jacket, and finally, to his brother's face, whose head cast a corona across the sky.

Kirk stared at him from behind his usual sunglasses, but it wasn't his brother. His eyes, normally cool and calm, were crazed and wild. His brother's face had a perpetual devious grin that replaced his usual stoic expressions.

Aidan recoiled and crawled backward. The roof was covered in graffiti. A rusted-out water tower lay a few yards away. Below, an L train whooshed by.

"What are you afraid of, brother?" Kirk asked, extending a hand.

This was the scenario that Aidan had always talked about with Kirk. One day, it was possible that he'd see his brother, but it wasn't his brother. Something sinister would be staring at him instead. Today was that day.

"Who are you?" Aidan asked. "You're not my brother."

"What's the matter, baby?" Kirk asked, holding his hands out. "You're just jealous of who I've become."

"What have you done with my son, demon?" Bruce asked. "To my knowledge, he made no deals for the right of possession."

"Yes, he did," the demon said. "Your brother entered a contract with me to save his life."

"His life!" Bruce cried.

"He was never in danger," Aidan said. "He was just doing reconnaissance."

"And then nature called," the demon said. "Oops. I guess you weren't supposed to know that."

Aidan stood. "Explain."

"See, you two made a deal with Axel Valentine, but it wasn't Valentine. You got played by a nymph."

The demon laughed.

"Nymph?" Aidan asked.

"A tree nymph called Oleandra," the demon said. "Anyway, things got complicated for dear old Kirk, so I'm commandeering him for a little while until he comes to his senses."

Aidan cursed. He could have summoned a demon of his own, but it would have been unreliable. This demon wasn't telling all the details.

"I need your assistance," the demon said. "Once I have it, I'll relinquish your brother."

"And if we don't cooperate?" Aidan asked.

The demon pulled out a gun and held it to his head.

"Bye bye, Kirk."

Bruce groaned. "State your terms."

Aidan listened incredulously as the demon gave them instructions.

CHAPTER THIRTY-SIX

Becca shifted uncomfortably in the soft theater chair and fanned herself with a program.

"This place is so nice," Aurora said. "Your brother is missing out."

The black box theater was cozy, and smaller than Becca thought. She had expected a Vaudeville theater, but this place was more like a college scene with a low budget. The stage was lit with an orange scrim that reminded her of sunset. Two stacks of boxes were strategically placed on stage, with spotlights on them. A sound machine played harsh wind.

"Any word from Cy?" Becca asked.

"He says he's on the way, but sometimes you never know with him," Aurora said.

Becca sensed the barbs in her mom's voice. Ouch. Cyrus was going to get eviscerated. At least it wasn't *entirely* her fault.

Aurora nudged her and pointed to her program.

"Oh, look—one of the actors in the play is from Wilmette."

Becca feigned interest. She just wanted to rest and not have to worry about putting on a show of her own with her mother.

Aurora nudged Becca again. "The actors in the play are coming out."

"The show doesn't start for a few minutes still," Becca said.

A line of actors streamed onto the stage, dressed in old-timey clothes. One man looked like newsboy with a tan vest, green pants, and a herringbone cap. He smiled as the lights hit him, and Becca thought it was the fakest smile she'd ever seen in her life.

A woman in a scarf and a white dress followed him, and she carried a basket of fake fruit. The newsboy offered his arm and they walked together down the stage and into the audience. They nodded to each row and welcomed them to the show.

Becca groaned. What was the name of this show anyway?

She turned her program over to read the name of the show, but something brushed against her. She caught a whiff of sewer and gagged.

Cyrus squeezed past her and plopped into the chair next to her. He leaned over Becca and kissed Aurora on the cheek.

"You reek," Becca said.

"Oh my," Aurora said. "Cy, where have you been?"

Cyrus laughed nervously. "Fontanelli called me in."

"Jesus, have you been rolling around in a sewer?" Becca asked.

"Maybe," Cyrus said. He leaned in toward Becca, giving her an extra whiff of rat urine. She recoiled from him, but he motioned her to come closer.

"I'm sorry, Bec, but I promise this is worth it. I found the giant rat and vanquished it."

Becca's eyes widened. "Seriously?"

He patted her leg and gave a doofus smile. "Enjoy the show."

The newsboy and fruit girl passed and said hello.

Cyrus said hello in a chipper tone.

The scent of his stink reached the fruit girl. She made a quick face of disgust and then smiled a look of pity at Cyrus.

Becca glanced surreptitiously at the row behind her. The couple sitting behind them quietly moved across the theater. They must've smelled her brother too.

Cyrus settled into his chair and opened the program, whistling as he read it.

"Hey, look, someone from Wilmette," he said.

His smug tone triggered Becca. She pinched him.

"Ow!"

"Say more words," Becca whispered. "You can't tell me you vanquished a giant rat and then not give me any more details."

"More words," Cyrus said.

Before Becca could say anything, Aurora asked, "So what exactly were you doing today?"

"Bunch of rats in Bucktown," Cyrus said. "I know why you were so afraid, Mom. Rats everywhere."

Aurora shuddered. "Don't share the details, please. I just wanted to know the generics."

"I just want you to take a shower," Becca said.

Silence. The newsboy and fruit girl made their way to the back of the crowd.

"The rats were the dead shifters that Murgalen killed," Cyrus whispered to Becca. "They were restless. I did what any reasonable paranormal would do."

"Reasonable and paranormal don't belong in the same sentence," Becca said.

"Will you two stop bickering?" Aurora asked. "I have no clue what you're saying, but it's obnoxious."

"We'll stop bickering after I kill him," Becca said. Then she turned to Cyrus and whispered, "Come on. Out with it."

"I told them to go home," Cyrus said. "Since there is no threat anymore, there's nothing to worry about."

"Excuse me?" Becca asked.

Aurora tapped them both. "They're changing the lights. I think the show is going to start. Knock it off, you two. Sometimes I think you're both six years old."

Above, the orange light shining into the scrim behind the stage turned to blue and white, emulating a sunny day. The harsh wind softened to an ocean wave with gulls.

"I just love the set," Aurora said.

"If only they had popcorn," Cyrus said. "I worked up an appetite."

Becca could have sworn she heard his stomach grumble.

She kicked her brother surreptitiously.

"You're telling me that you told a bunch of zombie rats to go home?" she whispered.

"Worked like a charm," Cyrus said. "Remember when we were in the van and Bruce MacLeod's spirit was there and we told him to get lost? Same concept."

He pointed at the program and spoke to Aurora. "Aww, man. They sell beer here and I missed it!"

"Sneak out at intermission," Aurora said, hushing them.

Becca kicked Cyrus again.

"There's no way that worked," she said.

Cyrus shrugged. "If you don't want to believe me, that's your problem. But given all the shit we've been through, I intend to enjoy a nice afternoon with Mom. Ssssssh."

Becca puffed as the lights dimmed.

Silence swept across the theater as the sound machine faded.

A female voice spoke offstage.

"This is the story of us."

A male spoke with her, doubling her.

"The power of us."

The actors walked slowly toward the stage, entering one by one, until they stood in a diamond. The spotlights lit them all up. There were four—two newsboys and two fruit girls.

"Things used to be so good," the two girls said.

"But somehow, things fell apart," the newsboys said.

"It used to be so simple," the girls said. They took hands and swung each other around. "But we let life happen."

The two newsboys pretended to fight. One of them took a box and hit the other with it. The lights in the theater flashed red as the hit actor fell dramatically and rolled off stage.

"I paid my price," the victor said.

"And we got by," the hit actor said, emerging from under the stage. The other actor grabbed his hand and pulled him up.

The four actors stood shoulder to shoulder.

"This is the story of how we fell apart," they said in unison.

The theater faded to black, but before the lights clicked off, Becca saw a faint outline standing on one of the boxes.

Her heart pounded as a pair of rat eyes glimmered before floating off the box and into the shadows.

Kirk, Aidan, and Bruce popped into existence in front of a theater.

Aidan panted, worn out from another demon deal to transport them here. A cold, enormous hand had plucked them off the roof and deposited them on the sidewalk in front of the theater.

"One-act plays," the demon said, reading the marquee. Kirk still couldn't get used to the demon speaking with his voice, with his lips. "Sounds accurate for what we're about to see."

"You're sure about this?" Aidan asked.

Of course he's sure, Kirk thought. *He's never been more sure about anything in his demon life.*

"You know your orders," the demon said. "Wait for the

noise, and then get it done. That is, unless you don't want to see Kirk alive again."

Aidan turned to the demon, looked it right in the eyes, and said, "Brother, if you're in there and can hear me, just know we're going to get you out soon."

"I appreciate it, brother," Kirk said in his mind, even though Aidan couldn't hear him.

Kirk watched Aidan and Bruce disappear along the side of the Fat Amphibian Theater. The building was three stories with a metal facade and a large digital marquee over the front doors. A red sign with the theater's name curved down the front.

Kirk wished he could tell his brother to summon a demon for protection, but that was what got *him* into this mess. But it might be the only thing that could get them all out of this demon's grasp safely.

The demon's voice popped into Kirk's mind.

"You should stop thinking about escaping," it said. "I'm almost done with you anyway."

"You're sending them off to die," Kirk said.

"Perhaps," the demon said. "But it's of no consequence to me. The only thing that matters is to maximize the suffering in this world."

"Suffering?" Kirk asked. "Haven't you caused enough with me alone?"

"Not nearly enough," the demon said, voice fading. "And there's still a long road of suffering yet for you, Kirk."

"What's that supposed to mean?"

But the demon's voice faded. He walked up the small steps to the theater, opened the glass door, and walked into a carpeted lobby. The lobby was enormous, replete with a coffee and beer stand and small kitchen. In the back, several black doors to the theater were shut, guarded by ushers. This was definitely not Kirk's type of place. You would have never caught him in a theater, but here he was—against his will.

An usher in a red and white vest called out to him.

"Sorry, sir, we can't let you in," the man said. "The show has already started."

"No biggie," the demon said, shrugging. "My girlfriend's in there. Mind if I wait in the lobby?"

The usher waved in assent.

Someone yelled in the kitchen.

"Rat!"

A brown rat scurried across the carpet, followed by another.

"We're in the right place," the demon said. "I can taste that girl's blood." He took off his denim jacket and sunglasses. He tossed them into a trash can and leaned against a tall glass window, waiting.

"Martha, I got a confession to make."

The crowd watched spellbound as one of the newsboys held one of the fruit girl's hands. The lighting was tender and pink. The other couple stood, pretending to be frozen on opposite corners of the stage.

"I'm going off to war," he said.

The girl shook her head. "No, you can't!"

The newsboy faced the audience and said, "If enough of us go over, then it'll be over soon. The French need our help."

Cyrus rolled his eyes at the cheesiness. These actors couldn't act their way out of a paper bag. But his mom seemed to be enjoying the show. She leaned in every now and again and pointed at things.

The newsboy stood at the front of the stage and reached inside one of the crates, pulling out a soldier's helmet and a camouflage shirt. As he put them on, he said, "I'll be back soon, Martha. You just wait."

He held the fruit girl's hand, they embraced, and then he ran offstage.

The spotlight lit up Martha and she wrung her hands together, trying to find the next words.

In the corner of his eye, Cyrus noticed something moving around her foot.

He nudged Becca.

"I see it," his sister said. "*Now* you believe me."

When Becca told him she thought she saw a rat, he dismissed her. It was impossible after what he just went through. Impossible!

Yet now, a rat was on stage, trying to steal the show.

"This was the beginning of the end," she said. "My happiness shattered four months later."

Sounds of machine guns and cannons rocked the room as the woman faded from the spotlight.

Bright white light filled the theater, making Cyrus put his hands in front of his eyes.

"They could turn the lights down a notch," Aurora said.

Everyone in the theater made noises of discomfort as the light intensified.

Then, the squabbling of rats intertwined with the guns and cannons.

The floor shook, and one of the lights above crashed to the ground in a magnificent explosion. Someone yelled.

Another light turned on, and the giant rat was standing behind the fruit girl as she continued her lines.

"I got the news that Billy stepped on a landmine."

The giant rat looked around the stage. Cyrus knew the little rats' eyes were adjusting to the darkness. The crowd murmured.

"Wow, this show took a turn," Aurora said. "That thing looks disgusting."

Becca kicked Cyrus.

"I told you!" she whispered.

"No," he said, shaking his head. "They left. I saw them."

"Yeah, they left to come here," Becca asked. "Well, genius, what do we do now?"

"Oh, Billy!"

The girl dropped to her knees, face twisting into a theater cry.

"If I could search my heart for the words," she said, putting her hand on her heart, "I would find rivers of grief that ran all the way across the Atlantic to him."

Footsteps ran across the stage. It was Billy. Martha looked up at him, confused.

"We have to go," Billy said.

A look of confusion and anger flashed on the actress's face.

"And despite what challenges may come," Martha said, pushing away his hand and trying to continue her lines, "I will never—"

"Annie, shut up and look behind you!" Billy cried.

The fruit girl broke character upon hearing her real name. She turned to see the giant rat, and it roared at her. She screamed, and Billy dragged her off the stage.

A loud *blam* erupted somewhere behind the theater.

Aurora turned toward the door.

A few people in the crowd let out noises of interest.

"Great sound effects," Aurora said.

"No, that was a gunshot," Becca said.

Screams erupted from the lobby.

Suddenly, everyone was clambering over the theater chairs, racing for the exit.

"We've got to get out of here," Aurora said, panicking.

Cyrus whispered to Becca. "Bec, take Mom and get out of here."

The three of them jumped out of their seats and ran. Cyrus let Becca and Aurora in front of him, and he intentionally hung back until more people passed him.

"Cyrus?" Aurora cried. "Cyrus!"

Cyrus watched as Becca grabbed her mother's hand and guided her out of the theater.

Soon, it was just him and the giant rat. The beast stood on stage, and its many rat eyes flashed red within its body. In unison, the rats arched their backs, bending the giant rat into attack formation. Their hair rose like electricity was surging through their jumps.

"I told you to go home!" Cyrus cried, running at the stage.

"Shit, we're late," Aidan said, quickening his pace up the fire escape leading to the third floor.

The gunshot had startled him, but not the immediate screams that ensued.

Bruce swirled alongside him. He was a ball of anxiety, and his voice was whinier than normal.

"Damn it," the old man said. "I told you that you didn't need to use that dumpster. You could have reached the bottom rung with a running start."

"Dad, let's not do this right now," Aidan said.

"Your brother is going to join me if we don't do something, fast!" Bruce said.

"We're all going to join you if we don't figure this out."

"I can't imagine what your brother did to get us in this mess," Bruce said. He moaned in pain.

"The demon's not telling, so why don't we focus on Kirk so he can tell us?" Aidan asked.

Bruce rocketed away, did a circle around the building, and returned.

"Dozens of people in the street," Bruce said. "Come up with an alternative plan, son, before it's too late."

Aidan grabbed another rusted ring and pulled himself up. "You're the supernatural one. I'll take your suggestions."

Aidan swung onto a landing on the third floor.

He remembered the plan: high-tail it into the building as quietly possible and make his way to the stage as soon as possible after he heard the gunshot.

Now the gunshot had happened and he had no clear path to the stage. He didn't even know which fucking stage he was supposed to be at because there were three of them in the theater.

He could only think of his brother as he kicked in the nearest window. With his foot, he knocked out the jagged corners and slipped through into an office with a few cubicles and a frosted glass door. The lights in the office were off.

Aidan stayed low to the ground as Bruce flowed in after him.

"I have an idea," Bruce said. "Forfeit your deal with me. Send me back to the world of the dead."

"So you can leave me all alone?" Aidan asked, opening the door and peeking down a quiet, carpeted hallway with picture frames of theater legends on the walls. "That's rich, Dad."

"If I'm gone, then the plan can't continue," Bruce said. The old man flowed through Aidan, forcing him to stop.

Aidan stared at the blurry image of his father's silhouette.

"It's that, or you summon another demon for protection," Bruce said.

"Let's consider Option A," Aidan said. "You abandon me and sabotage the plan. Kirk dies."

"Well, maybe not if you can stop it," Bruce said.

"Option B: I summon a demon and have to twist my soul into pretzels to save Kirk," Aidan said. "Any demon would sense my desperation. The stakes are too high, Dad."

Bruce sighed. "I'm trying to look out for you. The afterlife isn't as glamorous as you think. You should both stay in the world of the living as long as possible. Trust me."

Aidan sidestepped his father and kept going.

"As necromancers, we're ready for anything at any time," he said. "You taught us the risks."

"Says one who's never tasted death."

"I'm tasting death right now," Aidan snapped. "And it tastes terrible."

A roar shook the floor below, quieting them. Aidan ran to a nearby stairwell and dashed down to the second floor, where the lights were turned off and things were a little too quiet.

"It has to be the theater on the first floor," he said, taking off into another run.

Bruce circled the stairwell.

"If you want it your way, fine, but think of the pain it will cause *me*," he said.

"We can't have it both ways, Dad," Aidan said, breaking onto the first floor. He passed several green rooms and arrived at a black door. The floor shook on the other side, and a hundred hisses filled the air.

Aidan didn't let his father say anything—he tore open the door and ran into the theater.

Becca grabbed her mother's hand as they ran into the theater lobby with the stampede of other guests. Transitioning from near-darkness to bright sunlight made her squint, and it hurt her eyes.

"Where's Cyrus?" Aurora asked. She kept looking behind them. "He's still not coming out."

"He'll catch up," Becca said. "It's not safe here, Mom."

"What the hell is going on?" Aurora asked.

Becca found an opening in the crowd and pulled her mother through it. The sound of rapid footsteps and frantic shouts covered the lobby.

"Help! Oh God, help me!" a voice cried.

A black man was on the carpet on his knees, with his back

to Becca. He wore a white shirt, which was covered in blood. His arm was bleeding.

Becca cursed at the sight of so much blood. Aurora let go of her hand.

"Someone help me!" the man cried.

"Someone call the police!" Aurora said, stopping.

"Can you come outside with us?" Aurora asked. "It's not safe here."

The man tried to stand but stumbled.

"Becca, let's help him," Aurora cried.

They needed to run. At any minute, the giant rat would be breaking through the wall and they'd be helpless.

Becca slid to the man and helped him stand. Blood smeared Becca's arm as she held him by the waist. Both women took him and helped him walk.

"Thank you," the man said. "Thank you so much."

Then, Becca finally got a good look at his face, but it was too late.

He was the necromancer who had attacked Cyrus in the alley.

Instinctively she pulled away, but Kirk grabbed her.

"Be cool, now," Kirk said. "This blood swap is only going to hurt a little."

In an instant, Kirk pushed Aurora to the floor and ripped a switchblade out of his pants.

A sharp pain tore down Becca's arm and she screamed.

Cyrus jumped out of the way as the giant rat barreled off the stage and through the audience area, sending chairs flying into the air.

The giant rat turned and ran after him again.

"None of this is your fault!" Cyrus cried. "Murgalen did this to you, and you deserve rest!"

His sister's voice echoed in his head.

"You're telling me that you told a bunch of zombie rats to go home?" she asked. "There's no way that worked."

He dashed for the doors, but he stepped on something.

A living rat. It lay smashed on the carpet.

"No!" Cyrus cried. Remorse struck him.

The floor was covered in rats.

"You followed me all the way here?" he asked incredulously.

They weren't the evil rats that comprised the giant one.

No, they were the rats from the sewer. The living ones.

Wham!

The giant rat crashed into him and he hit the wall and slid down with a bang, landing on a chair.

The giant rat laughed. Below it, the living rats gathered around it and hissed.

The giant rat screeched and aimed for Cyrus again.

Cyrus could barely breathe as he climbed off the chair and onto the floor.

The giant rat beelined for him.

He shifted into a rat and dove into the shadows.

The beast's big steps made him unsteady on his rat feet, but he ran under the seats and away.

A blanket of hissing covered the air above Cyrus. The hairs on his hump stood up.

Wham!

A hundred dead rats rained on him. One landed on his back and dug its incisors in. Cyrus tried to shake it off but couldn't.

Another bit his tail.

Soon, he was surrounded with punching, biting, and pushing.

No.

He wasn't going to let it end like this…not like the woman in the condo.

He shifted back into a human, screaming as his lungs grew to their human shape. The dead rats went flying off him. He plucked the remaining ones off and threw them down like firecrackers.

Bite marks burned all down his back and he grimaced in pain.

The giant rat was gone. It must have broken apart to attack him.

Below him, more squabbling.

The living rats were charging the dead rats. All over the floor, they stood on their hind legs, grappling each other and baring their incisors.

"They're fighting," he said, amazed at the sight. "They're following my lead."

And then he heard Becca's voice in his head. "Geez, you're such a doofus. You couldn't catch a clue if someone handed it to you."

So it was war, then.

The dead rats sensed Cyrus's shift and streamed into the big rat again.

Cyrus found a maintenance broom just offstage.

"Follow my lead, guys," he said. "Let's go!"

He ran as fast as he could at the forming beast, waving the broom. The rats charged behind him.

But he tripped over a rat and crashed to the floor.

"Damn it," he said.

The giant rat stomped toward him.

Someone ran onto the stage.

Aidan.

He pointed at the giant rat. "Showtime, Dad!" he cried.

The giant rat turned around, sniffing. The dead rats followed something in the air.

Quickly, Cyrus shifted to a rat.

Bruce was shooting across the air. Cyrus saw him in his pure form—giant bald head, a necklace covered in screaming souls. Runes swirled on his head like animations. He stared with eyeless sockets as purplish-black energy shot out of his body.

"This gives me no pleasure," the old man said, "but it seems to me that you dead rats aren't dead rats at all! You're souls who are lost and looking for a leader."

Bruce hovered over the stage.

"And so it's a leader you'll get! Aaaaaaaaaagh!!!!'"

Bruce gritted his stained teeth. The dead rats turned to him and shrieked at the top of their lungs.

Bruce kept screaming, and the energy pulled the dead rats toward him. Soon the giant rat broke form and the dead rats were all in the air, legs and tails flailing.

The rats gathered in a pile on the stage.

"I command you!" Bruce yelled wildly.

The rats gathered, clambering over each other until they formed the giant rat again.

Cyrus gulped.

"A necromancer in life, and a necromancer in death," Bruce said. "Ha ha ha, I've still got it!"

"Let's get this done," Aidan said. "Get the rat shifter like planned. He's in here somewhere."

Cyrus's heart pounded and he dashed under a chair.

"No," Bruce said coldly.

"No?" Aidan said.

"I'm breaking our deal," Bruce said. "That rat boy was never anything special anyway. I'm going to save my son!"

"Dad, stop!"

Bruce let out a war cry, and the giant rat obeyed the old man and rampaged toward the door.

Metal sheared open and the beast grunted as it threw the theater doors behind it.

Cyrus transformed into a human. Bruce's spirit form and voice disappeared to his human eye, but he still sensed the crazy old man there.

Cyrus dashed into the lobby. A few yards away, Kirk and Becca stood.

Kirk removed a switchblade from Becca's arm, and she screamed.

Cyrus yelled as his sister dropped to the floor.

CHAPTER THIRTY-SEVEN

BECCA MOVED AS if in a dream.

She felt herself falling down, yet she hit the floor faster than she thought it was coming.

Voices slurred around her like soup.

Kirk's head danced around hers, his mouth open in a vomiting position, like he was coughing something up. His bloody hands were clamped on the small gash in her arm. Her wound sizzled like lightning.

Her feet tingled, then her arms.

Something passed through her—no, entered her—through every inch of her skin.

Her body went ice cold, then burning hot.

She couldn't move her arms, and the feeling of paralysis freaked her out.

Her thoughts echoed through her skull until her voice doubled on itself, hard to understand.

Once, when she was six, she had almost drowned. Her mother took her to a pool party, and Becca, having just watched Olympic swimmers on TV, thought she could win a gold medal. She dove into the pool, expecting to fly through the water, but she flew down, down, down—like a rock. She couldn't swim. She couldn't pull herself out of the water.

Somehow, she broke the water, and she remembered calling for her mommy, but the words came out garbled before she went under again. She thrashed and thrashed and threw her arms about until she realized it was useless. Two hands wrapped around her chest and pulled her up—her father. That pool party was ruined.

Now she was reliving the same feeling.

She didn't know why, but she called for her mother.

"Mom!"

But her head hit the floor, and the impact rocked her vision as the theater lobby went horizontal, then up and down as her head bounced and hit the carpet again.

"Mom…"

Then she realized her lips weren't moving, and she screamed.

It was just her inside her mind, watching everything through eyes that might as well have been drunk.

More garbled voices filled the lobby. Becca shrank inside of herself, feeling smaller and smaller in her mind.

Suddenly, someone was with her, taking up space in her mind. Absorbing her thoughts and resting with her.

A low, growling voice spoke.

"Hello, Rebecca."

Hysteria struck Becca, but she could not move her body.

"Who's there?" she asked. Still, her lips did not move.

"Consider me a friend," the voice said.

Her thoughts raced. Whoever this person was, he was not a friend.

"You doubt me?" the voice asked. "All humans do in the beginning."

It read her thoughts.

"Of course I can," the voice said. "Nothing is private anymore. I am absorbing all your memories, and soon I will know you more intimately than you know yourself. Do you see what is happening, Rebecca? Do you see the *insanity* out there?"

Becca's head rolled to the side, but she didn't do it. She *watched* her head roll to the side.

Cyrus ran by in slow motion, a furious look on his face. He raised his hand back, yelled something, and punched Kirk in the face.

Kirk toppled. Then Cyrus was on top of him.

The room rocked. Was Cyrus's punch that hard?

No.

Her head rolled to the other side.

The wall where the theater doors had been had crumbled and the giant rat was running at her.

She wanted to scream, but she knew her lips wouldn't move.

"Just relax while this plays out," the voice said. "Your dear demon friend Garamanthus has looked out for you and your brother."

"Demon?"

The demon laughed, and Becca screamed, stuck inside her head.

Aurora couldn't process the rapid-fire sequence of events.

The tower of rats that formed on stage.

The gunshot in the theater.

The man lying in a puddle of his own blood and bleeding profusely who desperately needed her help.

The switchblade in her daughter's arm. Her daughter on the floor, lying unresponsive. Cyrus appearing out of nowhere and attacking the man.

And then, the wall crumbling and the tower of rats running at them.

Time had slowed down.

She rolled over on the floor and tried to stand up.

The bleeding man hit the floor next to her. He still had the switchblade in his hand. Cyrus landed on top of him.

"Cy!" Aurora shouted, her eyes on the blade.

The man raised the blade.

Aurora dashed and landed on top of the man's arm. She tried to pry the blade from his fingers. Aurora became aware of every breath as she moved.

This guy was strong. She could barely move his index finger.

She adjusted her hand into a chop and karate chopped the man right in the middle of his forearm.

"Aaah!" the man cried, dropping the switchblade.

Aurora scooped it off the carpet and threw it as far as she could.

The giant rat screeched and turned her blood cold as it approached.

"Cy, we've got to go!" she said.

She slid to Becca, who lay, eyes open and staring at the giant rat. A superficial cut ran down her shoulder. It probably hurt, but she'd be okay.

Why wouldn't she move? Fear struck Aurora at the thought of Becca suffering a neck injury.

"Becca, honey, we've got to go," she said, tapping Becca's cheek.

Her daughter didn't move. She looked paralyzed.

Her heart raced as she feared the worst.

"Cyrus, we've got to help her!" Aurora called.

Cyrus, who was still wrestling with the bleeding man, glanced over and his eyes widened. He landed a final punch and ran to Becca.

Then he saw the giant rat barreling at them and cursed.

Aurora fell backward as Cyrus jumped on her, covering her and Becca.

"Stay down, Mom! We'll be fine."

The giant rat screeched and picked up the man, inspecting him.

Aurora got a better look at the beast—it wasn't just a single rat—it was hundreds of rats with glowing red eyes.

The man hung like a bleeding rag doll in the rat's arms, and then it set him down gently, all its rats growling.

The beast stopped as if waiting for a command.

A man in a track suit came running out of the theater.

"Kirk!" he cried. He dropped to the floor.

"Aidan, I'm…free," Kirk said.

"About fucking time," Aidan said. "Let's get you out of here. Dad was about to go medieval on that demon."

Kirk pointed a finger at Becca. Aidan shook his head.

"It doesn't matter now," Aidan said. "Let's get you out of here, brother."

Aurora pushed Cyrus off her. He tried to grab her, but she bolted to her feet.

"Excuse me," she said angrily. "Your *brother* just stabbed my daughter."

"It wasn't him, lady," Aidan said. "You'll have to forgive him. He wasn't himself." Then he cracked a wry smile. "But you might want to take your daughter to an exorcist."

Cyrus charged Aidan, but the giant rat intervened and knocked him halfway across the lobby.

"My dad says to butt out," Aidan said. "You and your sister aren't in any more danger. Fortunately, we don't need to finish our deal anymore. Old Bruce is sparing you."

"You…bastards," Cyrus said.

Cyrus talked to them like he knew them. *Did* he know them?

Aurora bent down and caressed Becca's hair.

"Honey, you've got to wake up," she said.

Becca's lips moved, but no sound came out.

Aidan helped Kirk up and slung his good arm over his

shoulder. Together, the two brothers walked out, and the giant rat followed them.

"I won't let you get away with this!" Cyrus cried, charging the brothers again.

The giant rat stepped in front of him, but Cyrus flashed and disappeared.

"Cyrus?" Aurora asked.

A brown rat landed on the floor and dashed around the giant rat and toward the door before doing a quick about-face. It morphed into a human shape, rat parts elongating into hands…feet…a torso…and then…her son.

Her son?!

Cyrus grabbed the switchblade that she had thrown across the lobby. He jumped into the air, screaming madly, aiming it for Aidan. His face meant murder.

"Cyrus, no!" Aurora cried.

The giant rat leaped into the air and barreled down at Cyrus.

Everything slowed down again. The hair on Aurora's arms raised as a subtle electricity coursed through the air. Outside, day shifted to night.

All of the windows in the theater lobby shattered. The floor filled with brown rats pouring in from the theater, and hissing and screeching drowned out Cyrus's mad scream.

A ferocious growl swept across the theater as another giant beast flew past and pushed Cyrus out of the way mid-air and slammed into the giant rat. This beast was a…hyena? But it was also a man, wearing a long trench coat and a gold chain.

The hyena slammed into the giant rat, knocking it off kilter. All of the rats fell like marbles on the floor, mixing in with the rats that poured out of the theater.

The hyena landed in front of Aurora, growling.

"Desmond!" Cyrus cried.

Two ravens flapped into the lobby and landed next to

Desmond. Aurora watched dumbfounded as they morphed into two people.

"Not just Desmond," a woman in a flannel shirt and jeans said. "And not just us."

A black woman joined them. Aurora recognized her as Letitia Frankland from Channel 100.

Why was the news here?

The ground shook.

Aurora turned. Outside, a seven-foot-tall winged beast fluttered into the building with enormous angel wings made from black feathers. Shining white chains jingled all along its legs and covered its torso.

It raised a sword, which gathered with light. In the other hand, it held a book. It looked at Aurora with oval-shaped eyes. She expected the beast to say something, but then she saw that it didn't have a mouth.

"Oh my God," Aurora whispered.

"How are you adjusting, Rebecca?"

The demon's voice echoed in Becca's head.

She had watched her mother try to revive her, and Cyrus turn into a rat to stop Aidankirk. She willed all of her energy and strength into her arms and yelled as she tried to reclaim control.

"Come on, come on, come on!" she said.

"Why fight it?" Garamanthus asked. "You could just ask me nicely."

"Let me go," Becca snarled. She still willed her body to move.

"Very well," the demon said. She didn't trust the sudden politeness in his voice. "I have more absorbing to do. I am becoming a student of Rebecca Marie Grant. Your life has been fascinating, hasn't it?"

The demon's voice faded. All her concentration surged into her arms, legs, and head.

She left the shaded attic of her mind and went back into herself, into the fullness of her body. She shot straight up, gasping.

"Bec!" Cyrus cried.

Cyrus held her head in his heads. "What happened to you?"

Becca wanted to talk, but her lips wouldn't move fast enough.

"I…Cyrus…Mom…"

Cyrus picked her up. "Let's go."

Becca set eyes on Axel, who floated into the lobby in nephilim form.

"Shit…" she said.

"Shit is right," Cyrus said. "Mom, your help!"

Aurora stared spellbound at Axel. Behind him, his son and assistant entered, holding white chains of light to contain him.

"Mom!" Cyrus cried again, breaking Aurora from her staring. She turned and saw Becca breathing and moving.

"Becca, what a relief!" Aurora said. She hugged her and started to cry.

"Mom, can you take Becca and get out of here?" Cyrus asked.

"No," Becca muttered. "I can't go. I have to stay…"

"No, you are *not* going to stay," Cyrus said.

Becca lifted her arm to punch Cyrus in the shoulder to get him in line, but her swing missed. She felt drunk.

Aurora grabbed Becca and she didn't protest as her mother led her out of the theater lobby. The patrons had all streamed out the door and into the street.

The last thing Becca saw was Axel, Desmond, Cyrus, Luna, Rocco, and Letitia Frankland in a standoff with Aidankirk and the giant rat, which had regathered next to the two brothers. The living rats darted across the floor, confused.

And then Becca gazed up at the sun blazing in the dark night sky. Axel's transformation had wreaked havoc.

The demon's voice popped into her head again.

"This will be our little secret, won't it, Rebecca?"

Becca startled. She looked around, but the demon wasn't there. Just the street with frozen cars. People on the street were frozen in mid-stride. Cars were stopped in the middle of the street.

"What is going on?" Aurora muttered under her breath.

"Mom…" Becca said.

"What is it, honey?" Aurora asked as she helped Becca down the stairs.

"I'm…sorry."

"Don't apologize," Aurora said. "There will be plenty of time for that."

A voice called Becca's name.

Gilberto was on the street, running toward her.

"Becca!" he cried, sliding to a stop in front of them.

"Gilberto?" Aurora asked.

"Sorry we have to meet again like this, Mrs. Grant," Gilberto said. He met Becca's eyes and his own widened.

"Ah, I lied," the demon said, its voice surging into her head. "Excuse me for a moment, Rebecca. It's time for a rondo with fate."

Becca uttered a cry, but it didn't escape from her lips. She could only watch as the demon took control of her body again and knocked her mother to the pavement.

"Hey, buddy," she said, standing tall. But she wasn't speaking now. The demon was.

"What the heck is up with you?" Gilberto asked.

Becca screamed inside her mind again as she watched herself tackle Gilberto to the ground and wrap her hands around his neck.

～

"It's over, Bruce!" Cyrus said. He couldn't see the old man, but he knew he was floating just behind the giant rat and that he could hear him. "You guys have meddled in our affairs enough."

"What are we all even fighting for anymore?" Kirk asked, straining.

"It doesn't matter!" Cyrus said. "You stabbed Becca and you're going to pay for it."

Axel waved a hand. Ezekiel stepped forward, encased in a column of golden light, holding the white chain of light attached to one of his father's legs tightly.

"The three of you need to surrender now," Ezekiel said. "We will take you into custody and you can explain why you framed my father."

Kirk laughed. "Framed?" He clutched his arm in pain. "That sounds about right, but I didn't do the framing."

"Let us go," Aidan said. "You're making a big deal out of nothing."

"You don't have anywhere to go," Cyrus said. "You're cornered and outnumbered."

"I have some information that might change the calculus a little," Kirk said. "Maybe we're all on the same side."

Desmond growled.

"You might be interested to know this too, big man," Kirk said, grinning.

Silence.

"Instead of attacking me, why don't you attack the nymph that impersonated you?" Kirk asked. "She hired me and my brother to kill Gilberto, but we thought you were the one who hired us."

Kirk winced. "When I found out it wasn't you, it was too late. But I got myself into a bad demon deal and got possessed."

"Why aren't you possessed now?" Cyrus asked.

"Ask your sister, bud," Kirk asked.

He and Aidan both laughed.

Cyrus balled his fists.

"What did you do to my sister?" he asked.

"Like I said," Kirk said. "It wasn't me."

Ezekiel made a look of disgust. "A nymph did this to us?"

Johanna shook her chain that was also connected to Axel's leg. The woman's face hardened. "Of course she did. They can never be trusted."

Axel shook with rage. His angel wings flapped, releasing black feathers.

"Go ahead, nephilim," Kirk said. "Do your worst."

Cyrus processed the words.

Nymphs…

Oleandra did this. He just knew the evil nymph was behind it.

A scream erupted from the street.

His mom.

Cyrus ran outside, where Becca was choking Gilberto on the street. Aurora was trying to pull her off.

"Bec, what the hell are you doing?" he asked, running for Becca.

Something whacked into him hard, sending him rolling across the asphalt. He looked up as leaves flittered down around him.

Two vines closed around his wrists and strung him into the air. He struggled against them but couldn't move.

He glanced up into a massive canopy of leaves and branches that blocked out the sun. He was hanging in a tree.

A feminine laugh sounded behind him.

"Let me go!" Cyrus cried.

"You're not going to ruin the plan," Rue said. He couldn't see her, but he knew that she was in tree form by the way her bark cracked as she spoke.

Oleandra stood in front of the theater in human form—

brown raincoat and blood-red high heels. "It's time to clean up the mess you made, rat," she said, walking in.

Cyrus cursed.

He looked at Becca and Gilberto. His mom was trying to throw Becca off, but she couldn't.

"Gilberto, Becca is possessed," Cyrus cried, remembering Kirk's cryptic words. "Pray!"

Gilberto heard him and uttered a prayer in Spanish.

Cyrus pulled at the vines, but Rue held him tight.

"I don't have time for this!" he said. He shifted into a rat, but Rue adjusted the vines and kept his arms bound.

The world shrank into his rat's eyes. He screeched as loud as he could, twisting himself in the vines.

He followed his instinct as he screeched, the hairs raising on his back like a buzzsaw.

Soon, a cascade of rats poured out of the theater, rushing toward Rue.

"You stupid rat," Rue said.

Cyrus kept screeching as the rats raced up Rue's trunk.

A rat chewed one of Cyrus's vines. It snapped, freeing one of his arms. He transformed to a human and, with his other arm, he yanked the other vine loose and dropped to the ground.

"Get back here," Rue said.

Cyrus sensed another vine shooting at him, but he jumped out of the way.

He turned to the tree woman. Rats covered her, swarming all over her trunk and branches. The nymph yelled as one of the rats bit her on the eye.

"Good job, guys," he said.

Nearby, Gilberto let out a gasp. He continued his prayer, speaking quiet and fast Spanish as Becca squeezed.

"Becca, let him go!" Cyrus cried.

He threw himself on top of Becca, but she must have seen him coming because she rolled him off. He tried to push himself between her and Gilberto, and then he saw her eyes.

It wasn't his sister's eyes. Sure, they were the same, but they were…evil. He had never seen such a murderous look in his sister's face. It wasn't possible.

He remembered Kirk's words.

"Becca, if you can hear me, fight it," Cyrus said. "Don't let it take over."

A wry smile spread across Becca's face as Gilberto's face turned blue.

Becca couldn't believe her eyes as the color drained from Gilberto's face.

She was killing him.

No.

The demon was.

"I told you to let him go!" Becca cried, her voice echoing in the walls of her mind.

"I'll let go soon," Garamanthus said.

"I won't let you use my body for murder," Becca said, focusing all her attention on her arms.

She tasted hot sweat, felt the cords in Gilberto's neck flexing as he spoke the same prayer in Spanish over and over and over, staring her right in the eye.

Gilberto completed his prayer and started again.

Becca's vision clouded with white, like someone gently poured milk on her eyes. A wave of relief swelled through her, and she became mindful of every thought. Every breath. The whiteness expanded infinitely across her mind.

All the while, Cyrus and Aurora's voices spoke, distant but persistent: "Becca, you can do it. You can do it."

Inhale, exhale. Heartbeat.

"Nuestro padre que estás en los cielos…"

Inhale, exhale, heartbeat.

"Let go of my body!" she cried.

She had to get the demon to let go. She would fight however she could. She wouldn't let her friend die…

"Stop wasting your energy," the demon said. "You'll have control of your body soon."

"Soon is not soon enough," Becca said. "I want it now."

"I will do further damage to your body if you do not shut up," Garamanthus said. "And I will kill your family."

"Leave my family alone!" she cried.

Becca kept straining, pushing with every inch of her mind.

Inhale, exhale.

"Move, arm, move," she said, focusing on the expanding whiteness across her eyes.

Her fingers wiggled. Had she wiggled them?

She couldn't see, but she trusted her intuition, focusing all of her being into her fingertips.

"No, you stupid girl," the demon said. "You're going to make a colossal mess."

Becca ignored him, insinuating herself into every fiber of her body.

The white cloud bubbled away and the demon screamed.

Becca was on top of Gilberto, in control of her body again. She saw his pale, dying face in full color now.

She let go and scrambled away from him, panting.

Gilberto rolled over, sucking in air. Quickly, the color returned to his face.

Becca crawled back, horrified at what the demon had done. What she had done.

Aurora tried to grab her, but she pushed her away.

"What have I done?" she asked softly, tears in her eyes.

"You've made a mess," the demon said, his voice so clear in her head, it was as if he were next to her.

"The healer was supposed to die," the demon said. "That was fate."

"Screw your fate," Becca said. "Get out of my head!"

She clutched her head, shook it, and screamed as the demon cursed at her in a language she couldn't understand. The syllables were harsh and vicious. Every word was a hot flame in her soul chased by poison.

"Never has a human defied such a clean possession," the demon said. "You beat me once, but I will take back control."

She didn't know why, but she sensed the white energy that had clouded her vision filling a well inside her soul that hadn't been filled before. Was it some kind of protection?

"You will not change fate," the demon said.

"Just watch me!" Becca said. "I will get you out, fate be damned!"

The demon laughed. "And how will you do that when I have you forever to hold?"

His voice faded into night air. She was on the street, cowering against the wall of the theater. She looked down at her palm and saw purple locks in her palm. She was pulling her hair out. Her scalp tingled with pain.

Cyrus and Aurora stood several feet away, staring. Gilberto was on his knees now, coughing.

"Bec?" Cy asked softly. "Or demon?"

"It's…me," she said, looking at him in the eye. Cyrus softened upon seeing her real gaze.

Becca hugged herself as Cyrus and Aurora approached.

"Stay away from me," Becca said.

But Cyrus and Aurora continued approaching.

"Why won't you listen to me?" Becca yelled. The words spilled out first, and then she realized the anger behind them.

"Bec," Cyrus said. "It's going to be okay."

"How did this happen?" Becca asked, more to herself than them. "Why did this happen to me?"

Cyrus grabbed her and brought her into a hug.

"Cy, what's happening to me?" she asked, crying.

Cyrus said nothing as he held her.

CHAPTER THIRTY-EIGHT

KIRK STARED at the nymph who had deceived him.

Oleandra stood at the front door of the theater, her brown raincoat rippling in a wind she seemed to create on her own. She wore blood-red high heels, and her hair was pulled back into a bun.

He hated her just as much as he did when he met her the first time.

The only thing standing between them was Axel…Kirk had never seen a nephilim before, and the thing was terrifying, but not the scariest thing he'd ever seen.

He wanted to charge her, but he was losing too much blood. He had to get to a hospital. Aidan held him tight.

"This is what happens when I wind you all up and let you go," the nymph said.

Axel gestured to his secretary. The woman stepped forward.

"Oleandra, is it true that you framed Axel?" she asked.

Oleandra burst into laughter. "Framed? You're putting it too lightly."

She pointed at Axel. "I thought we could settle the score, love."

Then she pointed to Desmond. "And I thought I might as well not stand in the way of what Murgalen started."

Kirk whispered to his brother, "What's the quickest way out of here?"

"Behind us," Aidan said.

"Say no more," Bruce said, swirling around them. "I'll cover for you, boys."

Axel hollered with rage.

"Holler all you want," Oleandra said. "What are you going to do about it?"

Ezekiel and Johanna pulled the chains that secured Axel. The chains rustled as Axel strained against them.

"Kill me and you'll have a reason for the paranormal world to seal you away forever," the nymph said. "Or, relinquish your hold on the paranormal world."

"Sounds like a loss either way," Rocco said.

"That's the point, raven," Oleandra said. Her arms extended into long branches. "It's about time this city truly understands the paranormal residents living within. When they find out, I don't think they'll like living with you all any more than they do roaches."

Oleandra's human face stretched out, and her body elongated into a giant trunk that tilted on curved roots that walked under her like feet.

Aidan pulled Kirk swiftly toward the theater.

They moved with urgency. Every minute was now life or death.

"Speaking of roaches," Oleandra said. "You have two racing away right now."

"Damn it," Kirk said.

Desmond landed in front of them, growling.

"No, you don't!" Bruce cried.

The giant rat tumbled into Desmond, knocking him into the dark theater.

"Run, boys!" Bruce said.

Kirk and Aidan broke into a run.

"I told you that you would regret crossing me, necromancer," Oleandra said.

Something hit Aidan and he went down.

A switchblade. In his shoulder.

Aidan yelled in agony.

Kirk stumbled and fell with him.

Aidan brought his hands up to his neck, to the switchblade. He convulsed as a river of blood poured out of his neck and down his blue nylon jacket.

"Aidan!" Bruce cried.

"No," Kirk said, stammering.

Aidan was gone immediately. His eyes stared at Kirk and at nothing at all.

Tears welled in Kirk's eyes as he grabbed his brother, saying his name over and over.

A psychotic wail drew his eye to the air, where Bruce swirled around furiously.

"My son, my son…"

Bruce swelled to several times his size, then began to shrink.

"Never trust a nymph," the old man said. He looked at Kirk and said, "Save yourself, Kirk."

Bruce exploded in a flash of light, and then he was gone.

Aidan had summoned Bruce. Now that Aidan was dead, so was the bond.

Kirk's stomach churned. His hands were covered in his brother's blood.

The giant rat swayed like it was sleepy. Now it was without a leader.

Kirk slunk into the shadows and slipped out an emergency exit as the giant rat toppled over, spilling dead rats all over the floor.

Letitia Frankland wanted to make a difference and avenge the paranormals who had died in the teeth of the giant rat.

Now she was standing in the middle of the fight, between Axel, the giant rat, and a tree woman talking nonsense.

At least the giant rat had fallen. Dead rats covered the floor. Letitia felt no sadness for them, not after what they'd done.

A hand grabbed her and pulled her back just as Axel slashed his sword in a vow to attack Oleandra.

Rocco. He smiled at her.

She was grateful to him and Luna for saving her.

A loud wail cut off her current thoughts.

All over the floor, the dead rats were exploding into translucent human silhouettes who cried in pain.

Letitia had never seen these silhouettes before. Were they the rats?

They had to be.

The empath voice in Letitia's head spoke.

So much pain. So much sadness. No closure.

Letitia grabbed her heart and stumbled backward. Rocco caught her.

"What is it?" he asked.

"They're undead," Letitia said. "They're asking to be sent to rest."

"How exactly do we do that?" he asked.

Letitia listened to the voices. They didn't speak—only cried. Every noise was a dagger to her sensitive empath heart.

"We have to exorcise them," Letitia said.

"How the hell do we do that?" Rocco whispered.

"Umm, hello," Luna said. "We only have a gigantic angel demon hybrid standing in front of us."

"Axel's got bigger problems right now," Rocco said.

"I can feel their pain," Letitia said. "I might be able to talk to them and hold their attention. But it won't work if we can't chase it with an exorcism."

"What about Gilberto?" Rocco asked.

"I'm on it," Luna said. She shifted into a raven and flew out, gronking loudly.

Meanwhile, Rocco stood in front of Letitia as Oleandra finished her transformation into a giant tree, busting the ceiling. She laughed at them with enormous triangular bark teeth. Axel dashed at her, his sword glowing.

Becca let Cyrus go and found the strength to stand, and stand tall.

Aurora embraced her.

"I don't know what's going on, but it's going to be okay," her mother said.

Becca didn't answer.

Gilberto sat on the curb now, still coughing and getting air.

"Can I sit with you?" she asked.

Gilberto nodded and she sat on the curb with him.

"I'm sorry," she said.

"It wasn't you," Gilberto said. "I knew it by looking in your eyes."

Silence.

"We're good, Becca," he said. "I forgive you."

Becca buried her head in her hands and massaged her temples.

"How do I get it out?" Becca asked.

"We can exorcise it," Cyrus said.

"It's not that easy," Gilberto said.

"Wait a sec," Cyrus said. "Axel is a half-angel, isn't he? Maybe he can do it."

"I told you, it's not that easy!" Gilberto said.

"Maybe, but I think Cy is right," Becca said. "We have to try."

"You can try, but you'll be disappointed," Garamanthus said. The demon uttered more curses inside her mind.

She shook his voice out and focused on Gilberto.

An explosion rocked the theater.

Becca helped Gilberto up.

"Axel and Oleandra are going at it," Cyrus said.

A loud gronk distracted them. A raven flapped down from the sky and morphed into Luna.

"Gilberto, we need your help," she said. "Can you perform an exorcism?"

"What is it with you guys and exorcisms tonight?" he asked.

Luna shrugged and grabbed his hand.

Oleandra flew out of the theater and slammed into a nearby building. Bricks and glass flew high and crashed to the ground. Desmond hopped out of the theater, growling. Axel flew out behind him, sword in hand, his son and secretary pulling his chains.

"Now is our chance," Luna said.

Becca started to the theater, but Cyrus grabbed her.

"Are you sure you want to go in there?" he asked. "You're not in a condition to fight."

"I'm not running away from this," Becca said.

Cyrus nodded.

Another hand grabbed Becca.

Her mom.

"You're not leaving me here alone," Aurora said.

They ran into the theater lobby as Axel and Oleandra warred in the street, slinging blows and tremendous flashes of light.

The lobby was almost empty now save for living rats that were running around and translucent silhouettes floating around.

Rocco and a black woman were standing in the middle,

watching the souls. She was Letitia Frankland from Channel 100. Weird to meet a celebrity during a time like this.

Becca watched the souls with amazement.

"They're asking to be sent away," Letitia said. "I can connect with them, but I need someone to help me send them away."

"This I can do," Gilberto said, following a soul as it circled him. "Much easier than I thought."

Letitia and Gilberto held hands.

"Teamwork of the highest proportion," Garamanthus said.

Becca tried to shake the demon's voice away again, but it didn't work.

"When they begin sending off the souls, watch your healer's back," the demon said. "That is, if you want him to live."

Becca gritted her teeth and grunted.

"Stop talking to me," she said.

Cyrus grabbed his sister's hand.

"It's all right, Bec," he said.

Letitia spoke to the souls.

"I'm here to let you know that you are dead," she said.

Gilberto prayed in Spanish.

The souls flickered, then flitted around the theater, congregating around Letitia and Gilberto.

"Whatever has happened to you, know that you were loved," Letitia said. "But it's time for you to go now. Go home."

Suddenly, the moaning changed to sighs of relief. The souls spun around Letitia and Gilberto like a centrifuge, white balls of light breaking off their bodies and drifting up to the ceiling.

"Go home," Letitia said again. "Go home and be at peace."

Gilberto raised his voice and continued his prayer.

"Go home," Letitia said again.

"Yeah, go home!" Cyrus said.

"Go home," Becca said.

Then, everyone was telling the souls to go home at once like a sports game chant.

The souls of the rat shifters broke apart and dissolved.

Garamanthus spoke again. "Becca, I'd check behind if I were you."

She turned.

A giant tree branch hurtled toward Gilberto.

Becca dove and pushed Gilberto out of the way. The branch slammed into her, knocking her down.

Gilberto looked over at her in fright.

"Don't stop," Becca said.

Gilberto continued his prayer, joining hands with Letitia again.

Rue glided into the theater, her roots tromping up and down like spider legs. She had rats all over her trunk, biting and scratching her.

"This can't continue," the tree nymph said.

Becca rolled to her feet. Cyrus jumped next to her.

"Stay out of this, Rue!" Cyrus said.

Rue plucked more rats out of her crown. The nymph screamed and sent gnarled vines out of her canopy. They flew at Letitia and Gilberto and wrapped around their arms.

"This is exactly why you needed to die, healer," Rue said.

Soon, everyone was encased in a tangle of vines. Vines strung Becca up.

Letitia's voice stopped. Vines covered her mouth.

"No!" Becca cried, but vines covered her mouth too, and she tasted flowers and dirt.

Cyrus, Becca, Rocco, and Luna hung suspended from vines in the lobby.

Meanwhile, the souls, who had been sighing in relief, moaned again, the translucent balls of energy coalescing back to them.

"They will live in eternal purgatory so they can keep plaguing this city," Rue said. "That was Murgalen's plan."

"Then why did you want me to kill the giant rat?" Cyrus asked.

"We had hoped it would kill *you*," Rue said.

"This is what happens when you don't listen to me," Garamanthus said. "I can be of help to you, Becca. Being possessed by a demon really isn't so bad. Let me take control and you might be surprised at what I can do."

Becca ignored him.

"If you ignore me, at least consider that you're going to get another break very soon. Don't waste it. Maybe then you'll trust me. It's in my best interest that you live, you know."

Fuck you she thought, feeling good about herself.

"Hey, tree lady!" a voice shouted.

Rue rotated just in time to see Aurora with a fryer tray of hot oil. Aurora hurled it straight into the tree's mouth.

Rue recoiled, and the vines around the group went limp instantly. The tree nymph screamed and screamed.

"Your opening," Garamanthus said as Becca dropped to the floor.

Letitia spoke to the souls to calm them again, and Gilberto resumed praying.

Rocco and Luna shifted into ravens and pecked Rue's eyes, making the tree swat at them.

"Nice job, Mom," Becca said.

"I saw the tree coming and ducked into the kitchen," Aurora said. "Fortunately, there was still food going."

Rue fell out of the theater lobby as Rocco and Luna pestered her.

"The prayer," Becca said. "We've got to keep it going."

"Go home," she, Cyrus, and Aurora said loudly as Letitia and Gilberto continued.

The souls sighed again and spun around the lobby,

breaking apart and changing from translucent into soft, white balls of light.

"Don't be scared, and don't feel like you need to return," Letitia said. "We'll be just fine without you. But your new destiny begins now."

A shimmering flash covered the lobby, making Becca cover her eyes. A collective exhale blew her hair about, like the sound someone makes when they drink the first sip of a cold soda. When it faded, the souls were gone.

Quiet settled in around them.

"It's done," Letitia said.

"Thank God," Gilberto said.

A brown shape on the floor drew her eyes.

The living rats were dispersing, scattering away toward the nearest sewer. A gang of them climbed into a catch basin.

"They're not scared anymore," Cyrus said. "The shifters *are* truly gone."

Cyrus waved to the rats as they scattered.

Becca shook her head. Only her brother would wave goodbye to a bunch of rats and thank them for their help.

A ferocious roar came from the street. Outside, Desmond landed on a car.

"Desmond!" Cyrus cried.

Meanwhile, Axel and Oleandra clashed. Oleandra dodged Axel's sword and lashed him with several branches, knocking him backward.

Cyrus dashed into the street.

Cy, you idiot, Becca thought as she ran after him.

CHAPTER THIRTY-NINE

Cyrus ran to Desmond, who lay in the center of a car hood. The werehyena groaned.

Across the street, Ezekiel and Johanna shouted commands to Axel, who ripped his sword out of the ground after missing a strike at Oleandra.

"Dad, remember that rage cannot consume you," Ezekiel said. "Fight well but don't overdo it."

"Who cares if she dies?" Johanna asked. "She killed Therese. She must die as punishment."

Cyrus scratched his head.

"That's Axel's punishment," Gilberto said. "Years ago, he fought Oleandra and went berserk after she killed Therese. Now he has to be bound with reminders of his true nature—light and darkness."

"The Regulators' way of regulating him, eh?" Cyrus asked.

Gilberto shrugged. "Maybe. He's still pretty freaking powerful if you ask me." He pulled out a pouch and palmed some herbs, working on healing Desmond. Green energy flowed from his fingertips into Desmond's torso.

Axel lopped off one of Oleandra's branches. Oleandra hollered and twisted her canopy at him like a drill, knocking the sword out of his hand. The sword flew through the air like a boomerang toward Cyrus.

"Look out!" he cried, pushing Gilberto out of the way.

The sword stuck in the ground next to him. It glowed a radiant white, and its braided leather hilt was as wide as Cyrus's body.

He got the urge to touch it.

He reached out, but when his fingers touched it, an electric shock sent them away.

"Ow!"

"Still an idiot as usual," Becca said. "You didn't seriously think you could wield that thing."

Cyrus wagged his wrist. "Guess not."

Gilberto ran to Desmond and kept rubbing the herb against one palm and healing Desmond with the other.

Oleandra drilled Axel into the wall of the theater, but the nephilim grabbed a few branches in her crown and twisted. Oleandra let out a piercing scream, and then Axel carried her into the air.

"Dad, no!" Ezekiel cried.

Johanna lost her balance on the chain that bound Axel, and she was lifted into the air. She lost her grip as Axel flexed his wings and spun.

Johanna disappeared over the rooftops.

"Crap," Cyrus said.

Johanna's chain sliced down and slammed into Ezekiel's head, lashing him into the concrete. The impact knocked him out.

"Cy, duck!" Becca cried.

Becca and Cyrus ducked as the shimmering white chain zipped over their heads and dragged across the sidewalk, dragging up asphalt.

"With Ezekiel and Johanna gone, there is no one to contain Axel," Gilberto said. "He's unbound now and he's going to go berserk."

"What does that mean?" Cyrus asked.

"He'll destroy her," Gilberto said.

"That's not a bad thing, right?" Cyrus asked.

"He'll also destroy the city until he regains his senses," Becca said. "That was what happened last time."

Cyrus stared at her slack-jawed.

"Er, at least according to Gilberto," Becca said.

"Then we have to stop him," Cyrus said.

Axel spun again, ripping out more tree branches from Oleandra.

The chains flew back toward them.

Cyrus had an idea.

He watched the chains intently.

"Bec, on the count of three, grab a chain," he said.

"Are you crazy?" Becca asked.

"Yes, so do it," Cyrus said.

One of the chains flapped across the street in their direction. Cyrus ran onto a car hood and jumped into the air.

He held his breath as he sailed through the air toward the white chain. Either he'd catch it or it would cut his head off…

"Come on," he whispered.

Success!

Both hands wrapped around the white chain and Axel pulled him into the air.

The chain diffused cool energy into his hands as he held on tight.

He looked back at Becca, who stared after him incredulously.

"I thought we had each other's backs!" he cried.

"Don't shame me like that," Becca said, getting a running start.

"If I die up here, it'll be on your conscience," he called, rising higher.

"Cy, I'm going to kiiiiill you!" Becca shouted as she latched on to her chain.

Seconds later, they were both flying high into the sky after Axel as he rose over the rooftops.

CHAPTER FORTY

Becca almost lost the contents in her stomach as she whipsawed over a roof.

Her chain crisscrossed with Cyrus's and then they drifted in different directions.

The wind blew her hair wildly and she was all alone up here. The only thing she could do was hang on.

The chain, despite looking white hot, was cool to the touch. The links pulsed with pure power that made them impossible to cut. Becca thought they'd make killer whips.

"You choose to fly behind the angel," Garamanthus said.

Becca held the chain close and the links rustled against her skin.

"Leave me alone!" she cried.

"A containment mechanism," the demon said. "Two lines: one light and one dark to keep the nephilim in touch with its true nature. Which line are we, do you suppose?"

"I said shut up," Becca said, trying to focus him away.

"You have the power to end this battle," the demon said. "Can't you feel the energy coursing through this chain? It's enough to make me giddy!"

Above, Oleandra screamed as Axel ripped out more of her branches.

Below, her roots elongated, forming sharp points behind Axel.

"Axel, look out!" she cried.

The roots grabbed hold of one of Axel's wings, tearing it back. The nephilim yelled and let go of the branches. Oleandra butted forward and bit Axel's face.

The nephilim began to fall. Becca held on tight as the demon laughed.

"I can work with the energy in this chain," he said. "It gives me strength."

Becca felt herself shrinking into her mind again.

"No," she said, shaking her head. She concentrated on controlling her hands, but she was losing.

The energy in the chain was drawing out the demon's power.

"Your brother is a genius," the demon said. "His idiotic decision gives me a rematch."

The chain shimmered in her hands.

She didn't know why, but she prayed.

"I pray that you leave me alone, and that you leave my body forever," she said. "Heavenly Father, if you exist, don't forsake me. Tell me what I have done to deserve this…"

"You useless girl," the demon said. "You would dare say a prayer when attached to an angel? And I thought you had faith."

Becca continued with her words. She just let them pour out, even though they sounded ridiculous.

Garamanthus uttered a curse in his demon language.

Together, they spoke against each other, competing. The demon raised his voice and Becca raised hers.

Above, Axel extended his hand. The sword came rocketing up and he grabbed it, slicing off two of Oleandra's roots. The tree nymph slammed into a roof.

Becca kept praying, and Garamanthus kept cursing.

The white chain sparkled as energy pulsated from it and into Becca's hands. It sparked and shocked her hands. It was too powerful to hold now.

"If I die, I'll bring you with me," the demon said viciously.

Garamanthus hollered as Becca's vision went white.

~

"Bec, what the hell are you doing over there?" Cyrus asked, as if she could hear him.

Becca clung to the chain, muttering to herself. She wasn't even watching the battle.

Axel swung him over a city street and he made the mistake of looking down.

Maybe this was a bad idea, he thought as a street loomed impossibly far below him.

On a nearby roof, Oleandra brandished more sharp branches and leaped up at Axel.

The nephilim raised his sword, ready for the nymph.

Becca kept muttering to herself.

"Bec, pay attention," Cyrus said. "We've got to keep Axel balanced."

He remembered his duty and then said, "Axel, keep your sword steady. Aim to wound, but don't kill!"

The nephilim groaned in response as it flew down toward Oleandra.

"Bec!" Cyrus cried again, watching his sister twirl on her chain, doing nothing. "Come on, get it together!"

Axel speared Oleandra with the sword, straight through the mouth. The nymph's brown irises widened as she realized her fate.

Axel grabbed her trunk, ripped the sword out, and jammed it through one of her eyes.

"Axel, you've got to stop!" Cyrus said. "The battle's over!"

Then, he looked over just as his sister let go of the chain and fell.

Becca picked herself off the ground. She was on a rooftop.

Above, Axel and Oleandra traded blows in the purple night sky, eclipsed momentarily by the night sun. Cyrus hollered in the sky, twisting like a bell in a wind chime.

Her chain slid off the roof with a quiet rustle as the fight shifted away.

She sighed, dusting herself off.

A cold breeze blew, and she shivered.

She traced Cyrus's path through the sky.

"I'm sorry, Cy," she said. "I know you can do it without me."

Her stomach churned as a wave of self-hatred rolled over her like a rainstorm.

She hated herself for not being able to fight. For not being able to be the big sister she was supposed to be.

She found herself weeping uncontrollably. She couldn't stop the tears, and she hated herself for shedding them. This wasn't what Becca was supposed to do. This wasn't the strong big sister. Strong friend.

Her inner voice spoke.

I hate myself.

I let my family down.

Cy is going to die because of me.

What kind of friend almost kills a friend?

She found a ledge and sat down, covering her face as Axel and Oleandra clashed over another rooftop.

A voice cut through her self-pitying introspection.

"Becca."

She knew that voice even at the lowest volume. She wiped her face and glanced up.

A few yards away, her father stood next to a triangular stairwell entrance. His back was to her. He wore a striped button-down shirt and green slacks. A cowlick stuck out of his bushy hair—usual Dad.

"I found Cyrus," David Grant said, scanning the sky. "He really got himself into a mess, didn't he?"

"What about *me*?" Becca asked, wiping the last of her tears with her forearm. "Didn't you see me up there?"

"You're here now," her dad said.

"Yeah," she said, sniffling.

"It's all right," he said. "I'm proud of you."

He started to walk to the stairwell.

She stood. A nagging feeling insinuated itself into the moment, a question she knew she needed to ask.

"Dad," she said.

David stopped and looked over his shoulder.

"When you told me not to follow, what did you mean?" Becca asked.

"Come, and I'll tell you," he said. "It's cold up here and you'll freeze."

"Don't walk away from me again," Becca said. "I…can't take it."

"Let's go, Becky," her dad said. Though his back was turned, she saw a sly grin. He always called her Becky when he teased her.

She'd missed his teasing. She felt herself pulled forward, but she stopped. She narrowed her eyes.

"Dad, why can't you answer it here?"

"Because Axel could fly back any moment and you could be injured," David said. "Let's get to safer ground."

Her heart stopped.

Becca, don't follow, her dad had said.

Her dad smiled again and extended a hand, nodding gently.

She didn't move.

"Bec, come on," her dad said.

"No," she said, shaking her head. "I won't follow you."

She took a step back. "You told me not to."

"That was different," David said. "And this is now."

She took another step back.

"Becca," her dad said, more impatiently.

She took another step and wobbled. She looked down twenty stories at a raging traffic jam. She gasped.

"Becca, get over here!" her dad yelled.

A pair of cattle horns grew from his head and his hand mutated into malformed claws covered with golden rings. Smoke poured off his body, stinking up the air like rotting, putrid breath.

Becca balled her fists as the demon's claws extended for her.

Why had she stopped praying?

It was a trick.

She resumed her prayer and Garamanthus, half-David Grant and half unspeakable demon form, writhed in agony. His claws fell limp and hit the ground.

Her vision filled with white again, and she sensed herself expanding in the entirety of the place…

Her mind expanded over the rooftops…over the streets… among the twinkling stars and the blazing night sun…with her brother flying at the speed of a car…and finally, against the walls of her mind.

She breathed in as she prayed.

Inhale. Exhale.

Garamanthus dropped to his knees uttering a demonic curse in his melting hybrid form. Her father's eyes flashed red as they began to melt.

Becca finished her prayer as her vision filled with a white flash. Then, she was falling through the night sky. She had never been on a roof. That place was somewhere in the furthest corner of her mind now.

The air whipped around her and she rustled, aware of her weightlessness.

A glint of white flashed in the corner of her eye followed by a sharp jingle. She reached out and caught the chain.

Above, Axel ripped a sword out of Oleandra's eye, and he threw the tree nymph down to the ground.

Oleandra screamed all the way down to the street and the city shook as she made an enormous crater in an intersection.

The nymph struggled to get up, waved her branches, and then stopped moving.

Becca panted as she held on.

Cyrus and Becca's chains crossed as Axel roared.

"So very nice to have you with us!" Cyrus yelled.

"Screw you!" Becca said as they passed each other.

"We gotta calm him down," Cyrus said, streaming away. "We have to appeal to his nature."

"What the hell does that mean?" Becca asked, but her brother was gone.

Axel raged through the sky, flapping his wings furiously. A ball of light appeared in his hand and he threw it at a nearby building. The rooftop exploded in a flash of white fire.

"He's losing control," Becca said to herself.

She flipped several times and regained control of her chain.

"Axel, you've got to stop this," she said. "You're going to kill innocent people. The battle is done. You've won and cleared your name."

The nephilim growled and shook Becca, trying to throw her off, but she held on tight.

"Axel, we can go back to normal if you stop," she said. "You can have as many drinks at the Wicked Cat as you want. I'll lift your ban. How does that sound?"

The nephilim shook harder this time.

Cyrus swung past. "Not woooooorking!" he said.

Becca remembered the first time she saw Axel transform into a nephilim.

Ezekiel was saying kind words to him, and Johanna was taunting him. Somehow, that worked. Would the same thing work now?

She closed her eyes and remembered her encounter with Garamanthus on the roof. Bitterness spilled up from the deepest wells of her soul, pure hatred for the demon, pure desire to exorcise him and vanquish him from existence.

"Destroy the city," she said, anger catching in her voice. "Destroy everything and let it all burn."

Axel didn't shake her. He slowed his flight and turned his head in her direction.

"What are you waiting for?" Becca shouted. "Or are you too weak?"

Axel shook his head. He roared and threw his sword at traffic below.

"More," Becca said quietly. "More death. More destruction."

Axel brought his wings in and went into a barrel roll between two buildings.

"Come on," Becca said. "Do your worst. Make everyone in awe of your power."

Inside her mind, Garamanthus laughed quietly. She winced at the realization that he was still there. She shook him away.

Axel slowed down on his way to the street.

He expanded his wings, and Becca's chain disappeared.

She was freefalling now. She closed her eyes as she landed on Axel's fluffy wings.

Cyrus landed on the other wing. Axel groaned and fell through the air, smashing into an empty street.

The impact sent a quake several blocks in all directions.

Becca bounced and rolled across the street. A parked truck broke her roll. Cyrus landed next to her.

The giant nephilim lay in the road. In a flash of light, the night transformed into day. Then, silence.

In human form, Axel lay in the middle of the massive crater, sleeping.

"We did it," Cyrus asked.

Becca punched Cyrus softly on the shoulder.

"What was that for?" he asked, rubbing it.

"For having crazy ideas," she said.

Cyrus threw his arm around Becca. Together, they stared at Axel as he slept.

CHAPTER FORTY-ONE

"I THOUGHT we'd never get to the bottom of this one," Cyrus said as he and Becca walked up to the destroyed theater. Desmond sat on the sidewalk in human form. Gilberto must have worked his magic.

Ezekiel sat in the middle of the street. His head was bloodied, but he seemed to be okay. Cyrus waved at him and nodded. Somehow, Ezekiel must have known that his dad was okay.

"Where's Johanna?" Cyrus asked.

A raven flapped down and morphed into Rocco. "She's on her way. She's a few blocks over. She got really lucky and landed on a roof."

Rocco gave Cyrus a fist bump.

"Another adventure behind us," Cyrus said.

Two hands wrapped around Cyrus.

"And another nymph is toast," Luna said, pecking him on the cheek.

Cyrus patted her hands.

"I gotta give it to you, Cyrus," Desmond said. "I've seen almost everything. But you're one of a kind."

"Does that mean I get a raise?" he asked, brightening.

Becca folded her arms. "He's still living in my apartment, you know. Help a girl out, Desmond."

Desmond pursed his lips. "No raise."

Cyrus and Becca let out a joint sigh.

Cyrus studied the area. The theater was unrepairable—its windows were blown out. The theater sign hung by a few bolts on the front of the building. The marquee was going to break off and shatter on the sidewalk any second. A huge tree lay in the parking spaces in front the building. Cyrus looked away from Rue's mangled body.

Aurora came out of nowhere and was suddenly standing next to Cyrus and Becca.

"Hell of a one-act play, eh, Mom?" he asked.

Aurora smiled at the two of them.

"Turns out it wasn't a one-act play," she said.

Cyrus's face went long. "Huh?"

"There's a second act where the both of you tell me just what the fresh hell is going on."

"Deal," Becca said. "Oh, and don't let me forget to tell you about Dad. He really came through for me tonight."

Aurora stammered. "W-what?"

Becca hugged her mom. "There will be plenty of time to talk."

Cyrus thought of his dad and looked up at the bright blue sky. Was he watching them right now? It felt like someone was watching…

He became aware of eyes on him. Many, many eyes.

A group of people had gathered in the street, whispering. Silhouettes watched from windows in the buildings above. Traffic lined up on the street a block down, unable to navigate the world's biggest potholes left behind from Axel and Oleandra's fight.

"Yikes," Cyrus said. "These people are gonna start talking, aren't they?"

Desmond hopped to his feet. "Fortunately, the giant rat

didn't kill all of the suppressors. Axel's network held, though barely. This will be neutralized by nightfall. Just don't say anything or do anything stupid and we'll be fine. We've got a few agents in the police who are on the way to contain the scene."

He looked up at the theater. "Poor place. I'll have to think about how we can make the owners and actors whole again."

"Better get on that," Rocco said.

Desmond groaned. "It'd be nice to have a weekend for a change."

Gilberto tapped Becca on the shoulder, his hands clasped. "Hey, Becca—"

His face was sad.

Becca smiled at him. "Why so gloomy?"

Gilberto was nervous, and his words didn't come out. "There's…something…I have to tell you."

Desmond put a hand on Gilberto's shoulder. "It's not your fault."

Gilberto looked at Desmond sadly.

"What is it?" Becca asked.

"Becca, the good news is that this conflict is over," Desmond said. "But we've also got some bad news about Cristián."

Becca held Cristián's hand as he lay on a hospital bed.

Cristián slept, hooked up to an endotracheal tube and a maze of catheters.

It was just her and him in the room amid a steady cadence of beeps. She insisted on being alone with him.

"Kirk shot him," Gilberto had said. "But it wasn't Kirk. He was possessed. He held me at gunpoint and told me to heal him from death."

A tear slid from Becca's eye.

"Why did he have you keep him alive?" Becca had asked.

"Because…"

"Because what?" she had snapped.

"He said he wanted you to you see," Gilberto said. "He wanted you to know it was him."

Becca scowled as she stared at Cristián's wounded, broken body. All he'd been doing was taking out the trash, and he got caught up in her problems.

"I'll avenge you," Becca said.

"Ah, now there's some of that anger I wanted you to feel," Garamanthus said.

"Why did you do this to me?" she asked.

"This boy was just insurance," the demon said. "Some collateral to let you know who I am. The question is, who are you, Rebecca Grant?"

"I'm not who you want me to be," she said. "And you'll pay for this."

"I would love to see how you make me pay," Garamanthus said, laughing. "It will probably involve a little of your dark side, don't you think? I still have a score to settle with you for wounding me on the rooftop. I'll heal, but while I do, I'll study your every memory, and next time, you won't be so lucky. You *will* fulfill the destiny I have planned for you, Rebecca, whether you like it or not."

The demon's laughter rang inside her head as she kissed Cristián's hand.

"Mr. MacLeod, we're going to let you rest for a while," the doctor said. "But there's an officer who will be here soon who has some questions about how all of this happened."

Kirk rested in a hospital bed, laying his head back as a doctor and nurse left the room. His arm hung in a sling.

The silence was welcome.

He almost didn't make it to the hospital. He didn't even remember walking into the ER lobby. He only remembered his current train of thought now—coming awake in this bed after surgery, seeing the fluorescent light in the ceiling come into focus, and the doctor's and nurse's voices floating to him.

A few minutes more, the doctor said, and he would have been a goner.

In his morphine hallucinations, he relived his brother's final moments as if he were still in the theater. The switchblade in Aidan's neck. Bruce's lamenting. His father's final advice to save himself.

Isn't that what he had done? Saved himself?

A feeling of rosiness swelled around him as another wave of morphine eased through his veins.

Screw the cops that would come in here asking him uncomfortable questions, and screw the squad cars they rode in on. It was Chicago…didn't people get shot all the time?

Yeah, he told himself. That was the angle…

Maybe there'd be a better way to spin it. Now was as good a time as any to find out.

He closed his eyes and thought dark thoughts.

Something was in the room with him now, hovering next to the bed. He knew it by its filthy, flesh-ridden breath. Jesus. He'd need more morphine after smelling this damn thing's mouth.

"Bring me my brother and father," he said, not opening his eyes.

"Your price?" the demon asked in a deep voice.

Kirk spoke it, and the demon disappeared in a quiet twister.

He opened his eyes and beheld the soft silhouettes of Aidan and Bruce. He sighed with relief.

"You followed my advice for a change," Bruce said.

"Turns out you spit hot wisdom from time to time," Kirk

said. He pointed to Aidan, whose new form was faceless and legless. "You cleaned up good."

"If that's what you want to call it," Aidan said.

"Tell me, brother—what was it like?" Kirk asked. "I want a play by play of everything that happened after your last breath."

He closed his eyes and rested as Aidan told him about his transition into the great beyond.

After the shooting, Desmond had closed the Wicked Cat out of respect for Cristián. The bar looked frozen in time from a few hours earlier; warm drinks were undrunk on tables. Silverware was unrolled on the bar, waiting for someone to wrap it in a napkin. The fans swung madly.

Cyrus gathered a few drinks off the tables and poured them down the sink at the bar. He watched as his sister mixed drinks. Ever since she came back from the hospital to visit Cristián, she wasn't the same, even though she tried to put on a smile. He knew his sister, and she was fighting a war inside her head. He swore to help her somehow.

Desmond, Rocco, Luna, and Gilberto sat around a table and raised their drinks.

"Cristián's in stable condition," Desmond said to the group as they sipped their drinks. "Axel's fine too. We'll probably see him in a few days."

Desmond smirked at Becca. "That is, unless he's still banned."

"No ban," Becca said.

Cyrus plopped down in front of an ice-cold beer. "At least we're done with Oleandra and Rue. If I ever meet a nymph again, it'll be too soon."

Cyrus took a big slurp of his beer and shook his head.

"They just played chess with us to get back at Axel. And they used Murgalen's curse to their own gain too."

"Typical nymphs," Desmond said.

"Sometimes it feels like we don't even matter," Cyrus said. "Like we're pawns in a bigger game that we don't understand."

"That's paranormal life," Luna said. "We just have to do the best we can, you know?"

Becca set down a yellowish-orange drink in front of Gilberto.

"Hey, uh," Gilberto said, "I asked for a Pacifico."

"It's a new drink in your honor," Becca said. "A splash of tequila, half a lime, some grapefruit juice, and, of course, a dash of your favorite beer. I call it Healer Man, and I predict it's going to be a hit."

Gilberto sipped the salt-crusted drink and grinned wide. "I like it. Can I get some of the profits?"

"Don't push our friendship, buddy," she said, laughing.

Cyrus downed the rest of his beer and got that nagging feeling that he was supposed to be somewhere. The revelation hit him like a punch in the gut.

Marisol…

"Oh crap!" he said, stumbling out of the chair.

He bolted out the door but then got a whiff of himself and tripped as he changed direction to Becca's apartment.

"Kid, whatever you did, I want you to do it again," Fontanelli said excitedly.

Cyrus took the call on his earbuds as the Blue Line let him off at his stop. His hair was still wet from a shower—wetter than he liked. He tried to remember if he put on deodorant. He had run out of the apartment in such a rush, it was a miracle he had clothes on at all.

"How did you do it?" Fontanelli asked.

"Do what?" Cyrus asked, zipping past a crowd of joking teenagers who were playing tag on the steps.

"You said you had an idea," Fontanelli said, "and then you ran off. Next thing I know, all the rats were gone. I couldn't believe my eyes. The customers are callin' me again like gangbusters! They want me to solve every little fly on their property. They said if I could clear out those rats, then I was a fella they could trust. How about that? Come on, tell me what you did."

"Come on, Font, do you think I'm smart enough to figure out a solution to a thousand rats? I can barely mix pesticide."

"You're bein' humble," Fontanelli said.

Cyrus laughed nervously. "Okay, Font. I'll tell you the secret. I did a little dance, sprinkled some pixie dust on the street, and told 'em to get the hell out of town, or else."

Silence. Then Fontanelli let out a burly laugh.

"Ah, okay. Real funny, champ. Anyway, I'll see ya tomorrow at nine?"

"You got it, Font."

Cyrus hung up as he ran down the covered steps of the L station and crossed the street to an ice cream parlor with a giant sign of a vanilla ice cream cone.

He stopped at the window. Marisol was waiting for him at one of the tables. She wore a white dress and had a red clutch purse. Her curly hair blew gently in the building's air-conditioning. She was just as beautiful as last night.

Could he do it? Could he tell her the truth about everything?

〜

"Hey," he said.

"Hey," she said.

He bought her a vanilla ice cream cone and they sat down.

"How are you holding up?" he asked.

She hesitated.

He waited.

"You can tell me," he said.

And then she told him everything.

They took a stroll through a nearby park. The sun was setting in the sky and it was going to be another hot summer night.

Marisol finished her story.

"Isn't that crazy? I know I'm not crazy. I know what I saw, you know?"

"Way crazy," Cyrus said. "And no, you're not crazy."

As much as he wanted to get to know her more, he couldn't. He had another job now. She was forever exposed to the paranormal world, and there was no going back.

"Marisol," he said. "I'm sorry you went through that. But there's something you should know."

They stopped in the middle of a path under a large oak tree.

He sighed and told her about Axel's team.

"You're telling me that their *job* is to make me think I'm crazy?" she asked.

"They're kind of assholes," Cyrus said. "Led by an asshole-in-chief. I wouldn't have handled it that way."

"And you're...a rat?" she asked, making a face of disgust.

"It's a long story," he said. "I just want you to know I'm sorry for what happened, and I've talked to my boss at the

Regulators and we'll arrange to get you all the therapy you need. I can't imagine how you're feeling right now."

SLAP!

Stars exploded across his eyes.

He brought his hand to his cheek just as Marisol slapped him again.

Little birds might as well have been singing in circles over his head.

He rubbed his other cheek and looked up just in time to see the rest of Marisol's ice cream cone smash into his nose.

"Don't ever talk to me again or I'll call the police," she said angrily.

Then she ran away.

Cyrus stood there, ice cream dripping from his face and his cheeks stinging and a pit opening up in his stomach threatening to suck his whole body in and invert him from existence.

She was running crazy fast. Like the people in the old *Addams Family* sitcom who bolted when they discovered how crazy the family truly was.

He sighed.

Yep, that's how it would go, he thought as he stared at Marisol through the window of the ice cream shop. She twirled a tangle of hair as she studied the ice cream menu posted behind the counter.

It was his job as a Regulator to help people exposed to the paranormal. He didn't know what she went through last night, but he knew that any encounter with Axel's team would have been crazy-making.

He couldn't move his feet to go in there and talk to her. He thought he could. The call from Fontanelli helped take his mind off his nervousness.

To think he could do it was one thing, but to be here, two

yards away and see how beautiful she was again and—either tell the truth and make her hate him forever or lie and never be able to look into her gorgeous eyes....

It was a conflict of interest.

He swallowed hard. He stepped away from the window and sent Marisol a text.

Sorry, something came up. Maybe another time?

She didn't reply right away. She was probably irritated. He would have been too.

But she finally replied.

Sure. Hope you're okay.

He hid in a nearby alley as Marisol left and passed by. His heart skipped as she passed the alley and he got a final look at Marisol—her eyes were sad and she had a semi-deflated look to her walk, like she was deep in thought.

If only she knew that he felt the same way. He just didn't have the heart to tell her.

He dug his hands in his pockets and walked the other way. Cyrus hated being a jerk to her, but he knew that in the end it was kindest thing he could do for her. Marisol Garza's life would go on without his drama. One day maybe she'd forget about all of this and the sting she must have surely been feeling right now would fade away. That gave him a little hope.

So much for dating. Maybe the next time he dated, he'd find a nice paranormal girl who could put up with his crazy life. Hopefully, she wouldn't be scared of rats either.

THE END.

GET BOOK 3

Cyrus's adventures as a rat shifter continue in *Book 3: Year of the Rat*.

What's next for Cy and Bec now that Becca is possessed by a demon?

Turn the page to find out, or grab your copy of *Year of the Rat* today at www.michaellaronn.com/yearoftherat.

Michael La Ronn has written many books of science fiction & fantasy.

In 2012, a life-threatening illness made him realize that storytelling was his #1 passion. He's devoted his life to writing ever since, making up whatever story makes him fall out of his chair laughing the hardest. Every day.

To get updates when he releases new work + other bonuses, sign up by visiting www.michaellaronn.com/fanclub.